HEARTCOIL
Daniel Sheley

Ashwake Press

Contents

Chapter 1
Ashmouth

The mist in Eastland didn't lift. Not even when dawn cracked the soot-laden sky and splashed weak light against rust-choked towers. It clung to every broken gutter and iron girder, thick as breath from a dying lung.

Link adjusted the scarf across his face. The cloth rasped rough against days-old stubble and the healed-over split on his lower lip. Every breath tasted like old ash and frozen iron. He drew it higher, instinct more than habit—protection not just against the cold, but against being seen. Scars patterned his jawline, pale against wind-bitten skin. Marks of old burns and broken days. Eyes sharp, gray-blue and narrow, flicked between alley corners.

His fingers flexed unconsciously around the leather grip of his belt knife. Not out of need, but habit. Out here, instincts whispered louder than reason. Especially in the quiet hours, when the city almost pretended to sleep.

They had come far already that morning. The back alleys behind them stretched in choking silence, littered with broken crates and the skeletal remains of forgotten market stalls. Iron grates hung loose like broken teeth. Each step toward Ironvale's edge had brought fresh dangers. Twice, they'd ducked between shattered walls to avoid the soft clatter of automata passing overhead. Once, they had passed a mural so old the colors bled into soot — a child's drawing, faded to near-invisibility. Link had paused then, hand brushing the brick, before pulling Eve forward. Sentiment was death out here. They had learned that too many times.

Even silence had weight. A weight that pressed heavier every year.

1

He knelt now behind a leaning water cistern, its riveted seams hissing faintly from residual heat. The metal surface radiated just enough warmth to sting his gloved fingers as he steadied himself. Beside him, Eve checked her pistol with cold efficiency. Fingers, slim and oil-streaked, clicked through the motions without wasted movement. Her eyes, sharp and pale green beneath a tangle of cropped blonde hair, flicked up toward the skyline.

She wore layers pieced together from salvage: a patched canvas jacket cinched tight, frayed scarf wound twice about her throat, and rusted boilerplate tied loosely around one forearm like makeshift armor. Despite the grime, she carried herself with taut readiness. A faint scar curved along her jawline, visible when she tightened her lips. Link knew every scar she carried. They both wore Eastland's teeth marks.

"You see it yet?" she asked, voice low, tight, and hushed.

Link shook his head. He could barely make out the silhouette of the Ironvale tram line through the haze, much less the automata patrol they were supposed to tail. Still, the Guild's metal hounds would come. They always did.

He pressed his palm against the cistern's side again. Heat seeped through thin leather gloves. It was faint, but undeniable — the city still breathed. Not strong, not clean. But alive in the way embers refused to die. Around them, steam hissed faintly from cracked valves overhead. Distantly, somewhere deep in the city's bones, gears churned in steady rhythm. That sound haunted him at night. The city's steady, uncaring heartbeat.

Eve exhaled slowly, watching the mist coil from her lips. "It's never quiet without reason."

"Movement. Upper rail." She nudged him with a gloved elbow.

Link followed her gesture. A faint metallic clatter whispered from above. Shapes emerged—three automata in patrol formation. Standard Light Infantry units. Humanoid frames, brass-bodied and jointed like crude marionettes, hissed softly with each step. Steam vented from their backs, rising in curling tendrils that merged with the ever-present mist.

He watched them carefully. Their heads turned in precise, mechanical arcs. Single-lens eyes glowed faintly, scanning alleys and doorways without pause.

2

Crude as they were, they were relentless. They walked with a weightless smoothness, balanced as though every movement had been calculated to waste no effort.

"Standard cycle," Eve murmured. "We can slip behind them."

Link nodded but hesitated. Something about the patrol's cadence felt... off. Too precise. Too rehearsed. Years of watching, of running, made him trust instincts over logic. Still, they couldn't wait. Free Steam didn't have the luxury of patience when rations and shelter ran thin.

He gestured forward, low and deliberate.

They moved. Quiet, efficient. Link's boots crunched softly over frost-laced rubble, every step calculated. Eve ghosted beside him, her patched jacket rustling quietly. Up close, he caught faint details—a faded badge stitched onto her collar, the initials of some forgotten brigade. Her scarf was frayed, but she wore it like armor, wound tight and stiff with soot. She moved with a slight limp — a souvenir from an older raid, never properly healed.

Eve broke the silence briefly as they edged along the wall. "Looks like Markov's batch. Slow, stiff. Still dangerous."

Link grunted softly. "They're Guild stock. Dangerous enough."

Their words died as they reached the service tunnel beneath the rails. Link paused. He listened—not just with his ears, but with his gut. The city spoke in sighs and groans. Automata hissed. Pipes clanked and strained overhead. Somewhere distant, a child cried out, only to be swallowed quickly by the void.

No alarms. No fast-approaching footfalls. Yet unease crawled beneath his skin like burrowed frost.

"Cut through here," Eve whispered, tapping the tunnel entrance.

They slipped inside. The darkness pressed in immediately, wrapping them tight in greasy cold. Link's hand found the wall, steadying himself against corroded iron. Water dripped steadily from cracked rivets above, staining his sleeve. They pressed forward in near-silence, broken only by the dull hum of steam lines vibrating through the walls.

"Feels wrong," Link muttered quietly.

Eve glanced back. "Everything does lately. Guild's changing tactics."

Before he could answer, a sound—a harsh, staccato hiss—cut through the stillness. Eve froze mid-step, pistol halfway raised. Link didn't ask. He knew.

A Hunter Class automaton clambered down the far wall. Multi-limbed, insectile, and twice the height of a man, it moved with predatory grace. Its sensor array pulsed faintly, scanning in rapid arcs. Unlike patrol models, Hunters didn't broadcast their presence. They hunted. Silently.

The Hunter's body gleamed faintly in the dark. Its limbs were long and jointed like skeletal arms, ending in wicked claws designed for speed and grip. Brass plating had been worn down to dark gunmetal in places, giving it the look of a thing accustomed to pursuit. Every movement it made stirred up flecks of dust and rust from the tunnel walls, like a shadow bleeding into the stone.

Eve tensed. Link reached to his belt, fingers curling around the smooth casing of a disruption mine.

Too late. The Hunter's array snapped toward them. A shriek like tearing steel split the tunnel as it surged forward.

"Run," Link hissed.

Eve fired—steam-spitting slugs peppering the machine's front—but the rounds glanced off reinforced brass plates. Link flung the mine. It clanged once, magnetized, then detonated in a plume of superheated steam. The Hunter staggered, hissing violently, but didn't fall.

They sprinted. Link's muscles burned as he vaulted broken pipes, heart hammering against his ribs. Eve followed, limping heavily—her teeth clenched tight against a hiss of pain. Her face was pale, strain etched deep across her brow, but she forced her legs to move. There was no other choice.

Ahead, moonlight spilled from a grating. Link lunged up first, grabbing Eve's arm and hauling her through just as the Hunter slammed into the wall behind them, its clawed limbs rending steel and showering sparks.

They collapsed onto frost-slick cobblestones. Eve coughed harshly, wiping grime and soot from her cheek with shaking fingers. Link's hands trembled—not from cold, but from the closeness of death. He could still hear the Hunter's screech echoing faintly through the tunnels.

"That's new," Eve panted, pushing matted hair from her eyes.

"Yeah." Link's gaze stayed fixed on the grating. The Hunter didn't pursue. Orders, maybe. Or territory limits. Either way, they were still alive.

For now.

Eve leaned back against the wall, her breath clouding in the freezing air. Her eyes—reflective, pained—searched the mist-choked sky above. "Next time, we need better routes."

Link's jaw tightened. He knew what she meant. The Guild adapted faster now. Every night, Eastland grew tighter around their throats. No alley felt safe. No route felt unwatched.

He wiped sweat and soot from his brow, sitting for a beat longer. His breathing slowed, but every muscle still thrummed with residual tension. From his belt, he unhooked the empty mine casing and inspected it silently.

"That was the last one," he muttered quietly.

Eve nodded grimly, flexing her sore leg. "No more mistakes then. Next time it corners us, it finishes us."

For a moment, neither spoke. Only the sounds of Eastland filled the silence—distant shrieks of steam, faint groans of shifting metal, and the heartbeat of the city pushing on. Somewhere nearby, dogs howled in chorus. Not friendly dogs. Not safe dogs. Even they knew something had changed tonight.

Link finally stood. "Come on. Let's get back to the lines before the patrols loop."

Eve hesitated briefly, then pushed herself upright with a faint grimace. Together, without another word, they slipped into the mist. Their figures dissolved like echoes swallowed by the hollow city.

The mist pressed down again, heavy and smothering. It swallowed their words, their shapes, their defiance.

Without another word, they vanished into it. Like ghosts that refused to die.

Chapter 2
Scars in the Steam

The cold bit deeper as they crossed from Ironvale's fringe into the Warrens.

This was the city's cracked lung—where the arteries of steam lines knotted tighter and even the automata hesitated to roam. Link's boots splashed through shallow runoff, thin as oil and black as old blood. Each step was a whisper too loud. The mist here did not move like before; it hung, viscous and sour, clinging to clothes and clogging breath.

Link's scarf had soaked through minutes ago. Moisture clung to his cheeks, threading into the rough stubble along his jaw. His face ached from the cold, from tension. Every muscle remained tight after the escape. His ribs still hummed with the thudding echo of adrenaline. He kept his shoulders hunched low, head slightly down—an old instinct from when the Guild patrols had been faster to punish.

The silence was oppressive, weighted. Every drip of runoff, every metallic creak above became amplified. The air felt too thick, the stillness too complete. Every instinct screamed at him that they did not belong here — and that the city knew it.

Beside him, Eve limped more openly now. She no longer masked it, not here in the dead channels of the city. Her lips were pale, eyes narrowed in focus as she clenched her teeth against every jarring step. Beneath her jacket, Link could make out the outline of a makeshift splint tied to her shin—thin copper rods, wound tight with frayed cord. Temporary, but it kept her moving.

Her breaths came shallow and quick. Each inhalation drew in the bitter, oily stink of the Warrens. Burnt rubber. Hot iron. Rust. The scents layered thick in the air like a shroud. Every breath tasted like industry and rot. Her eyes glistened faintly—not from tears, but from the constant sting of chemical residue hanging heavy in the mist. The city marked them both — in grime, in ache, in exhaustion.

"Give me ten," she rasped, leaning heavily against the wall of a crumbling brick stack. Her breath hitched faintly, turning to mist that drifted and died against the stone. Even her voice had grown rough, rubbed raw by too many cold nights and too many desperate runs.

Link glanced back. No sound of pursuit, no gleam of optics scanning the mist. Still, his stomach twisted tight.

"Five." He crouched nearby, his boots grinding softly in frost-laced dirt. "Can't risk it. Not here."

Eve didn't argue. She pressed her head back against the bricks and shut her eyes, shoulders heaving slightly. The fatigue was raw and heavy. Link could see her fingers flex unconsciously, working through the pain, refusing to let it take hold.

His gaze drifted to the wall beside her. Old posters peeled in thin curls, their ink half-eaten by damp and time. **"GLORY TO THE GUILD — UNITY THROUGH INDUSTRY."** The words clung on, faded and ironic in the hollow dark. He almost laughed, but the sound stayed trapped in his throat. Eastland's promises always turned to rot.

A faint vibration stirred underfoot. Link stiffened immediately. The sound was distant — a low hum, constant and steady. Not patrols. Not Hunters. A transport, maybe. Or worse, the furnace drudgers moving through midnight cycles. He couldn't tell.

He glanced at Eve again. She noticed too. Her eyes flicked open, sharp and alert despite her weariness.

"Time's up." She pushed off the wall with a grimace and nodded toward the narrowing alleys ahead. "We need to cut through Tinrow or we'll miss curfew drop. We stay out here when the bell tolls, they'll send sweepers."

Link rose silently, nodding once.

They moved deeper into the maze.

As they passed into Tinrow, the city's heartbeat shifted. Here, the cold carried new smells — burnt oil, spoiled rations, the faint metallic tang of dried blood somewhere hidden. The alleys twisted tighter, hemmed in by collapsed awnings and makeshift barricades. Somewhere nearby, low voices murmured in a tongue born from desperation and trade, punctuated by the clink of bottles and distant coughs.

Link's eyes scanned rooftops instinctively. Tarps fluttered, held aloft by ropes and scavenged metal poles. Shapes moved behind thin cloth—families huddled together, feral children watching strangers pass with hollow eyes.

A cry broke the stillness briefly — hoarse, human — and then was abruptly cut off. Link froze mid-step, hand drifting instinctively to the grip of his blade. Eve tensed beside him. But no alarm followed, no rush of footsteps. The city swallowed the sound like it always did. Here, death was so common it didn't echo for long.

They passed a collapsed carriage, its wheel rims stripped to jagged metal. Inside, a skeletal figure lay slumped in faded rags, untouched and ignored. No one bothered with the dead here. Not when survival left no time for ceremony. In Tinrow, the dead became part of the backdrop, indistinguishable from the decay.

A small gang of youths crouched around a barrel fire as they passed. Faces hollow-cheeked and eyes wary, they followed Eve and Link's progress in tense silence. One boy, no older than ten, clutched a long iron rod sharpened to a vicious point. Another gnawed absently on a piece of hard tack, eyes darting nervously. The others sat with knees hugged tight to thin bodies, radiating mistrust. Survival, Link thought bitterly, had no age limit here.

Further down, an elderly woman sat alone beneath a torn awning, sewing what looked like scraps of leather together with frayed wire. She didn't look up as they passed. Her movements were automatic, practiced, indifferent. Surviving, not living. She would sew until she starved, and the city wouldn't even blink.

No one spoke. The streets here didn't tolerate weakness — or questions.

Link kept his head down, pulling his scarf higher. Eve followed his lead, careful not to limp too noticeably here. Not all dangers wore brass and steam. In Tinrow, hunger and desperation were far crueler enemies.

By the time they reached the rendezvous point — an old boiler hatch tucked beneath a broken tram arch — dawn threatened on the horizon. Not that it mattered. Light in Eastland was a pale, gasping thing. It revealed nothing but rust and ruin.

Link crouched low, running gloved fingers across the hatch's seam. Warmth radiated faintly from the other side. Someone was home.

He knocked twice, then paused. Three quick taps followed.

A metallic scrape answered. The hatch split with a hiss of steam, revealing the grim face of Rett, one of Free Steam's quartermasters. Thick-necked and broad-shouldered, Rett looked carved from the same stone as the city's foundations. His beard was singed in places, his left eye slightly clouded from an old chemical burn. He wore a heavy riveted apron smeared with soot and grease.

"Late," Rett growled, voice like gravel rolling through old pipes. He stepped aside, letting them in.

Eve slipped past without a word. Link followed, pulling the hatch closed behind him.

Inside was warmth — not comfort, but something close enough. Pipes lined the walls, throbbing faintly as steam coursed through them. The smell of iron and sweat clung thick in the air. Small groups of rebels — men and women wrapped in scavenged layers — crowded around makeshift tables covered in maps, schematics, and half-eaten rations.

They were a hard lot. Scarred faces, missing fingers, eyes sunken from malnutrition. Some looked up as Link and Eve entered, their expressions guarded. No one spoke, but nods passed between familiar faces. In Free Steam, survival was camaraderie — fragile and worn thin, but still real.

Rett handed Link a cracked mug filled with something hot and bitter. Link took it gratefully, though the taste hit his tongue like burned coal. He drank anyway. Warmth mattered more than flavor tonight.

"Your route went bad?" Rett asked, already knowing.

"Hunters." Link didn't elaborate. The word was enough.

Rett grunted, gaze darkening. "They're pushing harder near Ironvale. Heard they pulled a Watchman squad out of Blackridge to reinforce."

Eve sat heavily on a crate, peeling back her boot to inspect the swelling beneath. She winced but said nothing. Link watched her quietly for a moment before shifting his gaze back to Rett.

"We can't keep running like this." Link's voice was quiet, but edged. "They're closing too many paths."

Rett looked at him, expression unreadable beneath grime and beard. Then, after a long pause, he nodded toward the far side of the chamber where a crude model of Eastland stood pinned with dozens of red markers.

"Then stop running." His voice dropped low, conspiratorial. "Tomorrow night, council's voting. Talk says we don't scatter anymore. We hit back."

Link's jaw clenched. Not fear. Not surprise. Something deeper. A mix of weariness and the faint flicker of something dangerous.

Hope.

But hope in Eastland always felt like handling unstable fuel. Too much spark, and everything burned.

He met Eve's eyes. She stared back, pale and hollow and hard. Beneath that cold stare though, he caught something else. The barest tremor of her fingers tightening on the edge of the crate. Not weakness — anticipation. A hunger that mirrored his own. Around them, the others murmured softly, the word 'hit back' hanging in the air like the first flicker of flame in dry brush.

Neither spoke. Not yet.

But in that silence, something shifted. Something inevitable.

Chapter 3
The Ghostframe

The Spines Awaken

Morning came slow and gray.

The mist hadn't lifted. If anything, it had thickened overnight, soaking the ruins in a dense, muffling weight that blurred edges and swallowed sound. Shapes lost definition. Shadows clung like tired ghosts. The world felt muted — wrapped in heavy cloth, unwilling to stir.

Link and Eve moved carefully through the alleys, boots slipping on stone slick with ash and rain. Each step became deliberate, each shift of weight calculated. Gravel crunched softly underfoot, drowned beneath puddles that mirrored the pale, dismal sky. They walked close, shoulder to shoulder now, each an anchor for the other, bodies tense but steady. The cold worked its way beneath their clothes, thin gloves doing little to block the damp seeping into their bones.

The city felt different now.

Alive — but not in any hopeful sense.

It was the kind of life born from tension. Vast and sleeping, yet coiled. Ready to crush should anyone draw its attention. This was not malice. The city did not hate them.

It simply did not care.

The deeper they moved, the more oppressive that indifference became. Drips echoed, not fast or rhythmic, but irregular — like something breathing slow and heavy in the dark.

Even the walls seemed to lean in, cracked facades arching slightly inward as though listening.

They left behind the skeletal shelter of the textile mill, threading through market ruins where rusted stalls leaned like weary old men, backs broken under the weight of time. Ivy and rot clawed at forgotten corners. Splintered wood broke beneath their boots, releasing sharp cracks into the fog-choked quiet. Above, shattered balconies hung like broken teeth, windows empty-eyed and watching.

Steam hissed faintly from ruptured pipes. The scent of boiled oil, mildew, and rust weighted the air. Each breath tasted like metal and regret. Every inhalation felt stolen.

Ahead lay the Spines—Eastland's old industrial heart.

Even at a distance, its silhouette dominated. Jagged smokestacks stabbed at the sky, blackened towers loomed like the ribs of dead titans. A graveyard of ambition left to rot.

No one sane ventured into the Spines.

Even scavengers gave it wide berth. Stories clung to this place — tales of collapsing floors, sudden bursts of steam that could skin a man alive, and gangs twisted by isolation. Darker still were whispers of the Guild's hidden sanctums, buried experiments that should have died with their makers.

Link did not know which stories were true.

He did not want to know.

But they needed parts. Not scrap. Not salvage. True relics. Only the Spines still clung to those.

At a broken bridge, they paused. The canal beneath lay dead — filled with rubble and jagged rails. The bridge's metal ribs thrust up through the mist like a beast's spine.

"We go down," Link said, already searching for purchase.

Eve simply nodded. Words felt wasted here.

Their descent was awkward. Boots scraped and slipped against slick metal. Fingers curled tight around girders and corroded edges. The mist pressed closer at the bottom, thick and cold. Link glanced sideways at Eve, watching her steady herself. She didn't complain — she never did. Not even now, when the weight of the air felt almost personal.

Every breath tasted heavier. Wet rust. Forgotten sorrow. Invisible fingers curling into their coats, tugging them deeper. It was a clinging, oppressive thing, as though the Spines themselves did not permit easy passage.

The path grew tighter. Machines twisted by collapse and age jutted from broken walls, forcing them to slide sideways or crawl beneath bent girders. Pipes hung low, dripping cold water that soaked through cloth and clung to their skin like unwelcome fingers.

Eve paused once, eyeing a rippling puddle where distorted faces seemed to form and vanish as though the mist itself remembered what had once been. Her eyes lingered too long. She touched Link's arm lightly before moving on. Just to make sure they both knew they weren't ghosts yet.

A wall greeted them. Graffiti clung to its face, faded and bleeding:
HERE BEGINS THE SPINES. TURN BACK.

The words were not just warning. They were truth.

Link rested his hand upon the wall. Faint vibrations thrummed beneath his palm. Not random. Not dead. They stood there longer than necessary, Eve's eyes following the uneven pulses as though trying to memorize them. In the silence, the city's slow breath felt closer — a giant just beneath the surface.

The Spines were awake.

And they were stepping willingly into its open jaws.

Beyond the warning, the city shifted.

Ruins no longer merely abandoned felt consumed. Massive gear housings cracked and twisted. Towers sagged as though crushed from within. Steam whispered softly through jagged seams. It sang quiet songs of entropy and slow death.

Eve moved closer, brushing Link's shoulder with her own. Not accidental. Not fear.

Survival.

They spoke no words. In this place, noise felt like invitation.

The corpse of an old crawler slumped ahead, melted and glassy. Scavenger glyphs scratched deep warned of danger long past. Eve paused to study them briefly, running gloved fingers across the symbols.

"Trap ahead," Link muttered, scanning the path for anything still alive.

"Still active?" Eve's voice was faint silk, but edged now with the sharpness of old instinct.

"Too old. Probably." He didn't like how hollow that sounded.

But probably wasn't safe here. Probabilities killed.

They pressed forward, surrounded by shifting fog. Every movement sounded near. Groans. Metal sighing. Their steps slowed. Eyes darted. The city pressed inward — every ruined vent, every broken beam watching silently. The air became heavy with anticipation, like the breathless moments before a predator pounced.

A deep grinding stirred the air. Heavy. Wrong.

Not Guild.

Older.

They froze. Breath shallow. Muscles taut. For several heartbeats, neither dared move. The sound passed like a judge sparing them, leaving only frayed nerves behind.

They continued. The mist closed tighter as they slipped into a collapsed tunnel, the entrance yawning dark and narrow beneath a leaning tower of boilers. Rust flakes fell as they passed beneath, dusting their shoulders in a fine, silent snowfall. Even their footsteps changed — softer now, more hesitant.

Shelter.

Eve pointed, and Link followed. They slipped inside, leaving the city's whispers behind.

The chemical torch spat to life. Pale blue light crawled over rust and ruin. Scarred walls bore stories of violence. Someone — long dead — had painted scavenger names here, as if they hoped to be remembered.

"There was fighting," Eve murmured, fingertips tracing damage softened by age.

Forward they pressed, crouched low. The tunnel narrowed. Shadows stretched, clawing up walls like desperate hands. Every step was deliberate, calculated. They breathed shallowly, afraid that even a heartbeat too loud might draw something closer.

Without warning, Eve slipped. Rotten metal gave way. She fell — Link's hands shot out, catching her wrist. No words. Only instinct and trust.

Her face twisted briefly in pain, but she masked it quickly. She squeezed his fingers once in silent gratitude before moving on, her hand brushing the wall to stay balanced. Link kept closer now, ready if it happened again. They were tethered together, even in silence.

Every inch forward felt like entering the throat of something long dead but still hungry. Even their torchlight struggled to pierce the gloom ahead, swallowed whole just a few feet beyond.

At the tunnel's end, they found it.

A reinforced bulkhead. Its edges bled pale green light — flickering irregularly, like breath caught between life and death. The glow was faint, sickly, yet still alive in defiance of everything else here.

Link stared. Hunger and unease tangled in his chest. This was what they needed. This was why they came. Still, hesitation tugged at him, the thought of what might wait beyond chilling his resolve. The handle was coated in grime and rust, untouched by any hand in years. He felt its age through his gloves — a roughness that seemed to whisper of sealed things best left forgotten.

Eve's hand found his shoulder.

"Careful," she said again, voice low — reverent almost, as though speaking to a shrine that might turn hostile at any moment.

That word again. More sacred than hopeful. He nodded faintly, knowing its weight.

They approached, twin shadows in a hollow grave.

Link wrapped his fingers around the handle, feeling the rust bite against skin. He paused, breathing once, twice — steadying himself in the thick quiet, where even the mist seemed to hold its breath. The silence pressed against them from every side.

And pulled.

Chapter 4
Breakpoint

B eneath the Iron Bones

    The rusted handle shrieked as Link pulled.

The bulkhead groaned in protest, heavy gears grinding reluctantly before unlocking with a shudder that vibrated through his bones. The door cracked open only a grudging few inches. From within, a wave of stale, metallic air exploded outward — so dense and sudden it slapped them both backward like a physical force.

The stink hit instantly. It clawed at their nostrils with layers of rot and ruin — old oil long soured, mold caked thick on forgotten steel, and something sharper beneath, acidic and violent, the sour tang of chemical burns. Beneath all of it lingered something older still, a ghost of burned flesh and ruined dreams.

Link winced, turning his head sharply aside. Eve did not. She merely narrowed her eyes, her nose wrinkling slightly but without a word. They had smelled worse. They had survived worse.

Without discussion, they slipped through the gap as the bulkhead groaned closed behind them — sealing with a weighty *clang* that sounded disturbingly final. The echo lingered like a closing tomb.

Inside, the world transformed again.

They stood upon the threshold of a collapsed maintenance bay vast enough to swallow entire city blocks. It yawned before them, hollow yet oppressive. Once, the space must have thrummed with relentless industry — steam presses,

19

conveyor belts, fabrication arms hissing and roaring in synchronized chaos. Now it lay broken and still.

Cracked gantries drooped from the ceiling like skeletal arms reaching for salvation that never came. Pools of still water carpeted the floor, mirror-smooth and unbroken until disturbed. Their surfaces reflected the fractured ceiling above — jagged shapes mirrored below, turning the bay into a doubled ruin, as though the past and present shattered together.

Only the faintest light clung to existence. Pale green emergency lamps, cracked and soot-blackened, flickered with tired defiance along the walls. Their dying glow cast long, hesitant shadows that shivered and danced as if afraid of the dark.

Every step became thunder in the silence.

Link and Eve moved carefully. Each splash of their boots echoed grotesquely, rebounding from the metal and water alike. Even breathing felt dangerous. Trapped beneath the iron bones of Eastland's forgotten heart, sound became a betrayer.

The cold deepened here. Dampness clung to their clothes and skin, beading in droplets along their gloves and lashes. Steam whispered faintly from fractured vents — the exhausted breath of machines too broken to die properly.

They worked methodically, falling back into the muscle memory of survivors.

Link stopped first at a shattered control panel. His fingers, stiff from cold, pried loose a cracked pressure regulator. He inspected the fractured housing. Not ideal — but usable. And usable was everything.

Eve knelt nearby, hands moving through a collapsed toolbox. She worked quietly, brushing aside twisted bolts and shattered bearings. When her gloved fingers closed around a still-intact coupling, she pocketed it with silent efficiency.

The devastation worsened as they ventured deeper.

Walls did not simply crumble — they had been obliterated outward by violent forces. Blackened scorch marks slashed across beams. Boilers gaped open along the far wall, ripped apart and hollow like punctured lungs.

"There was a fight," Eve murmured, breaking the stillness.

Link said nothing but nodded grimly. This was not entropy. This was not time. This was violence. Sudden. Ruthless.

They climbed carefully up a warped staircase, handrails corroded and bending beneath their weight. The steps whined faintly, threatening collapse, but held. From this higher perch, the bay sprawled like a battlefield seen from above.

Debris lay everywhere — but some had been arranged. Barriers hastily constructed. Scavenger symbols scratched into walls like fading prayers. Directions. Warnings. Final words.

Someone had fought here.

Someone had lost.

At the far end of the bay, Link spotted it.

A machine hulking half-submerged in black water — massive, crooked, heavy. Unlike the others, it retained some shape. A fabrication rig, or what remained of one. Once it had assembled great steel beasts. Now it slouched broken and abandoned.

But not dead.

The mist curled around it, recoiling like wary animals. Nearby emergency lamps flickered violently, as though the machine drank greedily from their light.

Link's chest tightened. He could almost feel it breathing — faint tremors, heat shimmers radiating outward in sickly waves.

Eve's hand brushed his sleeve, fingers cool and tense.

"Something's wrong." Her voice was thin, hollow. The bay swallowed her words before they reached full weight.

Link's hand found his coil blade without thought.

"We don't have a choice."

Necessity was cruel. It gave no mercy.

They approached carefully, steps cautious and deliberate. Boots broke the mirrored stillness of the water, which clung to them like grasping hands. Beneath the surface, hidden vents exhaled softly, steam curling upward to kiss their faces in damp, cloying threads.

Every movement magnified.

Then —

A sound.

Low. Mechanical. Alive.

They froze mid-step.

Not decay. Not random collapse.

Deliberate.

From within the rig, something stirred.

A convulsive hiss of pressure burst forth. Panels sheared aside. And then the thing pulled itself free — not birthed, but vomited from ruin.

It shambled forward, broken and brutal. Half its face was gone — metal shredded away to reveal weeping pipes, exposed pistons, and fluid leaking in steady, rhythmic pulses. What remained of its face glowed dimly, a cracked lens swirling faint light. Like an eye... or something that remembered how to see.

Link's stomach lurched. He seized Eve's arm, dragging her back beneath a collapsed catwalk. Shadows clung to them, but did little to ease the primal tension vibrating between them.

The thing moved slowly but surely. Limbs stiff. Servos shrieking faintly with every pulse of motion. Steam bled constantly from its shoulders, hissing softly into the surrounding mist.

It did not hunt them specifically.

It hunted anything.

Clicks. Pulses. Sensors twitched like nostrils, tasting the air for vibration and presence.

They held still.

Link felt his heartbeat press up against his throat, shallow and violent. Eve's hand hovered near her blade but never dared unsheath.

The machine limped forward. Left leg dragging, uneven. Yet its pace remained steady. Purposeful. Hungry.

A narrow mezzanine path offered thin escape. Link gestured subtly.

Eve read him instantly. Together they slid along rusted rails, shoulders tight against corroded steel. Every nerve screamed not to make noise.

Below, the thing paused.

Its ruined head cocked. The cracked eye flickered.

The tension shattered when luck, for once, intervened.

Far above, a chunk of ceiling surrendered to gravity. It fell with a deafening crash.

The machine reacted instantly, shrieking in mechanical fury as it charged toward the collapse. Steam vented wildly as its legs tore through water and rubble.

"Go," Link hissed.

They ran.

The stairwell loomed ahead — half-collapsed and treacherous.

Eve surged up first, boots scraping and slipping. Link followed, gasping as wet metal betrayed his footing. Below, the creature shrieked again — raw, discordant — and slammed into the gantry with terrifying force.

Steel screamed and buckled.

They reached the upper levels, lungs burning. The mist hung thinner here, but the cold bit harder, settling into bones and slowing muscles already fatigued.

The ruin above offered no comfort. Just shattered cranes and skeletal pathways.

They crouched behind a half-melted control booth, drawing shaky breaths. Link's hands ached as they pressed against cold iron. Eve trembled faintly, steam curling from her in lazy, ghost-like wisps.

Below, the monster raged.

It slammed the ground repeatedly, unleashing screeching pulses through fractured steel.

Eve leaned in close, her words barely wind against Link's ear.

"We can't outrun it."

He knew.

But then he saw it.

A crane — still hanging, still intact. Its claw loomed above the bay, suspended directly over the thing.

If they could drop it —

Eve followed his eyes and nodded sharply.

"Do it."

Link moved fast and low, racing along the unstable gantry toward a corroded control console. The machine below snapped its head up, sensing movement.

Eve bought him seconds.

She grabbed a hunk of rusted scrap and hurled it wide. It clanged loudly into the shadows. The monster twisted violently and charged.

Link seized the manual override lever. It refused at first — rusted and jammed — but desperation lent him strength. He drove his knife deep into the mechanism and wrenched hard.

The cable screamed.

And the claw fell.

For a heartbeat, silence held. The machine below seemed to look up, as though dimly aware.

Then the impact came like divine punishment.

Steel crushed steel. The bay shuddered as the machine was obliterated beneath the massive claw. A burst of steam shot skyward, howling like a dying animal.

Link stumbled back. The gantry sagged dangerously, threatening to collapse entirely.

He spun and grabbed Eve's hand.

Together, they fled deeper into the ruins, their boots pounding against shaking walkways as the bay let out one final groan — the death rattle of Eastland's forgotten heart.

And behind them, as they vanished into the mist, silence fell once more.

Chapter 5
Engrams

A sh in the Blood

They ran until the mist swallowed the bay entirely, and the shrieks of shifting metal faded into dead silence.

When they finally stopped, bent double and gasping, their breath came out in white plumes that instantly froze and drifted like ghosts, curling and unraveling in the bitter air. The silence that followed wasn't peaceful. It pressed close. Claustrophobic. Every heartbeat sounded too loud, every breath dragged too sharp against raw throats.

Link slumped against a buckled steam pipe, the cold iron biting cruelly through his gloves and seeping into raw, aching hands. The chill gnawed through sinew and skin alike. Every inch of him protested. Muscles torn, nerves shredded, lungs ablaze from the freezing, chemical-laced mist that clung to his throat like a parasite.

He winced as he flexed his fingers — stiff, pale, trembling. They didn't feel like his anymore. Numb. Fragile.

Eve wiped grime and sweat from her face with the back of her sleeve. A shallow cut ran across her temple, leaving a thin line of blood that mingled with soot. The blood traced down the curve of her jaw, turning dark where it mixed with the filth, disappearing into the frayed collar of her jacket. Her eyes, glassy yet vigilant, darted constantly, scanning the gloom as though expecting the city itself to lunge forward and devour them whole.

Neither spoke.

What words could survive the aftermath of what they'd seen?

Around them, Eastland muttered in its sleep. A hollow groan passed through the wreckage — steel beams twisting with invisible weight, ancient pipes wheezing out exhausted breaths. Steam slithered through shattered arches and skeletal frames, curling against frost-bitten stone like pale serpents. The sounds didn't comfort. They reminded. The city lived, even if only in hunger and spite.

The manufactories pressed close here. Towering wreckage and iron beams formed a jagged, suffocating maze. Narrow alleys choked with boiler stacks and twisted bridges overhead clung like ribs to a rotting leviathan. Above, the sky had ceased to exist — only smothering gray, oppressive and heavy, lowering like a lid on a coffin.

Eastland wasn't dead.

It was dying. Slowly. Vengefully. Every breath a curse, every shifting girder a warning.

Link and Eve limped forward, bodies stiff and reluctant. Damp clothing hung from them like chains, and the air pressed heavy with soot and invisible poisons. Every step they took felt wrong. An intrusion into sacred, malignant ground. Their footsteps sounded too loud, foreign against the whispering ruin.

Then came a crack — sharp and cruel.

A scaffold overhead, rusted through and betrayed by time, surrendered with a shriek. It collapsed in a storm of pipes and soot. The clanging metal scythed through the fog with violence that felt deliberate — like the city itself had snapped.

Reflex ruled them. Link and Eve dove sideways as debris rained down. The storm roared past, pipes clanging and ricocheting dangerously close. The heavy stink of rust filled their nostrils, burned their eyes. They pressed tight against the cold spine of a buckled tramline. Dust and powdered rust invaded their mouths as they breathed shallowly, lungs coated in bitter metallic grit.

The ground beneath them gave a warning tremble.

Eastland wasn't done.

The tremor faded slowly, leaving behind a breathless tension. Link adjusted his satchel, the strap biting deep into bruised flesh. He hissed through his teeth and cursed softly. "Another day under the Guild's lords," he muttered, his voice a mix of venom and fatigue.

Eve didn't answer with words. She spat into the soot, her face hollow with exhaustion. The words didn't need to be said aloud. They hung in the air, thick as the choking mist, shared and understood.

Ahead, open ground stretched before them — barren, exposed, cruelly wide. A cracked expanse between skeletal towers and rust-choked supports. Crossing it would make them vulnerable.

But staying still would make them dead.

"Fast," Link said quietly, already bracing himself.

Eve gave a small nod. They ran.

Their boots slammed against fractured stone and rust-streaked rail ties. Each step echoed cruelly, cruelly loud in the oppressive emptiness. Midway across, Eastland grew hungry again.

A deep groan surged up from below.

Without warning, the earth fractured beneath them. Pavement split, tore, and caved inward. A void yawned — deep, jagged, eager.

Link felt it tug at his legs like grasping hands. Panic flared. He shoved Eve ahead roughly, her boots scraping for purchase. His own legs churned against the crumbling surface.

They dove — barely.

Landing hard on the far edge, they slammed into the carcass of a rusted gear housing. Eve let out a ragged gasp. Link lay still for a moment, throat raw as he sucked in the bitter air, staring upward into featureless gray.

Mist rushed in to reclaim the collapse. The gap vanished.

Behind them, the abyss became nothing but gray. Like the earth had simply... forgotten they were there at all.

"This city's trying to finish what the Guild started," Eve rasped. She sounded more resigned than angry now. Almost cold.

Link gave a humorless laugh. "Might get the job done faster."

A weak breeze stirred the fog, revealing fractured horrors in glimpses.

Steam carriages reduced to skeletal husks. Sagging sky-bridges drooping like snapped limbs. Towering buildings collapsed inward, coughing faint steam from their broken lungs.

And beyond them — vague but terribly real — a silhouette.

Standing. Watching. Silent.

Eve's fingers curled tightly around the strap of her satchel. Her voice broke softly through the heavy air. "Shelter?"

Link's stare lingered. "Maybe. Or worse."

He extended his hand to her. Fingers scraped and bloody. She took it without hesitation. No need for words. Silent agreement passed between them.

Standing still wasn't survival.

The shape resolved as they neared. A service entrance — bent and blackened, hanging crooked on ruined hinges. Link forced it closed behind them. The groan of tortured metal echoed like a closing tomb door.

Silence clung inside.

Link paused. He heard something — or thought he did. A whisper, faint and hungry, threaded faintly through the steam. Not words, but memory. This place remembered.

On the wall beside them, a message surfaced through the grime:

VALTOR FEEDS. WE STARVE.

The letters sagged and wept. Eve traced them slowly, her fingers hesitant. Her voice came faint and sharp-edged. "The Guild's pet lord."

Link offered no reply. Valtor's shadow didn't require words. It was carved into every stone and silence.

Further inside, propaganda clung stubbornly to soot-stained walls.

A figure in ornate steam armor stood defiant above stylized towers.

ORDER THROUGH STRENGTH. LORD VALTOR PROTECTS YOU.

Someone had gouged out the eyes.

Eve tore the poster down with disgust. The curled remains crumpled at her feet.

"Protects," she muttered bitterly, "himself."

The ruin swallowed them whole.

Fans overhead spun lazily. Click. Click. Click. Their dying rhythm echoed faintly, the heartbeat of something too large to kill easily.

The manufacturing bay stretched ahead — conveyor belts twisted and torn, ruptured boilers looming like broken gods. Their shadows felt deeper here. Watching.

Movement stirred the mist. Both froze.

A scavenger automaton limped through the gloom. Half-dead. Cables trailing behind like entrails dragged from a corpse.

"Roland's toys," Eve whispered darkly. "All gold. No guts."

Link's face hardened, his lips tightening.

Roland — Valtor's golden mask. A commander of banners and empty speeches. Shiny boots and sharper teeth.

Eve's eyes burned with scorn. She didn't need to see him to know him. Men like that wore power like tailored suits.

The deeper they pushed, the worse it became.

Oil clung to everything. Rust flakes drifted down like dead snow. Ash clung to their skin, layered on every breath. The city coated them in its decay, claiming them inch by inch.

Then came the clang.

They froze. Not footsteps. Not voices. Just Eastland stretching and yawning, testing its intruders.

Beyond a crumbling archway, graffiti glared red and raw through the fog.

FREE STEAM RISES

Eve hesitated, her hand near the painted mark. Then she withdrew slowly, as though afraid to disturb a ghost.

Link studied it. Free Steam — rebels, martyrs, terrorists. Heroes or monsters. Their stories spun wild depending on who whispered them.

Hope and danger wore the same face here.

"Could be a trap," Link warned softly.

"Could be hope," Eve countered, her words steady, fierce despite the weariness dragging at her frame.

Link hesitated.

Stillness was death.

Without more words, they pressed deeper. The mist closed in once more, greedy and suffocating, and behind them Eastland seemed to exhale slowly, content to let them wander further into its quiet, waiting jaws.

Chapter 6
The Coil Burns

———◆———

Lord of Ash and Steel

The council chamber steamed like a dying engine.

Pale vapor curled lazily through the vaulted room, coiling around iron beams and pooling in the hollow spaces between gaslight sconces. It moved with the sluggish grace of something alive and half-asleep—too heavy to rise, too stubborn to dissipate. Even the air itself seemed reluctant to move, clinging to walls heavy with age. The heat and moisture clung to skin and cloth alike, turning even breath into something heavy and wet.

Lord Valtor stood immovable at the head of the ironwood table, his presence as rigid and unbending as the steel supports that framed the walls. His uniform was immaculate—dark, tightly fitted, trimmed with silver thread that caught the weak light and refracted it coldly. Not a single crease marred its surface. Every button gleamed like a tiny sentinel. Perfection maintained with ruthless, almost fanatical precision. His gloves, stretched taut over long fingers, flexed slightly every few minutes—his only concession to discomfort. His hair, thick and iron-gray, was combed back in rigid, controlled waves, revealing a severe widow's peak that cast faint shadows over deep-set eyes. Those eyes—pale steel-blue—burned quietly beneath heavy brows, sharp and unsparing even in stillness. His face, pale and severe, was carved with lines of strain and sleeplessness, the years of command etched deep into his skin. Beneath the collar of his uniform, the faintest trace of veins stood out, blue and taut, like stress frozen into flesh.

The faint scent of oil and old parchment clung to him like an aura of inevitability.

But beneath that flawless exterior, pain throbbed quietly. His spine ached from hours of stillness. His temples pulsed with pressure, a dull iron weight settling deeper with every passing moment. Deep within, he felt the slow crawl of weariness pressing against resolve. Behind his unmoving features, the weight of fatigue loomed like an old enemy.

The banners above sagged. Crimson and gold turned ruddy and muted by soot and moisture, the symbols of order hanging like faded memories. Condensation clung to them like a funeral shroud. Everything here—stone, steel, silk—seemed caught in the slow collapse of purpose, strangled by history.

"...loss of control in Sectors 9 through 12. Increased graffiti activity. Suspected Free Steam cells possibly mobilizing..."

Valtor's expression remained carved from stone, yet a subtle tension pulled at the corners of his jaw. To untrained eyes, it would pass unnoticed. But the councilors—seated like uneasy vultures—knew better than to comment. They watched with careful detachment, masks of duty veiling private doubts.

Decay. Everywhere.

They surrounded him now, the so-called architects of stability. Men and women whose robes masked ambition as surely as the soot masked the city below. Their murmurs were like gnats, circling over dwindling carrion. Resource requests. Jurisdiction disputes. Petty concerns dressed up as necessity. Behind each politely phrased suggestion lurked selfish preservation.

Valtor inhaled deeply. The air tasted of rust, copper, and faint traces of stale oil. Familiar. Comforting, even. It was the perfume of Eastland's slow suffocation—and the fuel of his iron resolve. He could almost taste the dust of crumbling towers in each breath.

Let them whisper. Let them circle. He did not need their words to sense the rot seeping through the cracks. He could hear it in their hesitations, see it in their averted gazes.

Weakness bred where fear lived unchecked. If left alone, it grew—subtle, cancerous—until even the strongest beams would snap.

He would not allow it.

"Reinforce patrols near the manufactories," Valtor ordered, his words crisp, honed, lethal. They sliced through the room, leaving no space for argument. "Double the sweeps. Quietly. We do not reward them by acknowledging their nuisance."

Muted nods followed. Garments rustled like dry leaves. No voices rose against him.

They never did.

Not directly.

But ambition festered beneath layers of etiquette and calculated smiles. He could feel it coil in the spaces between words.

Valtor adjusted his cuffs with deliberate precision. The faint creak of leather broke the fragile quiet, followed by the subtle snap as his gloves tightened over pale knuckles.

Discipline was ritual. Ritual was survival. He lived by it, ruled by it, became it. Every small act of control—button, cuff, collar—was another brick mortared against chaos.

The councilors filed out in well-rehearsed order. Boots echoed sharply across the tiles, rhythmic and hollow. Their breath left faint clouds in the cold air, brief ghosts vanishing into nothingness as quickly as their resolve.

He remained.

Silence folded in on itself. No words, no distractions. Only the low, patient hum of steam trickling through iron veins hidden deep within the walls. The heartbeat of Eastland's dying glory.

Valtor closed his eyes briefly, fingers pressed to the side of his head where the ache sharpened, carving lines of pain through bone and thought.

The chamber sagged around him. Once a monument, now a mausoleum.

Cracks spidered unnoticed along the ironwood panels. Banners hung tattered, too proud to fall yet too faded to matter. Every stone seemed to sigh under the weight of years unkind.

He turned to the wide window overlooking Eastland.

It stretched beyond, choked in eternal twilight. Towers leaned like drunkards whispering conspiracies to one another. Steam hissed endlessly from broken pipes, curling into the sky as if begging release. Far below, winding alleys drowned in mist and silence, smothered beneath generations of soot.

And yet, through that gray expanse, something moved.

Free Steam. A rebellion made of whispers. Ghosts who still dared to dream.

Children.

Foolish children playing with sparks they couldn't control.

Valtor's lips twisted faintly, though not with humor. His reflection—half-lit and warped in the glass—regarded him coolly. The deep creases around his mouth and brow told of sleepless nights and decisions made with steady, unforgiving hands. His steel-blue eyes, hollow yet fierce, seemed to accuse him of every compromise carved into the city's bones.

They did not understand. They never would.

The city did not need freedom.

It needed chains.

And only one hand remained steady enough to hold them tight.

His thoughts strayed, reluctantly, toward Roland.

His son.

Polished. Pristine. Crafted for the stage and adored for the veneer. The Guild's darling. The propaganda machine's perfect prince.

But too smooth. Too soft.

Roland would inherit an empire he could not comprehend. Not truly. Not in his blood or his marrow. Not when he had never felt the bite of hard choices or carried the dead weight of inevitability on his back.

Valtor imagined him here—filling this chamber with false smiles and empty speeches, adored by the masses too blind to see they were worshiping weakness.

Loved.

The word tasted sour.

Valtor's fingers tightened instinctively against the cracked surface of his desk. The old leather gave faintly beneath his grip, whispering beneath skin worn raw from years of command.

No. Not yet. Not while he still stood.

He released the desk slowly, rolling his shoulders until the tension unwound by degrees. His bones popped faintly in the stillness.

Duty did not permit indulgence.

A knock shattered the quiet.

Valtor's spine straightened, his face smoothing instantly into practiced severity.

"Enter," he commanded, voice carrying with cold authority.

A junior officer entered briskly. Frost clung faintly to his boots. Saluting sharply, he recited his report:

"My lord. Eastern ruins patrols. Fresh graffiti. Arms caches uncovered in maintenance tunnels. No confrontations—yet."

That final word hung heavy. Pregnant with inevitability.

Valtor regarded the boy coolly. The younger man did not meet his gaze long. None ever did.

"Good," Valtor replied. Each syllable fell like a hammer tapping iron. "Let them think themselves clever. Let them build quietly."

His eyes gleamed faintly, sharp and unsparing.

"We will remind them who holds the flame."

The officer bowed swiftly and departed. The door hissed closed behind him with a finality that seemed absolute.

Valtor stood alone once more.

No witnesses.

No masks required.

Only then, when the echoes faded fully and the city fell silent again, did he relent.

Eyes closed, he let the exhaustion slip through cracks in the armor he wore so well. It wrapped around him softly, clinging like the ash falling endlessly beyond the windows.

Cold. Quiet.

He let it settle, like embers in a hearth slowly surrendering to the night.

And as the last of the council's voices faded into distant corridors, Valtor stood silent in the hollowed chamber, aware of a truth too poisonous to voice:

Eastland did not need heroes.
It needed monsters.

Chapter 7
Static Lines

---◆---

S plinters in the Fog

The mist hung thicker now, dense enough to bead on their clothes and cling like a second skin. It wound like wet gauze around every ruined corner, smothering sight and sound alike. Buildings melted into vague outlines. Pipes, broken carts, and shattered masonry softened until they felt like the fading bones of some ancient, hollow beast. Nothing here stood untouched — rot gnawed at stone, and even rust had begun to curl and peel as if trying to escape the slow death of Eastland.

The air was heavy and wet, carrying the bitter taste of iron and the sour reek of oil long spoiled. Every breath clung tight to the throat, sluggish and unwilling, coating tongues with soot. Beneath the quiet, something hummed — faint and deep, the heartbeat of a city too broken to die cleanly. Even the sky above, veiled entirely by low gray clouds and drifting particulate ash, pressed low enough to feel oppressive, barely fifty spans overhead in this district. Eastland did not breathe freely anymore.

Link crouched low behind a shattered wall, his gloved hand pressed against cracked stone slick with condensation. His dark hair clung in damp strands to his temples, plastered there by sweat and mist alike. Sharp cheekbones cast hollow shadows across his face beneath the low light. His gray-green eyes — tense, sharp, unblinking — scanned the shifting void ahead with the intensity of a hunter whose own blood beat too loudly in his ears. His breath came slow and controlled, misting faintly in the frigid air, each exhale thin and fragile against the oppressive stillness.

His legs burned from the crouch, knees pressed to cold stone that radiated moisture into his joints until every tendon ached. He ignored it. Pain was part of the city now. Every muscle throbbed beneath his worn, layered coat, now heavy with moisture. He shifted slightly, leather straps creaking faintly as he resettled the satchel on his back. Around them, distance was measured not in steps but in endurance—each block a battle, each alley a gauntlet.

A crooked steam tower wheezed faintly somewhere distant—at least thirty spans ahead, the skeletal structure barely visible in the haze. Its voice was thin and strained, leaking exhausted vapor into the air like a punctured lung. The sound was soft, yet it set Link's teeth on edge. Too exposed. Too open. He adjusted his crouch subtly, his fingers flexing against the damp wall. Cold, damp stone pressed against his knees, numbing them slowly.

Eastland pressed on them from every side. It wasn't just ruin. It wasn't passive. It whispered slow, broken promises—that hunger would find them, that collapse would outlast them. It felt personal. Like a predator learning patience.

Beside him, Eve shifted. The movement was small but loaded with tension. Her coat rasped faintly as she pulled it tighter against the damp, the motion tugging at her injured ankle. Strands of dirty blonde hair clung stubbornly to her blood-smeared cheek, curling around the cracked, dried wound at her temple like crimson threads. Her face was pinched with pain, pale against the grime and faint bruising. She didn't complain. She never did. But her jaw flexed tightly, her teeth grinding faintly every time her foot twisted wrong.

Her breaths came short and quick through parted lips, steaming faintly in the thick air. She glanced sideways at Link, silent, but the strain in her eyes was plain. She would keep moving. But only just.

They had no shelter. No friends. Only a satchel full of desperate hope—and Eastland's hollowed-out corpse standing against them.

Link adjusted the satchel. The Heartcoil inside pressed firmly against his spine. Not just metal—possibility. Or failure. It felt like a loaded gun with no safety, or a live ember smothered under thin cloth. Waiting to burn through.

Mist flowed like liquid around them, turning close sounds foreign. Drips became sharp notes. Groans stretched oddly, reluctant to fade. Link jerked his chin toward a crooked alley below, perhaps twenty spans down a cracked incline — just barely enough to vanish into if something came hunting.

"Move," he said, voice low and gravel-rough. Eve followed without argument, limping but determined. Each step was calculated, deliberate, and strained. The mist swallowed them hungrily, closing like fingers around fleeing prey.

Their boots scraped over wet stone and moss patches, every step sounding too loud. The ruined city seemed to listen. The alley twisted sharply, forcing them through tighter spaces. Above, rusted balconies sagged like broken ribs, their supports groaning faintly under invisible weight. Thin streams of water dripped steadily from cracked pipes, the droplets cold as needles where they splashed against their skin. Link's shoulders hunched instinctively as if expecting the world above to collapse at any moment.

Decay here felt alive. Moss. Rot. Rust. The city was eating itself. The scent of mold and wet iron clung thick in the air, mixing with the sour tang of old steam. Their breaths tasted of metal and mildew, burning faintly in their throats.

It had taken them nearly fifteen minutes to cross the first five blocks since the last hideaway. Distance meant nothing when every step felt watched.

The alley fed them into a wide courtyard—a battlefield after the dead had rotted away. Collapsed warehouses loomed, cracked like broken jaws. The silence here was deeper, heavier, as if memories themselves weighed down the air. At the courtyard's heart stood a dry, cracked fountain, its base scarred with graffiti:

VALTOR FEEDS. WE STARVE.

Eve stared hard at the words. Her lips pulled tight, her gloved fingers brushing briefly against the vandalized stone. Anger simmered beneath her stillness, deep and heavy. The words seemed alive in her eyes — not just defiant, but desperate.

The fog shifted, curling tighter, and a sudden clatter broke the quiet. Both dropped instantly behind a cracked support beam. Hearts hammered as they pressed into the cold stone. Link's pulse roared in his ears, loud and primal.

Metal scraped stone—quick and sharp.

A figure darted through the fog—small, fast. Not Guild. Not organized. A runner, vanishing before they could see more. The shadow left behind only unsettled silence and shallow footprints already softening in the mist.

Link's blade hand slid down, fingers brushing his coil blade. A choice hovered.

Stay still and risk being hunted. Or press forward.

He looked to Eve. Her narrowed eyes flashed with fierce resolve. Forward.

They advanced, weaving through skeletal manufactories. The ruins groaned softly around them—a slow, exhausted breath. Above, tram lines sagged like veins, heavy with rust and fraying cables. Steam hissed softly from ruptured valves. The city felt closer now. Watching. Holding its breath.

Their footsteps rang hollow on broken catwalks and scattered debris. Every pipe they passed whispered faintly, like the city itself gossiping to unseen ears.

The runner's trail ended at a collapsed boiler house about a hundred spans ahead, half-swallowed by rubble and overgrowth. Green light flickered faintly from within—sickly, unnatural. Not torchlight. Not floodlights. Something older, malfunctioning but stubborn. It bled faint shadows across the rubble, making every corner seem deeper, every jagged shape like a crouched figure waiting to lunge.

Eve frowned, unease tightening her features. Link paused, muscles tense. Hope and danger clawed at him equally, but instinct made the decision for him.

Inside, voices murmured:

"...move the last cache tonight..." "...if they find the coil—"

Link froze. Coil.

These weren't scavengers. They were survivors. Rebels. Or something worse.

Eve locked eyes with him—no fear, only readiness. Her free hand hovered near her weapon, knuckles pale beneath the grime.

Crawler treads groaned distantly, maybe five city blocks behind—close enough to feel in their bones. Time bled away. The faint vibration rolled through the stone beneath their feet like the city itself warning them.

Link hesitated. Old betrayals whispered. Faces of those who sold him out for bread. But Eve never hesitated. She never would.

Together, they stepped forward—into the broken mouth of ruin. Toward voices, fire, and whatever fragile future waited in the choking fog.

Chapter 8
Smoke and Thorn

The mist clung to the broken bones of the boiler house, slipping in through shattered vents and twisted girders. It oozed along rust-slick walls like something alive, wrapping around beams and machinery like a serpent too tired to strike but too stubborn to release its coil. Every inch of ruin sagged under the weight of it, bleeding rust and ash into air so thick it scraped the throat raw.

Link hesitated at the threshold. One boot rested on cracked stone slick with oil and condensation. The cold radiated up his leg like fingers closing slowly around bone. The next step forward felt heavier than the mist itself, as though Eastland was daring him to commit.

Beside him, Eve leaned against the warped frame. Her breath came in sharp bursts, her ribs bruised deep with sickly blotches of purple and red where the coat could not hide them. Her eyes — dark, sunken, but burning — stayed locked on the space ahead. Blood had dried at her temple, curling into her dirty blonde hair like a thin, clotted vine. She never winced, but Link saw the pain in the way she kept perfectly still, as though movement itself had become expensive.

They stood as shadows in the rotted belly of the ruin, half-swallowed by gloom. Inside, greenish light flickered unevenly—chemical torches strapped to cracked columns, flames coughing in defiance of the damp. Shapes moved around them — silhouettes that broke and reformed like memories, quick and quiet.

Not Guild.

Not patrols.

Survivors.

The air tasted of desperation. Unwashed bodies, boiled leather, rusted pipe smoke. It pressed in on their tongues like biting into copper, heavy as the long kilometers they'd crossed just to reach this fragile harbor. Link estimated at least twelve—maybe fifteen—kilometers since dusk, winding through alleys and industrial veins to get here. His legs felt every one of them, tendons burning and ankles raw inside damp boots.

A voice cracked through the haze.

"That's far enough."

Link froze mid-step, raising his hands. Eve mirrored him, but her weight shifted subtly. Her hand, gloved and steady, hovered near the hilt of her coil blade — ready, always ready.

A woman stepped from the haze, rifle already leveled. Captain Marrow. She wore the torn and soiled remains of a Guild officer's longcoat, insignia ripped free and replaced with crude stitches forming the cracked gear and thorned vine of Free Steam. Her hair, cropped brutally short, clung to her head in sweat and soot. A scar pulled her mouth into a permanent half-snarl, shadowing sharp cheekbones and hard, flint-colored eyes.

She did not lower her rifle.

"You're not from here," Marrow said flatly, voice scraping like gravel.

Link's reply came cool and even. "No one is anymore."

Her eyes flicked briefly to Eve — seeing the limp, the crusted blood, the stubborn stance of someone who had been running too long. Her expression tightened, unreadable.

"Carrying?" she asked sharply.

Link hesitated, tasting the weight of the truth.

"Scavenge," he offered carefully. "That's all."

The rifle remained up. "You scavenge into patrol zones? Into Free Steam ground?"

Tension cracked invisible in the air. Link's arms trembled faintly from holding still so long. Eve didn't move, but her fingers flexed minutely on the blade's grip.

"Saw your mark," Link said simply. "Seemed safer than freezing."

Marrow watched them for a long breath. Then, finally, she lowered the rifle a fraction.

"Maybe you're stupid. Or desperate." She gestured with her chin deeper inside. "Move. Slow."

They followed without hesitation.

Inside, the ruin bloomed into a nest of survival. Oil drums burned weakly, leaking thin warmth. Dozens of hollow-eyed survivors gathered close — gaunt faces, tangled hair, hands clutching weapons patched together from bone, scrap, and fury. Barricades ringed the camp, built from crawler carcasses, shattered conduit beams, and rusted steam pipes twisted into cruel spikes.

Hope here wore the shape of old, broken things.

Eve stumbled slightly as they passed a barricade, biting off a grunt of pain. No one asked if she was alright. In Eastland, pain wasn't remarkable.

Marrow crouched by the largest fire, cradling a battered tin cup. She stared at them, calculating like someone sorting scrap into useful or worthless piles.

"Names," she said simply.

"Link," he answered.

"Eve," she added after a moment.

"Captain Marrow. What's left of her." She tossed the title like it tasted sour.

She handed them the tin. The broth inside was barely more than warm water with bitter herbs, but it filled Link's mouth with something precious — warmth.

Across from them, a boy no older than ten clung to a broken coil-blade, cradling the dead weapon like a talisman. The blade's core was cracked and the coils sagged uselessly, yet the boy's grip never loosened. His ribs jutted painfully against his oversized shirt, eyes hollow but fierce. The blade was almost half his size, yet he clung tighter each time boots echoed outside the shelter walls.

Marrow's eyes stayed sharp. "Two days ago, you'd be dead already."

Link raised a brow. "What changed?"

Marrow's smirk was bitter. "Bullets don't grow back."

Movement stirred around them as the survivors worked. Rusted crates dragged. Rifles checked. Barricades reinforced. All too quiet. All too prepared.

Eve asked softly, "You're Free Steam?"

Marrow barked a joyless laugh. "What's left of it. Burned, gutted, and stepped on. Southpoint burned last. Three districts at once. Roland led it. Made it a show."

The name hit the camp like cold steel. Link felt Eve's posture stiffen as the words settled. Roland — the polished propaganda darling. The blade disguised as silk.

Marrow's voice darkened. "You want to stay, you work. You bleed."

Link met her stare without flinching. "We work."

No thanks. Just acceptance. The survivors shifted subtly, making space but offering no welcome.

Night fell like a stone dropped into a well — heavy, choking. Link and Eve rested close to a barrel fire, its embers barely fighting the cold. The Heartcoil pressed against his hip, humming faintly with its own secrets. He closed his eyes.

Not to hope. Just to endure.

✻✻✻

Eve shook him awake, urgency cutting through the fatigue.

"Guild patrol."

No alarms. No shouting. Just cold inevitability. Outside, crawler lights pierced the mist. Silently, Marrow gestured — split up. Confuse. Survive.

Without a word, Link and Eve followed those heading down into the maintenance tunnels — a graveyard of sleeping machines and cracked pipes. The descent was steep, easily fifty meters before leveling out — every step pressing tighter on their lungs as stale, moist air thickened.

Their footsteps whispered against old stone, guided only by rusted signs and fading graffiti:

VALTOR FEEDS.FREE STEAM RISES.

The enforcers passed like ghosts. Their glowing visors swept deadly light across the walls. Link held his breath until his chest screamed. Eve pressed against his back, breath ragged, heartbeat trembling through his coat.

When they were gone, Marrow did not slow. They kept moving, pushed by necessity until the tunnel widened at a collapsed pumping station. Gas lamps flickered against rusted machinery towering like dead titans. The ceiling here stretched at least ten meters above them, lost in mist and crisscrossing beams.

Marrow turned, face hard. "Tram gate's dead. No way through without it."

Her eyes locked on Link.

"You said you can work."

Link swallowed. The Heartcoil throbbed quietly against his ribs.

"We can."

No thanks. No ceremony.

Eastland did not give rewards.

Only the chance — if you earned it — to keep breathing.

Chapter 9
Gears in the Ash

T he mist choked Eastland's broken veins.

It slid through every crack and shattered duct, winding like greedy fingers through the city's rotted bones. No matter how deep they pushed, it followed—cold, wet, clinging. The farther they went, the more it felt alive. Not sentient — but hungry. It filled the empty spaces like breath held too long, pressing against their throats and lungs. Link swore it whispered, or maybe that was only his frayed nerves inventing voices in the cold.

Every step echoed like an accusation. His boots scraped against uneven stone, slipping at times on slime-slick patches where water had pooled and long ago turned stagnant. The satchel on his hip thudded with every stride, the Heartcoil inside feeling heavier than steel. He adjusted the strap for the hundredth time. It dug into his shoulder like iron teeth. Every movement tugged on already-sore muscles.

Behind him, Eve limped badly but refused to fall behind. Her breath came sharp and shallow, each inhale a hitch that betrayed how much pain lived beneath her stubborn mask. The wound beneath her coat had bled through everything — cloth, bandages, even her inner shirt — staining the fabric an angry black-red. Her long, dirty blonde hair hung limp around her face, matted to her temples with sweat and grime. She kept pushing. Kept moving.

Her eyes — fierce, rimmed with exhaustion and framed by dark shadows — stayed locked forward. Not pleading, not desperate. Determined. Quietly, furiously determined. When she caught Link glancing back at her, she didn't speak.

Instead, she shot him a look that told him plainly not to ask if she needed help. She would ask when it mattered. Until then, she'd carry the pain.

The survivors of the boiler house followed in grim procession, huddled shapes swallowed by mist and fear. They moved like broken shadows, ducking low, clutching what weapons they still had left. Marrow led them like a ghost of war, her scarred face tight, her coat drawn close to her body as if holding herself together through sheer will. She didn't flinch. She didn't slow. Every hand signal she gave was sharp and immediate — no hesitation, no wasted motion.

No one spoke. Not anymore.

Words were too heavy. Too risky. Even breathing felt like sacrilege against the oppressive silence.

The tram hub's gutted frame stretched around them, wide and dead and filled with the detritus of forgotten purpose. Rusted rails sliced through cracked concrete like arteries clogged by centuries of decay. Puddles of stagnant water shimmered with floating oil slicks, colors bending faintly where chemical runoff still bled from ancient piping. Crawler husks loomed above them, half-collapsed titans hanging from broken supports. Their twisted limbs sagged downward like rotted ribs, and their gutted chassis gaped wide, picked clean long ago.

Graffiti scarred the iron girders, drawn in soot, blood, and desperation: VALTOR FEEDS. WE BLEED. FREE STEAM NEVER DIES. BREATHE FIRE, NOT FEAR.

Eve passed one of the slogans, brushing her fingers over the faded words. The ash smudged her fingertips black. She didn't clean them. Didn't flinch. Her lips pressed together slightly — tight, but not cruel. She carried something old in her silence. Not hope — hope had long fled Eastland's bones — but memory. The weight of those who came before and who were no longer there to speak for themselves.

"Almost through," Link whispered — more to himself than to anyone else. His voice felt small in the vastness of the ruins.

They pushed deeper. The walls narrowed, and the oppressive weight of the mist thickened. Link felt his gut twist tighter with every footstep. Something felt wrong. Too quiet. Too still. The city around them wasn't simply dead — it was watching.

Being herded. He couldn't shake the idea. The Guild didn't move like animals. They moved like predators. They let prey exhaust themselves before tightening the noose.

Marrow gave another signal — up. A spiraling stairwell loomed ahead, twisting sharply through fractured stone. Its steps were broken and slick with condensation, carved by years of rot and negligence.

One by one, they began to climb.

Marrow went first, movements sharp and deliberate. The survivors followed, slower, more uncertain. Eve moved stiffly, her limp worsening, each step sending a tremor up her body. Link stayed directly behind her, one hand hovering near her back in case she slipped.

At the halfway point, she faltered. Her foot missed the step, and she staggered, nearly pitching backward. Link caught her immediately, his grip strong and steady as he braced her weight.

"I'm fine," she hissed, though the pain cracked through her voice. Still, she leaned against him for half a heartbeat longer than necessary before pushing forward again.

Link stayed closer after that.

They emerged into another maintenance corridor — narrow, slick, and barely lit by flickering bulbs. The walls sweat moisture, leaking from overhead valves that groaned and whispered softly. Every footstep sent echoes chasing down the tunnel ahead, bouncing back distorted and strange.

The low hum returned — not mechanical exactly, but rhythmic, like the city itself was breathing. Link knew better.

Crawler patrol.

Marrow motioned sharply. Instantly, they flattened against the walls, weapons drawn tight to their chests. The tension in the air thickened like steam under pressure. Link's skin crawled as the distant thump of heavy treads grew louder.

Moments later, they passed.

Five Guild enforcers. Their exo-frames gleamed faintly beneath the emergency lights, visors dark and cold. Rifles swept the mist lazily but with deadly purpose. Their boots hit the floor with mechanical precision, every movement coldly rehearsed. Machines in human skin.

No one dared move until they passed fully out of sight.

Only then did Marrow give the signal again.

"Keep moving," she mouthed, and the survivors obeyed.

They pressed onward through the maze until they hit a collapsed service door. Half the wall had caved in, steel beams tangled like snapped struts. Marrow cursed softly.

Link didn't wait for orders. He dropped his satchel and began hauling rubble aside. The others joined quickly — even Eve, though her hands shook faintly as she worked. They worked quickly and in tense silence, shoving aside sharp-edged debris with raw palms. Blood mixed freely with grime.

Finally, after long minutes, they forced a narrow crawlspace through.

"Go," Marrow ordered.

They slipped through in single file. Link took up the rear, dragging Eve's limp body forward by the arm when she started to falter. She bit down on her lower lip hard enough to bleed, but she didn't complain.

Beyond was a freight corridor stretching into dark infinity.

Guild crates towered along the walls, their stamped seals cracked with age. Link's throat tightened as they passed untouched rations — supplies meant to outlast sieges left to rot while people starved above.

"This city eats its own," Eve muttered hoarsely as they passed. It was the first thing she'd said in nearly an hour.

Link didn't answer.

The survivors filed into a loading platform near the corridor's end. Marrow motioned for them to hunker down. They did so quickly, crouched low between crates and broken pallets.

Eve sagged heavily against the wall. Link dropped beside her and checked the satchel. The Heartcoil still sat heavy inside — dormant, dangerous, and necessary.

He rested his palm on it. He could feel the cold pulse beneath his fingertips. Still there. Still waiting.

It hadn't been meant for this. Not originally. It was just supposed to be a new kind of power source — something cleaner, something smaller. But like everything in Eastland, it got swallowed by what the world needed it to be. Still, part of him wondered — if they ever made it out, if the city ever breathed again — maybe it could be what it was meant to be after all.

A dull clang echoed from deeper within the ruins.

They all froze.

Then came another. Closer.

Marrow stood immediately. "Go. Now," she whispered harshly.

No questions. No hesitation.

Something heavy moved behind them. Something not Guild. Not human.

The clangs grew louder, uneven and broken — like a machine walking on shattered legs.

Eve's face went pale.

Link pulled her upright and half-carried her toward the narrow hatch Marrow had pointed to. The survivors scrambled through like rats fleeing a burning ship.

The tunnel beyond shrank further — tight, suffocating, alive with the wet stink of ancient rust and chemical decay. Pipes bled moisture onto their heads. The steam hissed with every heartbeat.

Behind them, the thing let out a sound like a scream — high and metallic, sharp enough to turn Link's spine to ice.

Whatever it was, it wasn't alive.

But it knew they were.

The survivors moved faster now, urgency replacing caution. They slipped and stumbled in the confined space, hands grabbing slick walls for balance.

Link stayed at the back, dragging Eve forward with him. Her teeth were clenched so tightly he could hear the grind of enamel. He held on like the tunnel itself might take her.

Ahead — faint light.

A shaft exit. Maybe salvation. Maybe death.

Link didn't care anymore.

Behind them, the thing howled again. Closer.

He squeezed Eve's hand tight and ran.

There were no words anymore.

Only forward.

Only away from the jaws of steel that followed.

Only toward what waited in the dark — teeth or freedom.

He didn't know.

None of them did.

But they ran anyway.

Because in Eastland, you either ran...

Or you died standing still.

Chapter 10
Ash Between the Cracks

T he tunnel narrowed until they were crawling on hands and knees.

Link grimaced as rusted piping tore at his coat, every movement sending knives of pain through his already bruised shoulder. The metal groaned faintly beneath him, each scrape feeling like a shout in the oppressive dark. Dust and grit clung to his sweat-slick face. His muscles trembled with effort as he dragged himself forward.

Behind him, Eve struggled along quietly, her breathing ragged and uneven. Her ribs still bled sluggishly beneath the crude wrappings they had hastily tied hours ago. Dark stains marked her coat, spreading wider with every painful inch she forced herself to move. Her long, dirty blonde hair hung in wet clumps against her cheek and neck, clinging to her skin like spider silk. She pushed onward anyway, jaw clenched so tight her teeth ached.

The others followed in grim silence, shadows half-swallowed by the mist. None complained. None spoke. They were past the point where words mattered. Each dragged themselves forward on raw instinct, driven not by hope but by the dull, hollow fear that stopping meant death.

Marrow led them, hunched low, rifle strapped tightly across her scarred back. The scarred woman moved like she'd done this a hundred times — each movement calculated, steady, slicing through hesitation the way her blade sliced through enemies when necessary. She offered no encouragement. Survival was encouragement enough.

The shaft twisted and curved downward sharply, the walls slick with condensation and oily runoff from decades-old leaks. The deeper they crawled, the thicker the air became. Rust and decay seeped from every surface. Pipes groaned softly, bleeding steam from unseen wounds. The air burned faintly in Link's throat.

Somewhere behind them — far behind now — the thing still hunted. Even when its shrieks had faded, its presence lingered. They could feel it. Like sickness, like hunger. Like the air itself had turned against them.

It didn't need to be loud anymore. They knew it would come eventually.

Finally, they spilled clumsily into a collapsed service junction. The chamber yawned wide but broken, half-destroyed by old shellfire. Concrete and iron were melted together in jagged formations, like bones fused and crushed beneath impossible pressure. Half the ceiling had caved in years ago, leaving them in a space more grave than shelter.

The survivors fanned out slowly. Some coughed violently, choking on the sickly chemical stink hanging in the air. Others simply sat or slumped where they stopped, hands shaking from exhaustion.

A single emergency beacon flickered weakly overhead — its cracked casing spitting sick light through the gloom. The shadows it threw danced wildly, giving the broken shapes around them a lurching, feverish motion.

Marrow crouched down near a broken pipe and spread out a battered map. The parchment was stained, brittle, marked with dozens of desperate scrawls from hands that had likely long since gone cold.

"We're here," she muttered, jabbing a gloved finger at a point near the eastern manufactories. Her voice was quieter than usual — dulled by fatigue, or maybe resignation.

"Nearest Free Steam node is about two miles from here," she continued. "If the rails still hold."

A bitter groan passed through the group. Two miles might as well have been two continents. Especially for those carrying wounds and for those like Eve, who now leaned back weakly against a slab of twisted conduit. Her face had gone pale under the grime.

Link knelt beside her quickly.

"You're bleeding through again," he muttered urgently, reaching for the wrappings that clung damply to her side.

Eve smiled faintly, though her lips barely moved."Better out than in."Her voice rasped. The words were light, but the weight behind them was heavy.

He shook his head. No words could make this less brutal than it was. She was fading, slowly.

Marrow straightened and pointed at another route on the map — a rough line that spiraled deeper into the maze of tunnels."Maintenance lines," she said. "Buried deep. Hidden. Adds distance... but safer than rail crossings under crawler patrol paths."

Link's eyes narrowed. He traced the route mentally. Longer, darker, harder. But safer.

Marrow read his hesitation and gave a single grim nod."Survival isn't about shortest. It's about not dying."

The group quickly divided without debate."Split into twos," Marrow or dered."Rails if you're fast. Sewers if you're bleeding."

There was no argument.Arguments belonged to people who still had choices.

Link immediately turned to Eve."Underground," he said simply.

Eve gave a tired, crooked smile."Home sweet home."

Before they could move, the tunnels trembled faintly.A sharp, metallic shriek tore through the distant dark.The thing.Hunting again.

Marrow's voice snapped through the tension."Move."

The groups split. The able-bodied sprinted for the rail tunnels, quickly vanishing into mist and ruin.Link, Eve, Marrow and the most injured dropped through rusted maintenance grates into the deeper earth.

The descent was sudden and cold.An iron ladder slick with grease and moss guided them down. Link gripped Eve tightly as she half-slid down beside him, breathing hard against his shoulder.

The bottom opened into sewer tunnels. Wide. Rotting. Half collapsed in places.The stink was immediate and choking.

Old mold. Rotting waste. Dead machines and dead men.

It didn't matter.It was shelter.Shelter was everything.

The group moved carefully now.Their boots sank into knee-high sludge, sucking at their ankles. Every step forward was met with resistance, both from the filth and from their screaming muscles.

Twice they were forced to backtrack — once at a collapsed pipe jammed tight with rubble, once at a flooded passage that reeked of chemical spills.

Each detour sapped more strength.

Ahead, the ceiling cracked sharply. Link reacted on instinct, shoving Eve forward just as a chunk of stone and rebar caved in. Dust and steam flooded the corridor behind them.

One of the wounded — Pett — wasn't fast enough.

The rubble pinned his leg cruelly, twisting it in a way bones shouldn't twist. He screamed — raw and high, breaking the silent resolve of the group.

Marrow was on him instantly. She dragged him free with ruthless efficiency just before more debris fell. His leg hung uselessly, ruined.

There were no words of comfort.

Two survivors immediately hoisted him between them without needing to be asked.

Eastland didn't give second chances.Neither did they.

They moved on.

Somewhere in the haze of exhaustion, Link's mind slipped.For just a heartbeat, he wasn't here.He was a child again, standing under clear skies in the market square. Watching his father haggle with a merchant over copper fittings. Smelling bread from nearby stalls.

A warm day.A safe day.

The memory crushed him as much as it comforted.

He shoved it down violently.This wasn't there.This wasn't then.

This was the sewers.This was survival.

Eve stumbled beside him again.Her knees buckled slightly before Link caught her, keeping her upright.

"I can't," she whispered."You will," he answered, not harshly, but as a command.

Her fingers gripped his sleeve tightly.She didn't argue.

Ahead, a faint whimper echoed.

A young girl — no more than fifteen — collapsed onto her hands and knees. Marrow reached her swiftly, yanking her upright by the collar with brutal efficiency.

"No second chances," she barked.The girl stumbled forward, half-carried now.

No pity.Pity got people killed.

They pressed on.The tunnels grew tighter, the ceiling lower. Pipes hissed softly in the gloom, bleeding pressure from places unseen. Rust and slime coated every surface. Steam clouded the air until vision became little more than shapes and colors.

Every step was a battle.Every breath tasted of iron and rot.

Finally — finally — they found an opening.

A cracked maintenance shaft led upward.Link helped Eve up first, his hands guiding her as she dragged herself toward the faint glow overhead.When he climbed after, the surface air hit him like knives.

It wasn't fresh. It wasn't clean.

But it was not the sewer.

They stood amidst twisted manufactories now — towers of black iron and skeletal gantries. Steam vents hissed, expelling poison into the stagnant sky. Guild banners hung in tatters, their once-proud symbols shredded by fire and wind.

The survivors gathered slowly, clustering near broken walls and half-buried crates.

Their breaths came hard. Their bodies sagged.But they were alive.

And that counted.

Link's eyes scanned ahead — past the rusted scaffolds and collapsed factories.

Beyond the ruin, against soot-streaked walls, symbols stood out in stark relief:

A cracked gear.Thorned vines wrapping tightly around it.

Free Steam.Still here.Still watching.

Still fighting.

Link felt Eve press weakly against his side as she stared too.

"Not gone," she murmured."Not yet."

And for the first time since the tunnels swallowed them whole, Link felt something loosen in his chest.

Maybe not hope.But something close.

Chapter 11
What Remains Beneath the Ash

The shelter creaked with every breath of the dying city. Water dripped from the collapsed stairwell — slow, rhythmic, like the ticking of a clock counting down toward oblivion.

Link sat against a cracked wall, motionless save for the restless shifting of his eyes. Eve lay beside him, curled weakly against his shoulder. She shivered beneath his coat, her body drenched in cold sweat though her skin burned with fever.

Her breathing came rough and shallow. Her dirty blonde hair clung to her face in wet strands, plastered across flushed cheeks and cracked lips. Link tightened the makeshift bandage on her arm again, hands steady despite the exhaustion dragging at every muscle. The cloth was damp—stained dark with blood and sweat. Not enough. Nothing was enough.

Still, he worked. Still, she breathed.

Outside the ruined office, Eastland pressed down. The mist clawed at every shattered wall and broken vent, pushing fingers of cold through the gaps. Beyond that: silence. Not peace. Never peace. Silence in Eastland meant waiting teeth.

Link forced himself up eventually, bones groaning with every movement. His legs ached. His shoulders burned. But survival didn't care how much it hurt. Su rvival was motion.

He scavenged what he could from the ruin. A rusted crowbar, pried loose from a shattered desk. A length of old chain coiled in a corner, links stiff with grime. A few pressure canisters still hissing faintly in forgotten corners — unstable, maybe useful if desperation called.

Near the entrance, he rigged another tripline — stripped wiring tied tight between broken furniture legs. Primitive. Sloppy. But it might slow something ugly for a heartbeat. And sometimes, a heartbeat was all that mattered.

When he returned, Eve stirred faintly in fevered sleep, her lips parting to whisper fragments of dreams. Link sat beside her again, spine pressed to cold stone, and listened to the ruin breathe.

The fight replayed in his mind. The automaton's claw. The metallic shriek as it died beneath falling wreckage. Eve crumpling in the dust, blood staining broken tiles.

He could still smell burnt oil on his sleeves. Still hear the silence that followed — heavier than screams. Still see the flicker of her pulse, fragile and thin beneath grime-covered skin.

A sound cut through his thoughts. Footsteps.

Measured. Controlled. Too steady to be anything but Guild.

Link's eyes narrowed. He eased Eve lower, covering her with his coat. She mumbled softly, but didn't wake.

He crept to the ruined window, peering through a crack in the rubble.

Guild soldiers. Gas masks. Iron-backed armor. Three of them, rifles slung low.

Worse — an automaton followed. Bent and broken, dragging a shattered leg. But its optics flickered hungrily as it swept side to side, scanning.

A scent tracker.

Link pressed flat against the wall, arm locked protectively around Eve. He counted slow, steady breaths as light from their lamps cut across the ruins — pale and hungry.

Closer. Closer still.

The automaton paused, head twitching. For a terrible second, Link thought it would turn toward them.

Then — mercifully — it moved on.

The sound of boots and gears faded slowly, folding back into the city's hollow lungs.

Only then did Link allow himself to breathe again.

Eve stirred weakly. "...gone?"

"For now," Link whispered back.

He didn't sleep the rest of the night.Not by choice.Necessity.

Every creak, every whisper, every gust of mist became a blade pressed against his throat. He stayed still. Watching. Listening. Counting every drip of water, every scuff of settling rubble.

Survival wasn't strength.It was endurance.It was staying awake when others couldn't.

Eventually, the fever broke.Eve shifted quietly in his arms, her breath soft and steady now.She clutched weakly at his sleeve, seeking warmth or reassurance.

He didn't pull away.

Somewhere beyond the ruin, a steam-whistle screamed thinly into the night. Shift change.The Guild's machine kept turning.Above them, orders were barked, crawlers hissed, and the city devoured another day.

But down here — in the cracks of that dead machine — two more ghosts still clung to life.

Pale gray light bled through broken windows when Link forced himself up again.His joints screamed as he stretched. Every bruise felt deeper. Every muscle, frayed.

He moved carefully, scouting the ruin.The upper floors were gone — shattered stairwells leading only to void.The ground level was barely intact.

He found it tucked away behind twisted girders and broken walls.A hatch.Old Guild-make. Reinforced. Sealed. Forgotten.

It took him hours to clear enough rubble to force it open.His hands tore open on sharp edges. His arms shook by the end.

But it opened.

Cold, stale air rushed up from the dark below.A tunnel.

Hidden. Intact. Dry.

Better than nothing.

When he returned to Eve, she was asleep again — shallow but steady.

Link knelt carefully and lifted her into his arms.

Her eyes cracked open faintly as he moved. "Where—?"

"Somewhere safer," he murmured.

She didn't argue. Her head fell against his chest as he carried her out of the ruin.

Down broken hallways.Over splintered tiles and collapsed beams.Through dust and dying echoes.

He carried her to the hatch, slung her carefully over his shoulder, and lowered them into the earth.

The dark swallowed them whole.

Above, Eastland whispered.

Mist rolled through the skeletal towers.Ash fell like slow, bitter snow.Footsteps faded.Hope, thin and brittle, dissolved into soot.

But beneath the surface — in the cracks between ruin and rust — two shapes pressed onward.

Still breathing.Still stubborn.Still alive.

In Eastland, that alone was defiance.

Chapter 12
When the Fog Burns Back

The sun never came.

Not truly. Not the way it was supposed to.

What passed for morning in Eastland was only a slightly brighter shade of decay.Gray on gray. The color of dust and memory.It seeped through broken roof beams and fractured ductwork like the breath of a corpse, washing over everything in cold, sticky layers.

Above them, the sky churned in silence. Not clouds. Not smoke.Ash.

The mist was heavier today, thicker than the night before, and colder in a way that went beyond simple temperature.It pressed down.It coiled and clung and whispered against exposed skin with greedy softness.

As though it had weight.As though it remembered.

Link crouched low in the dark, his back and knees stiff from too many hours without rest.The metal floor beneath him radiated chill like a dead thing. Every joint screamed quietly in protest when he shifted his weight, but he ignored them all.His attention was on Eve. Always on Eve now.

She lay curled beside him, head resting lightly against his shoulder.Her breath came shallow and uneven, ghosting out in faint ribbons that dissolved instantly into the mist.Her face had gone pale — pale enough that the grime and ash that clung to her cheeks seemed almost like bruises.Her lips were tight, cracked in places, pressed thin as she battled the pain in silence.

The makeshift bandage wound around her side — a strip of his own coat, torn hastily in the tunnels — was soaked dark.Not fresh. Not anymore.But it hadn't stopped.

Link swallowed against the rising lump in his throat.

She hadn't complained. Not even once.Not through the climb.No t through the crawl.Not even when her legs trembled so violently earlier that he was sure she'd collapse right there in the debris.

That frightened him more than any bleeding wound ever could.

People who were winning could afford to cry out.People who still had fight left could curse or scream or push back.

But Eve — Eve only leaned quietly against him, teeth grinding together as though clamping down on weakness itself.Her silence made the danger sharp and clear.She was slipping.And they had very little left to give.

Link adjusted her bandage again with slow, deliberate care.His fingers were stiff — blood circulation lost to the cold and to how tightly he gripped the edge of control.Still, he worked with focus, tightening the fabric to stem what little bleeding he could, mindful not to pull so hard it became agony.

Eve's eyes fluttered. Barely open. Barely there.

Still, when they met his, she smiled faintly.Just enough to tell him she was aware.

"Better out than in," she whispered, her voice little more than a brittle ghost of sound.

Link forced a smile back, but it didn't reach his eyes.

He didn't answer her.Not because he couldn't.But because words wouldn't help.

Instead, he leaned back, pulling her gently with him, tucking her more securely under his half-shredded coat.The only warmth they had left was stolen from each other.

The mist pressed close.Heavy. Slow. Watching.

Somewhere deeper in the ruins, beyond the skeletal walls and splintered beams, Eastland groaned.

The sound rolled through the ducts and broken floors like the snarl of a dying god.Metal grinding against metal.Pipes rattling with loose pressure.Supports shifting under unseen strain.

Link's pulse jumped.

That sound wasn't distant.The city didn't just sigh.That was motion.

Something was moving beneath them.Or worse — something hunting.

He listened, motionless, for what felt like hours in the space of mere minutes .The tension wound tighter until even his breathing slowed to nothing.

No follow-up sound came.Not yet.

But they both knew it would.

"We need to move," he murmured softly into Eve's hair, his voice swallowed instantly by the ruin's oppressive quiet.

Eve nodded slowly, her eyes heavy and reluctant, but resolute.No protest.No argument.Just quiet resolve.

Together, they pushed upright.Every motion was work.

Eve leaned heavily on Link as they staggered forward into the depths of the foundry.Her steps were uneven, dragging slightly.Each footfall left faint scuffs in the ash, which quickly blurred away under the restless shifting of the mist.Like Eastland itself couldn't stand to remember their passing.

The interior was worse than the outside.

Twisted conveyors formed skeletal arches overhead.Enormous vats sat tilted and burst open, bleeding rust in long, streaking patterns down cracked ceramic linings.Once, molten iron had flowed freely through here — hot enough to burn men to cinders in seconds.Now, only cold remained.Cold and silence.

The gantry leading to the upper floor sagged dangerously ahead.It was the only path left.

Climbing it felt like asking death for permission to proceed.

The twisted incline groaned underfoot.Eve bit down against a sharp cry as her wounded side flared.Link helped her again, his grip steady, but his heart sinking lower with every step.

At the top, they froze.Voices.

Harsh, clipped.Guild.

"Trail ends here.""Eyes sharp. They're bleeding. They won't have gone far."

The words hit Link harder than gunfire.Eve stiffened, her breath catching.

He shoved them both low, tucking behind melted support beams.His mind raced, already calculating.No exits. No cover.A single narrow path forward, and now enemies above and below.

Footsteps echoed.Louder. Closer.The automaton's metal gait was unmistakable.

Link knew they were cornered.And cornered people had only two choices.

Wait to be crushed.Or make something out of nothing.

His eyes flicked over the ruin, scavenging options in seconds.

Rusty hooks.Snapped chains.A length of copper wire.A sagging crossbeam.

Nothing designed for killing.But desperation wasn't picky.

He moved fast and silent, rigging a crude trap even as his pulse pounded like a war drum.No elegance. No guarantee.Just the hope of chaos.

The enemy arrived just as he finished.

The trap worked — barely.

The first soldier fell.The second hesitated.

That was enough.

Link burst from cover, coil spike slamming into the exposed knee vent of the automaton.Steam shrieked as the machine faltered.He didn't stop.A vent fell loose and crushed the third soldier.The others screamed, disoriented.

Link ducked and swung, each movement reckless and ugly — nothing but instinct and survival driving him.He killed fast, without grace, without thought.

Silence followed.The dead didn't shout.The steam vent hissed softly, as if mocking the brief violence.

Link stood there, panting, staring down at the mess they'd made.His knuckles burned.His muscles shook from effort and terror.

Behind him, Eve's voice broke through the thick haze.

"Link...?"

He turned fast.

She was upright, pale and exhausted, but alive.Her dirty blonde hair clung to her cheeks, and her eyes gleamed faintly despite the pain.

He crossed the ruined space to her in three quick strides.

"You good?"

Eve gave him a lopsided smile — tired but stubborn."Better than them," she whispered.

Link exhaled hard, and for a second, relief made his legs weak.

Together, they limped forward into the fog-choked city once more.

Not heroes.Not victors.

Just survivors.

Because survival here wasn't about winning.

It was about stealing moments.Stacking them together.Minute by fragile minute.

Until maybe — just maybe — they could carve out something more than this broken existence.

But first, they needed another breath.And Eastland... Eastland was always stingy with those.

Chapter 13
The Bones Beneath

The sky over Eastland soured into deeper shades of gray, bruising with dusk as they crossed into the southern ruins. The light faded not into night, but into something heavier — as if the city itself exhaled ash and swallowed the sun whole. Above, skeletal towers loomed. Once proud steel and ferrocrete monoliths, now reduced to ragged spines that jutted skyward like the ribs of something long dead and forgotten. Jagged girders speared empty air where windows had long since shattered. Every gust of wind made them moan quietly, hollow songs lost to rust and erosion.

Underfoot, the streets became worse. What had once been industrial avenues were now flooded ravines, where oily black water sat stagnant between piles of broken concrete and collapsed roadways. The slick surface rippled only slightly as they passed — disturbed by falling debris or the occasional ripple of unseen vermin below. Rats, maybe. Or worse. Mist crawled thick and slow along these lower places, gathering like hungry tendrils against their ankles and curling up through broken drains. It clung to everything — coats, skin, weapons. It turned every breath into a damp, metallic drag. Every inhale tasted faintly of iron filings and rot.

Link shifted his grip on Eve, steadying her. She leaned into him without argument now, her body betraying its limits. Each of her steps dragged slightly, and though her lips were set in a hard line, sweat darkened the edges of her collar and soaked strands of her dirty blonde hair to her neck and temples. Her pride kept her silent, but Link could feel the tremors beneath her skin. Not weakness. Not yet. But close.

Neither of them spoke. Words, here, would only be wasted breath and draw more attention than comfort.

The further they pressed into the city's dying heart, the worse the ruins became. Structures slumped against each other like drunken giants, leaning heavily on fractured beams and one another for support. Street signs lay broken in gutters. Bridges sagged from half-collapsed anchor points, their cracked tiles dangling precariously like rotten teeth ready to fall.

Crawler tracks scarred the old roadways — gouges carved deep into stone, now filled with stagnant runoff and flecked with sharp bits of twisted rebar and spent casings. Everything felt heavy, as if Eastland itself pressed down here with intent.

High above, sagging tramlines stretched across the skyline like snapped veins. Their cables frayed and drooping, swaying gently with the stale wind. Every so often, they knocked together — faint metallic chimes echoing through the gloom, soft but ominous.

Link caught sight of movement — fleeting shapes far overhead. Probably Guild scout drones, too distant to identify, too high to care about ghosts crawling through the gutters. And they were ghosts, here. Small, slow, vulnerable.

A splash caught his attention. He looked down. A chunk of broken ferrocrete, displaced by his boot, had fallen into one of the oily puddles. Ripples spread outward, distorting the reflection of the tramlines above into jagged waves. He stared for half a second too long, unsettled by how little light remained.

Their pace slowed again as Eve's legs gave a slight buckle. She hissed softly, grabbing the rusted handrail of a collapsed stairway they were passing.

"You sure about this?" she asked at last, her voice hoarse and dry like parchment rubbed against stone.

Link didn't waste time thinking. His jaw clenched as he adjusted the weight of the Heartcoil on his back and said only: "No."

The alternative wasn't worth speaking aloud.

He found the entrance halfway down the stairwell — a maintenance shaft, wide enough for small crawlers and long-abandoned service carts. Half-buried now under rubble and rusted piping, only the faint outline of the hatch remained visible beneath flaking paint and smeared soot.

Eve leaned on the wall nearby, catching her breath. Her breath steamed faintly in the cold.

"This is it," Link muttered, mostly to himself.

The shaft yawned below them, breathing out stale, cold air. It smelled of trapped steam and ancient rust, clean compared to Eastland's surface rot but sharper — invasive in its own way.

Without hesitation, he slipped inside. The steel rungs groaned faintly under his weight as he descended slowly, carefully. Every clank of boot against metal seemed deafening in the tight confines. The walls wept with condensation, thin streams tracing old grime patterns down to meet the stagnant pool collecting at the bottom.

When he reached the floor, it splashed faintly under his feet — ankle deep, cold enough to bite through his boots and numb his toes instantly.

Eve followed moments later, slower, and Link steadied her as she stepped off the final rung. She sagged slightly in his grip, letting her forehead rest against his shoulder for the briefest second before pulling herself upright.

Ahead, the tunnel stretched forward, illuminated only by a dying pressure lantern bolted crookedly to a collapsed duct. The light it cast was sickly yellow, flickering weakly as though struggling to hold back the gloom pressing in from every side.

Pipes lined the walls like ribs in an iron lung, hissing quietly from hairline fractures. The ground beneath them was littered with scrap — broken gears, torn wiring, and old service panels scattered in chaotic disarray.

One of the engineers ran a hand along a rusted pipe. "Still warm," he muttered, almost with reverence. "This line used to heat half the south ring."Link didn't respond. But part of him wondered — if the bones still remembered heat, maybe the heart could remember light.

Link spotted it immediately. Footprints. Fresh. Small boots, quick strides, heading deeper.

"Not Guild," he muttered. Too light. Too fast.

His grip on the coil knife tightened instinctively anyway.

A shadow darted ahead. And then — a voice.

"You're not Guild."

High, young, but sharp. Intent.

A girl stepped out from behind a stacked pile of rusted steam fittings. She held a steam pistol with both hands, the weapon slightly shaking, though her jaw was set firm. She couldn't have been more than twelve. Her hair was cropped short, uneven, and her jacket hung off her thin frame in patchwork tatters.

The bruising across her cheek and temple told a story all its own. Survival, not luck.

"You're not Guild," she said again, eyes narrowing.

Link raised his hands slowly. Eve did the same, though her arm trembled with fatigue.

"No," Link said calmly.

The girl glanced at Eve, taking in the blood-soaked wrappings around her ribs.

"Guild doesn't bleed for each other," she said flatly. "You do."

Without another word, she lowered her weapon and jerked her head down the tunnel. "Follow."

And so they did.

The passages wound tighter. Crude barricades appeared — broken crawler frames positioned as makeshift defenses, tripwires rigged to fire old coil charges or drop jagged plates from ceiling rails. Children with scavenged rifles stood guard, barely old enough to remember anything but war.

They weren't hiding. They were preparing.

Signs of desperate existence saturated everything. Beds rolled out of scrap and tarp. Cookfires burning in corners, their smoke barely venting through cracked exhaust fans. Workstations rigged with salvaged tools and stripped Guild equipment.

Free Steam wasn't gone. It had simply gone underground.

The girl finally stopped before a reinforced door, massive and scarred with blast marks. A sentry stood nearby — a grizzled man with thick arms and patchwork armor, his rifle cobbled from spare barrels and scrapstock.

"Names," he demanded, voice flat and unreadable.

"No names," Eve whispered harshly, leaning heavily against Link. "Not yet."

The man hesitated only a moment before nodding slowly. "They bleed," the girl confirmed, stepping aside.

With that, the bulkhead screeched open.

What lay beyond stole Link's breath. A cavernous expanse, lit by hundreds of jury-rigged lanterns, stretched into the dark. Makeshift fires dotted the space, each surrounded by tired figures — young and old — hammering, repairing, or eating quietly. Children ran between workstations carrying parts. Guards stood watch atop piled scrap towers.

Banners stitched from torn flags and old clothing hung overhead, each painted with Free Steam's broken cog emblem — crowned with fire, choked with thorn.

This wasn't an army. It was something rawer.

A heartbeat. Alive. Battered. Relentless.

The girl looked back, eyes shining faintly beneath soot-streaked cheeks.

"Welcome to the bones beneath," she said.

Link felt the words hit him like a slow realization, heavy as the air around them.

Because this place didn't survive on speeches. Here, survival wasn't given. It was forged. One scar, one bolt, one act of defiance at a time.

Chapter 14
Gilded Chains

R oland stood before the mirror, still and perfect.

The gilded armor that clung to his frame was ceremonial—useless in combat, but breathtaking in its gleam. Engraved filigree ran along the shoulders and cuffs like curling flames, polished so precisely the gaslamps overhead shimmered twice: once in the air, once in him. Not a speck of dust dared cling to him. Every edge gleamed as though even the air itself feared his disapproval.

He smiled at himself.

But it was not a happy smile. It was hollow, practiced. The kind a painter might give a statue before dusting it off and calling it lifelike. The reflection looked the part—young lord of the Guild, handsome, composed, every lock of golden hair sculpted into place with ruthless precision. A warborn savior, they whispered in the upper towers. The face that would inherit the empire carved from soot and steam.

He tilted slightly, examining the angle of his jaw, turning just enough to admire his side profile. No blemishes. No flaws. Not even fatigue in his eyes, though he hadn't slept well in days. Perfection, crafted and curated.

Only control.

Until the knock.

A sharp, clipped rap at the door—two precise taps, timed like clockwork. Yet still, it broke the stillness. His eyes twitched slightly, annoyance surfacing just beneath the surface. He didn't look up.

"Speak," he said, coldly watching his own lips form the word.

The heavy oak door swung open on near-silent hinges. A steward in pressed dark cloth entered with deliberate haste, his polished boots faintly scuffing against the marble. He carried a brass-tipped scroll and a thin stack of trembling papers, cradled like fragile glass.

"Lord Roland," the steward began, voice thin with caution, "the patrols report continued resistance in the eastern corridors. Graffiti has returned — Free Steam's mark. They say it was scrawled boldly over your father's banner."

The boy's voice wavered noticeably at the word *father*. That word always lingered too long in these halls.

Roland turned his head then, deliberately slow. The air seemed to tighten as he pivoted, a single hand adjusting his cuffs as though the report itself were nothing more than lint on his sleeve.

"You mean to say," he said, voice silk-wrapped steel, "that the rats have defaced my crest. Again."

The steward's eyes flicked down nervously, throat bobbing. "Yes, my lord."

The silence that followed pressed down like the weight of a held breath. Even the gaslamps seemed quieter.

Roland moved. Not quickly, not with rage—just precise and steady. His steps echoed faintly on the polished floor as he crossed the chamber.He took the scroll smoothly, not sparing the words a single glance. The script mattered less than the insult it described.

His smile returned—colder now. Sharpened. He ran his thumb idly over the scroll's brass tip, as though testing a blade's edge.

"Dispatch the crawler units," he said softly. "Use the Flameborn engines. If they resist, burn the tunnels. If they flee, collapse the exits."

A bead of sweat rolled down the steward's temple. "But my lord—civilians—"

Roland's hand flashed. Fast. Precise.

The back of his gloved palm struck the steward's mouth with a flat, cracking *smack* that echoed sharply off the chamber walls.The boy dropped, a muffled cry slipping from bloodied lips as he crumpled sideways onto the marble like discarded cloth. The papers scattered, fanning across the floor in a brittle whisper.

Roland didn't glance down.

"You mistake me," he said calmly, almost conversationally, "for someone patient. Or weak."

The words hung in the room, heavy and unmoving. The steward, lips split and bleeding, scrambled silently to gather himself, eyes lowered and breath shaky.

Roland turned back to the mirror. His reflection awaited—unmoved, unblemished. As if the violence had not occurred at all.

"They think we are soft," he murmured to himself, fingertips trailing lightly across the glass. It felt cool, smooth, obedient beneath his skin. "They think this city belongs to them. That they can carve it from my father's spine and build their kingdom on the bones."

He leaned in closer. His breath fogged faintly across the glass, marring perfection for half a heartbeat.

"I will gild every chain they throw at me," he whispered, his lips curving faintly, "and make them kiss it."

Behind him, the steward had risen, wiping blood hastily from his chin, clutching the fallen scroll to his chest. He dared not speak.

Roland did not care. The servant might as well have been part of the wallpaper now—an object, not a presence.

He pivoted crisply, cloak fluttering faintly with the motion, and strode from the chamber without hesitation.

In the hall beyond, servants and minor officers parted instinctively as he passed, their faces kept low. None dared to meet his eyes. Some pressed to the walls, others faded into alcoves, all whisper-thin in their attempts to avoid notice.

At the grand staircase, a hulking automaton stood sentinel—Roland's personal model. Polished to mirror perfection, its brass plating gleamed with careful maintenance. It bore his crest upon its chestplate: twin gilded hounds curled around a burning tower.

Roland paused before it, reaching out idly to trail his fingers across its cool metallic knuckles. The automaton hummed faintly in response, pressure engines flexing under gilded armor. The moment hung strangely intimate.

"Soon," Roland whispered, almost tenderly.

In his mind's eye, he saw it—armies of these metal titans, marching shoulder to shoulder down Free Steam's narrow alleys, gold and brass glinting in the ruin's gloom. Faces pressed against shattered windows, watching in horror as their rebellion drowned beneath a tide of shining inevitability.

"March them into the ruins," he murmured, more to himself now, "Let the smoke of their dreams stain the sky."

Memories twisted with fantasy as he walked. He saw again the scroll's words in his mind—Free Steam daubing slogans across his banners. Words like knives. Symbols like mockery. *Free Steam rises.* No. They would not rise. They would drown in molten metal and ash. He would bury them so deep not even memory would survive.

Descending into the lower halls, Roland entered the war chamber where the true machinery of power ground mercilessly on. The air was colder here, denser. Tacticians and officers hunched over sprawling maps, breath visible in the chill. They straightened sharply as Roland entered.

Dominating the center of the chamber sat the brass model of Eastland—blackened and scarred, yet still intricate. Tiny flags marked disputed districts. Whole sectors had been replaced with crude soot-streaked tiles—places too ruined to repair.

Roland approached it slowly. His polished boots echoed softly across the iron-tiled floor. He let the quiet linger.

Once, long ago, he had stood here—smaller, wide-eyed, his father's towering shadow stretched long and unyielding across the war table. He had listened intently as Valtor's voice barked orders and promises, spoken with ruthless conviction. *Strength first. Mercy later. Love never.*

Roland's jaw tightened faintly. That boy—the one desperate for a nod of approval—was gone. Ashes in the wind.

He set his gloved hand upon the brass city model, pressing his palm against it until the edges dug slightly into his skin. The metal sang faintly under the pressure. Cold. Unfeeling. Loyal.

"Prepare the automata for street sweeps," Roland ordered, his voice slicing clean through the murmurs. "Crush every mark, every rebel, every whisper."

He let his gaze sweep the council, daring them to flinch. Some bowed their heads quickly. Others, older and grayer, hesitated before following suit.

Roland's eyes gleamed faintly, catching the light like daggers."Free Steam believes they can rise from the ash," he said softly.He smiled. Not kindly.

"We'll bury them under gold."

The words sealed the room in iron certainty.

As the officers dispersed to their tasks, Roland remained still, staring down at the city model beneath his fingertips. His reflection—distorted in the tarnished brass—stared back up at him. Not his father. Not anymore.

Only him.

And the city would learn that name soon enough.

Chapter 15
Scars on the Ledger

T he chamber was silent, save for the ticking of the gyroscopic clock embedded in the far wall — a whispering cadence of time measured not in seconds, but in calculations.

Valtor sat alone at the obsidian desk, sleeves rolled to the elbow, eyes fixed on the scattering of field reports that covered the surface like a disassembled map of human failure. The room, deep beneath the Guild's central tower, was sealed by three layers of magnetic lock. No aides. No guards. Just him, the scent of old paper and heated copper, and the task at hand.

He turned the page with the same deliberate care he used to disarm explosives.

Collapse of District Four confirmed. Free Steam automaton sighted — unknown configuration. Heat bloom inconsistent with Guild cores. No retrieval. Scout unit decimated.

That was the fourth report to mention it.

A soft knock broke the silence.

Valtor didn't look up. "Enter."

The door creaked open. A Guild runner stepped in — soaked to the knees, uniform scorched at the sleeve, eyes sunken with fatigue. He held a sealed case in both hands like it might bite.

"Report from Eastland perimeter, sir," the runner said, voice too loud in the stillness. "Scout unit seven, partial survival."

Valtor gestured without turning. "Leave it. Go."

The runner hesitated — perhaps expecting questions. Or orders. Or thanks.

He got none.

The door shut again. Quiet. Efficient.

Valtor waited until the footsteps faded before opening the case. Inside: a battered folder, hand-penned sheets, two of them scorched at the edge. He unfolded the top report slowly, eyes catching on the lines that mattered.

"...automaton classified as non-standard. No visible exhaust. No valve cycling. Movement inconsistent with known steam pressure patterns. Core emission registered at low-frequency pulse — not heat-based. Origin undetermined."

"Designation overheard: 'Heartcoil.' Pilot identified by locals as 'Link.' Secondary field leader: 'Eve.' Names confirmed via multiple intercepts."

Valtor's finger hovered above the word Heartcoil.

Not steam.

Not fire.

Something else.

That mattered more than names. More than rebel positions. More than the Procession's collapse.

Because the Guild's empire wasn't just built on machines — it was built on scarcity. On coal burned in rationed piles, taxed by weight, by soot, by the air it fouled. Factories bled black smoke not because they had to — but because that smoke proved allegiance.

If Free Steam had found another way...

If the Heartcoil proved stable, replicable—

The Guild's economic supremacy would fracture. Their entire doctrine — control through consumption — would rot from the inside.

A machine that ran without them.

He stood, slow and cold, and stared at the schematic wall across from him — the glowing model of Eastland. At the center, a faint pulse. Too regular. Too quiet to be steam.

"Innovation," he said aloud, the word tasting like poison. "That's the real insurgency."

He walked back to the desk and circled the names in red wax — Link, Eve — not because he feared them, but because the world might learn them before he erased them.

He took out a fresh sheet, wrote two orders with surgical precision, then sealed them in black-laced tubes for priority delivery:

Directive 1: Expand internal tracing network. Flag all passive intercepts for the terms *Link*, *Eve*, and *Heartcoil*. Cross-reference with non-thermal energy signals, engineer-class anomalies, and sector-wide resonance fluctuations.

Directive 2: Deploy Sable unit to the Eastland perimeter. Observation only. No contact. If target identified, report. Do not engage.

The wax seals cooled fast. He pressed the brass bell. A different runner would collect them. No words exchanged.

He didn't sit again.

He simply stood there in the stillness, eyes on the circle of names — but thought only of what they'd built.

"Names don't concern me," he murmured. "But tools that shape them do."

Chapter 16
Echoes in the Undercity

The mist thickened as they pushed deeper, clinging to every surface like mold-fed breath.

It pressed against Link's skin, heavy and wet, worming into every seam of his coat. It coated his eyelashes, soaked into his hair, and crawled down the back of his neck like cold, invisible fingers. Even breathing felt like drawing sour water straight into his chest.

The tunnels beneath Eastland weren't just abandoned—they were *hollowed out*, devoured by rust and haunted by the echoes of a thousand forgotten machines. Drips echoed like ghost footsteps. Every groan of warped metal above and below felt too deliberate, too alive, like the exhale of some unseen, dying giant that resented every intruder in its carcass.

Link led the way, hand dragging against the wall for balance. The stone was slick beneath his palm, leaving his glove dark with grime. His boots pushed through stagnant water that rippled outward with each step—black and murky, knee-deep in places, clinging to their legs like heavy hands.

The smell hit harder down here.

Rot. Metal. Oil thickened with age. It was the scent of old blood that had long since dried and been replaced by rust. Decay sat in the air like a crouched beast, unblinking.

Above them—layers and layers above, past collapsed infrastructure and suffocating debris—the city still groaned faintly. Eastland lived, somewhere. But not here. This was its belly. Forgotten. Hungry.

Eve limped beside him, biting down on every flinch. She was silent—but that silence was sharp, like a blade too proud to bend. The bandage around her thigh had turned dark with blood and runoff. Infection had crept in, silent and cruel, leaving angry red trails up her leg like warning veins. Her breathing was shallow now, cut short by pain she refused to voice.

Link noticed. He noticed *too much*.

That was the danger of strong people, he thought grimly. They didn't cry out. They didn't ask. They just *carried it*—until they couldn't anymore.

He remembered someone else like that. Maybe his brother. Maybe a worker at the old mill who fell dead at the wheel one day without ever once asking for relief. The memory was vague, dulled by years of ash and war. But the lesson was sharp now.

Strong didn't mean invincible.

"We stop soon," Link muttered, his voice raw against the oppressive quiet.

Eve didn't argue. She just nodded once, too tired to pretend otherwise.

They pushed forward until the tunnel widened into what must have once been a switching yard—only now, it resembled a broken ribcage more than anything made by hands.

A domed chamber spread out, filled with rust-choked tracks submerged beneath a sick, gray-green slurry. Collapsed catwalks hung overhead like jagged ribs, barely attached, swaying faintly in the mist-heavy air.

In the center, a raised platform of cracked stone offered the only dry ground. They climbed toward it in slow, painful steps. Eve nearly collapsed twice before Link pulled her arm over his shoulder and hauled them both up together.

As soon as they reached the top, Eve let herself fall sideways onto the cold stone with a ragged groan. Her hands trembled visibly. The strength she wore like armor was fraying badly.

Link crouched beside her without a word. He pulled off his gloves and gently unwrapped her bandages.

The wound had worsened. The edges were angry, inflamed, with dark streaks running up toward her hip. Heat rolled off it in steady waves. Not just fever. *Fury.* The body's quiet scream beneath skin.

He wiped it clean as best he could with water from his flask—his jaw tight as Eve hissed softly, eyes squeezed shut. He didn't speak. There was no comfort here, only necessity.

She opened her eyes slowly when he finished, her voice hoarse but dry.

"Doesn't look good, does it?"

He didn't lie. "It's bad."

"Be honest," she pressed again, her lips curling faintly with grim humor.

"We've seen worse," he said.

She barked a short, brittle laugh. It was not joy. Just survival's bitter joke.

"Yeah. Just never on me."

Link said nothing.

Instead, he sat beside her and stretched his numb fingers. The cold had sunk deep. They tingled painfully as he flexed them open and closed again, trying to bring some sensation back.

Across the chamber, beyond the broken catwalks and churning puddles, the mist twisted with subtle malice. Drifted slow, lazy, like smoke waiting for breath to return. Occasionally, the groan of shifting metal echoed faintly—distant, but never gone.

Link shifted his satchel forward, hesitating for only a heartbeat before unwrapping the Heartcoil.

The device was warm in his hands—unreasonably warm. Faint coppery light traced the engraved conduits, pulsing steady and slow. Almost like it was breathing. Or listening.

The feeling unsettled him.

It was supposed to be a tool. A key. A dead thing meant only to power or destroy.

But it wasn't dead.

Not anymore.

Eve noticed his hesitation. Despite the pain, her curiosity cut through. Her voice, softer now:

"I dreamt about it last night."

Link looked at her sharply.

"The Heartcoil," she continued, her eyes half-lidded but distant. "I saw it lighting up the sky. A tower made of glass and steam. Everything clean. Everything... easy. People smiling. No ash."

Link stared down at the device in his hands.

"That's not how this ends," he muttered.

"No," Eve agreed quietly. "But maybe it should be."

A faint vibration ran through the floor—subtle, but real.

Link stiffened. He packed the Heartcoil quickly, strapping it tight. Danger never gave speeches. It just *arrived*.

A rumble. Louder now. Steady.

He moved fast to the platform's edge, motioning Eve to stay low.

In the far tunnel, something huge emerged from the gloom.

A crawler—bulky, heavily modified, armor pitted with burns and scavenged plating welded at odd angles. Steam hissed violently from cracked valves as it trundled forward, its movements labored but deliberate.

No Guild markings.

Instead—just a faded sigil half-obscured on its flank.

A broken cog clenched in a fist.

Free Steam.

Link's muscles coiled tight. He pulled Eve deeper into the shadows as the crawler rumbled by, its massive treads sending dirty water churning into black whirlpools.

Through gaps in the hull, he glimpsed shapes inside. Faces. Gaunt. Armed. Human.

They didn't stop.

Didn't slow.

Didn't see them.

When the noise finally faded into the belly of Eastland, Link eased out of hiding and exhaled.

"We're not alone down here," he whispered.

Eve pushed upright, her voice fraying with both exhaustion and something harder.

"Good," she rasped. "Maybe we'll finally meet someone who hates the Guild more than we do."

They moved again.

This time following the crawler's trail deeper into the tunnel network—where fresh scorch marks marred the walls. Bullet casings floated in oily puddles. Craters chewed through concrete like gnawed bones.

Signs of fighting. And not long ago.

Halfway down the route, they passed the remains of a mangled automaton. Its body twisted and torn apart, joints snapped like twigs. The Guild's faceplate had been painted over crudely—mocking eyes and a lolling tongue drawn in black oil.

A warning.

Eve stumbled more frequently now. Her weight grew heavier, sagging against Link until every step was a burden they both shared. He didn't complain.

Eventually, they found refuge—an alcove cracked into a collapsed wall.

He barricaded them inside with scavenged scrap and pipe lengths. Not secure. But safer than open ground.

The space was tight, littered with old maintenance equipment. Control panels lined the walls, long dead and draped in spiderwebs thick with dust. Eve collapsed first, curling into herself as Link rummaged for anything useful.

He found little.

Cracked antiseptic bottle. Expired rations. Useless manuals faded beyond recognition.

Still—enough.

They ate mechanically, without ceremony. Every bite was a dry, dusty ritual—fuel, nothing more.

And when they finished, silence ruled.

Until Eve broke it softly, her voice barely audible:

"I wonder... has anyone ever made it out? Past all this?"

Link stared at the dead panels.

"If they did," he answered eventually, "they didn't come back for us."

Eve's eyes darkened faintly.

"No," she said. "They forgot. People always forget the ones they leave behind."

Link didn't argue.

He couldn't.

Not when he could feel Eastland pressing in around them like an old, cruel god.

Outside, faint voices returned. Shapes in the mist. Not Guild. Not sure.

Link snuffed the light and watched through a crack. A figure passed—masked, scanning walls with a strange clicking device.

Not scavenger.

Not soldier.

Something else.

The tension wound tighter in his chest.

Eve whispered, barely audible in the dark.

"They're tracking."

Link nodded grimly.

"Maybe us."

"Maybe the Heartcoil," she said, eyes sharp despite the fever.

Link unwrapped the device again, studying its pulse. Faster now. Almost hungry.

"I don't think this thing is just a battery anymore," he admitted quietly. "It's listening. Maybe calling. Or being called."

Eve's face twisted.

"What the hell did you make?"

Link didn't answer.

He didn't know anymore.

Outside, something thudded. Distant, but deliberate.

Link tightened his hold on the Heartcoil, feeling Eve's hand brush faintly toward her knife, even half-conscious.

The darkness outside the maintenance room shifted again—breathing, watching, *waiting*.

Eastland never slept.

And tonight, it seemed... neither would they.

Chapter 17
Fractured Alliances

The tunnels birthed them into a hollow that felt like the lungs of the city. Above them, the broken vaults of the old depot stretched wide and high, ribbed girders cutting sharp diagonals through the fog-choked air. Strands of torn insulation and rusted wiring drooped like vines left to rot in the sunless dark, swaying faintly with each whisper of underground wind.

That wind tasted foul. Metallic and heavy with stagnant decay, it coated lips and tongues until even breath felt like swallowing old coins. Each inhale scoured Link's throat raw, the taste of dust and rust becoming indistinguishable from the ache of exhaustion.

He pushed forward through the mire regardless, one hand trailing the wall — knuckles brushing over old rail bolts half-submerged in wet corrosion. The grit caught beneath his nails as he steadied Eve through the waist-high puddles of slush and sludge that filled much of the broken thoroughfare.

The depot wasn't silent. It breathed.

Somewhere above them, metal groaned with the slow, lazy complaint of a corpse being disturbed. Chains rattled intermittently, shifting as unseen drafts tugged them from one direction to another. Every so often, a single drop of condensation plummeted from the ribbed ceiling, smashing into the water below with a sharp plip that echoed far too loudly in the dead space.

Eve stumbled, nearly losing her footing as her wounded leg gave out for a heartbeat. Her fingers dug into Link's shoulder, clutching tight. He felt the tremor there—not weakness, but desperation holding the body together long after common sense would have surrendered.

"Rest," Link muttered.

"No." Eve's voice came tight. Strained.

But even as she refused, her body leaned heavier against him, her cane dragging through the sludge behind her like a banner lowered in defeat.

Around them, broken crawler husks sat like butchered giants. One lay on its side, ribcage panels split open by old explosions, its innards stripped bare. Pipes jutted from it at sharp angles, tangled like snapped bones. A bird—gray-feathered and half-dead—nested in the hollow of its eye socket, watching silently as they passed.

Farther in, the walls bore the marks of violence layered upon neglect. Guild insignias scorched black. Propaganda posters sagging under moisture, slogans faded to ghosts. FREE STEAM LIVES, written bold and jagged across a sheet of torn bulkhead.

A hollow laugh clung to Link's throat. If it lived, it was quiet.

Eve glanced at the symbols too, her lips barely parting. Her face didn't soften. Her eyes remained cold, distant — trained toward every darkened archway and collapsed side tunnel. Trust didn't exist here.

When they reached the loading platform, Link knelt, studying the blood-stains hidden in shallow pools of brackish water. His gloved fingertips came away sticky.

"Recent," he murmured.

Eve said nothing. She merely scanned the angles—checking exits, counting hiding places. Her face had settled into something fierce and detached, the soldier beneath the fatigue rising up as instinct demanded.

Through the blasted-out doors, the world opened and shifted.

A forge city reborn beneath stone and rust.

The foundry floor hummed alive — a low thrumming underfoot that vibrated through Link's boots and rattled faintly in the joints of his teeth. The walls were stained black from decades of exhaust, and yet new fires had already carved fresh scars into them.

Floodlights sputtered overhead, uneven and lazy, casting jittering halos across moving figures. Everywhere was motion. Motion layered atop motion.

Rebels moved in dozens — some pushing crude handcarts stacked with scrap, others hauling broken automaton limbs slung across their shoulders like fallen comrades. A trio of men dragged heavy chains in loops across the floor, swearing softly in cadence as they secured crawler plating to an armored scaffold. Sparks burst overhead as welders crouched precariously along narrow beams, balancing on makeshift planks while torches hissed.

The noise was not uniform.

Children whispered as they sorted copper wiring into neat piles by the wall, eyes hollow and faces half-hidden beneath scarves too big for them. At a nearby forge, a woman with a scar running from scalp to cheek shouted rhythmically as she hammered, each strike of metal-on-metal sending clang! clang! clang! in a brutal heartbeat through the space.

Somewhere deeper, gears turned slowly—ka-thunk... ka-thunk.. . ka-thunk—marking the passage of something massive, unseen but very much alive, nested deeper into the guts of Free Steam's hidden domain.

Above them, layers of scaffolding crawled with shadowed figures stringing cabling and securing fresh sheet-metal barricades. Some carried rifles slung loosely on their backs, others balanced precarious crates of chemical fuel that sloshed dangerously with every step.

An old man with oil-streaked gloves barked orders in clipped bursts—his voice hoarse, cracking as he cursed in three different dialects when a scaffolding beam slipped sideways, catching on a stray boot.

Not far from him, a woman stood on a steel crate, clipboard in one hand, shouting assignments over the hiss of machinery. Her hair was graying but pulled into a clean braid, her coat patched but neatly mended.

"Section five needs protein packs, not filament scraps. And someone tell Reggie we don't forge with wishful thinking!"

A runner nodded and sprinted off.

Link watched her for a moment. She moved through the noise like she owned it — calm, direct, too sharp to argue with.

Eve noticed too. "Who's she?"

A nearby worker answered without looking up. "Vessa. Quartermaster. Doesn't fight, doesn't run. Keeps the whole west sector fed. They say she once out-rationed three Guild supply officers with half a shipment and a broken rail line."

Eve raised an eyebrow. "Council material."

Link didn't answer, but he silently agreed.

Link and Eve moved in tight. Link kept one hand always at the strap holding the Heartcoil close, feeling its warmth pulsing faintly through the canvas.

It throbbed differently here. Faster. More eager.

Eve's head tilted slightly, her ear turning toward the coil even as she limped.

"You feel that?" she muttered quietly.

Link only nodded. No need to say more.

By the time Cutter arrived, everything around them had narrowed in — movement slowing, gazes sharpening. Dozens of eyes cut toward the newcomers as they stood before Free Steam's commander. Conversations dulled, laughter faded. Even the children working along the upper rails paused. A ripple of silent tension spread through the forge floor.

Cutter moved like a boulder being shifted only when necessary. His armor groaned faintly with every step, the welded-on layers scraping audibly in the heavy air. Sparks cascaded nearby from a welder finishing an armored shoulder plate—each spark reflecting in the faint, wet shine of Cutter's breastplate.

His stare carved right through Link.

They spoke, briefly, sharply. Cutter's words clipped but carrying weight that resonated even above the growing hiss and hammering that marked the forge's eternal rhythm.

When Link showed the Heartcoil, something in Cutter's weathered face cracked — not in fear, but recognition.

He did not smile.

He simply nodded, as though acknowledging a grim inevitability.

"You brought it here," he said quietly, tone unreadable over the subtle crackle of welding torches overhead.

And that was all.

Later, as they sat in the scaffolding alcove where Cutter left them, the forge resumed its relentless grind around them — as though nothing, not even fate's arrival in the form of the Heartcoil, could interrupt work already in motion.

Above them, feet thudded softly over metal. To their right, men whispered in low voices, trading names and rumors of Guild advances. To their left, an older woman coughed violently as she stirred boiling leather scraps into a makeshift dye pot, her ragged breathing lost beneath the deeper roar of exhaust fans kicking on overhead.

Eve leaned her head back against the crate, eyes half-lidded, hand slowly curling and uncurling at her side. She was watching it all. Absorbing. Calculating. Her pain dulled but not absent — masked beneath the soldier's mask that war and loss had long since burned onto her face.

Link felt the coil still humming quietly at his side. More eager now. More alive.

Far above, beyond the cracked ceilings, Eastland churned unseen — heavy, patient, and waiting. Waiting for the moment when steam, ash, and rebellion would finally collide.

Chapter 18
Sparks in the Dark

The quarters Cutter gave them weren't more than a hollow carved into the wall behind a collapsed boiler vault, but it had a curtain, a flickering lamp, and enough floor space to stretch without weapons drawn. That alone made it luxury in Eastland.

The stone was cold beneath Link's boots as he entered, scraping faintly despite his cautious step. Above them, iron pipes throbbed with faint knocks — the heartbeat of steam running uneven through long-abandoned arteries. Every few seconds, the wall hissed softly, releasing pressure like a sleeping giant muttering in restless dreams.

Eve collapsed onto the wool mat. Her coat sagged over her frame, hiding little of the exhaustion radiating from every tendon. Her leg gave an involuntary twitch as she settled. A sharp, shallow hiss escaped her lips, more reflex than complaint, and she clenched her jaw tight enough that Link saw muscle jump along the edge of her face.

He knelt beside her, shifting carefully to avoid rattling the scattered tools and broken bits littering the floor. The air was heavy, dust mixed with old oil. When he uncorked the salvaged antiseptic bottle, the sharp bite of chemicals tore into the room like a slap. Eve turned her head slightly aside, eyes fluttering as she braced.

"It's going to sting," Link muttered, though both knew it wasn't a warning. He poured slowly. The liquid hissed faintly as it met raw skin. Eve stiffened, breath catching in her throat as her back arched briefly. One hand shot up, gripping the torn edge of her coat, knuckles white. She never made a sound.

"You're getting good at this," she managed after a long pause, breath shaky but words laced with a thin smile that didn't reach her eyes. Her lips trembled slightly as they shaped the syllables.

Link glanced at her, the corner of his mouth twitching in return but never quite forming a smile. He stripped another section from his shirt, running fingers along the frayed edge before dousing it. His shoulders shifted subtly, tight from hours of carrying her, fighting, running. The bones in his back cracked softly when he leaned forward again.

Outside the thin curtain, the foundry murmured without end. Not loud — but deep. Hammerfalls sounded dull and rhythmic, softened by stone and soot. Pipes shrieked in irregular pulses, like metal beasts waking and dying again in slow succession. Voices murmured constantly beneath it all, low and thick, like a dozen whispered arguments tangled together.

Eve's head tilted lazily toward the gap in the curtain. Her lashes hung heavy over half-lidded eyes, watching the flickers of shadow that passed like ghosts. A heavy boot clunked past, followed by the rasp of someone dragging a chain. Another figure — barely more than a silhouette — paused near the entrance, shifting weight from foot to foot before moving on with a faint grunt of effort. No one lingered.

Link finished binding the wound tight, his fingers brushing against her skin only briefly, but both of them flinched slightly at the closeness. His fingertips came away sticky and warm despite the cold.

He leaned back, spine grinding softly against the uneven wall. His shoulders sagged as he pressed his palms into the cracked stone floor, feeling its coolness leech up through his skin. Above them, dust sifted silently from an unseen vent, drifting in faint spirals through the hot lamplight. When it landed, it was so fine it coated their arms and hair like ghost-ash.

Outside, voices rose again. Laughter this time — genuine but edged. Someone shouted about scrap weight. Another barked back, the words cutting through like iron scraping glass. Further still, a deeper voice yelled across the forge floor, followed by a metallic clang that vibrated through the walls and rattled Link's teeth faintly in his skull.

Eve's breath grew shallow. Not with sleep — not yet — but with discipline. She folded herself small against the wall, her fingers resting loosely near her blade. Not gripping, but near enough. Ready without showing readiness.

"Not like the old bands," she murmured softly after a minute, voice nearly devoured by the forge hum.

Link's eyes flicked toward the curtain again. He saw shapes — rebels gathered tight around barrels, sharing rations. Others hunched near weapon racks, sharpening lengths of scavenged pipe into makeshift spears. No one looked relaxed. No one had their backs turned.

He nodded faintly. "This has roots."

The two of them chewed the scrap of bread slowly, jaws tight. It wasn't food — just fuel. The stale crunch echoed oddly loud in the small hollow. They chewed faster to silence it. Crumbs stuck to dry tongues.

Then came the knock — sharp, direct.

Cutter's silhouette broke the flickering curtain light. The moment he entered, the air grew heavier — not from noise, but from his weight in the doorway. Eve's fingers flexed toward her knife. Link saw it. Cutter saw it. Nobody said anything.

"There's someone you need to meet."

The sentence hung a beat too long, like a nail half-driven. Cutter's head turned slightly, already ready to walk before Link could agree. That wasn't a request.

Link rose. Eve's eyes tracked him with faint worry, but she said nothing. Her hand stayed near her blade even after Cutter left.

The path Cutter led was tighter than before — narrower. Pipes pressed closer now, their skins sweating heat and faint streaks of condensation that ran in slow rivulets down the metal. The walls sang — not melodic, but subtle, a high warble of stressed metal vibrating under constant pressure.

They passed through intersections alive with the dense energy of too many bodies crammed into too little space. Men and women leaned against walls, talking in hushed voices while rolling lengths of stripped copper into coils. A pair of mechanics passed dragging a heavy sheet of plating between them — their boots splashing through water and leaving long, smearing trails.

Children flitted between legs — carrying belts, carrying bowls, carrying whispers.

One girl — couldn't have been older than seven — stumbled near the edge of a tool pit, arms wrapped tight around a gearbox half her size. Her knees buckled. The weight slipped.

Nobody helped. They were all too busy or too tired.

Link stepped toward her without thinking. Crouched. Lifted it for her.

Her eyes darted up, wide and too old for her face. One cheek was streaked with ash.

"Thank you," she said, voice barely audible over the hum.

Then she ran — barefoot, limping slightly — toward a tented alcove where a woman crouched over torn metal, holding a baby on one hip.

Link stared after her until Cutter nudged his shoulder.

"They don't stop," the big man muttered. "Not even the kids. No one does. We can't afford to."

Link said nothing.

But something in his jaw clicked tighter as they walked on.

At every junction, Link felt eyes crawl across him. Not hostile — yet. But not welcoming either. These were eyes that measured. That catalogued. Cutter seemed immune to them — his bulk parting them like stone breaking water — but Link felt each glance scrape against his skin like filings drawn to a magnet.

They passed the automata graveyard again. Link slowed unconsciously. A half-disassembled torso lay askew near his boot. One hand still attached, curled in a half-clutch — fingers fused together by rust. It looked frozen mid-reach.

"Guild didn't care about broken things," Cutter muttered over his shoulder, his voice low, nearly swallowed by the throb of forging hammers beyond.

In the next chamber, they passed the barricades. Half-welded crawlers stood sentinel, their plates covered in names and jagged teeth emblems. Steam hissed overhead from cracked vents, clouds thick enough that Link briefly lost Cutter in the dense swirls. Shadows moved within it — rebel crews working without pause, sparks bursting and vanishing before they fully lit the gloom.

Everywhere: heat. Motion. Humidity thick enough that it hung on Link's skin. His shirt clung to his back, and his jaw clenched against the constant thrum vibrating up through his boots. He shifted weight subtly with every step, the instinct of someone who felt watched.

Finally, they reached Mara's chamber. The shift was immediate.

Cooler. Denser. Tighter.

The moment the hatch sealed behind them, the foundry's roar dulled to a distant, muted groan. Link's ears popped faintly, and even Cutter's bootfalls softened.

Mara turned — face stern, eyes sharp as heat-tempered steel. Her fingers twitched as she approached, not quite resting at her sides — flexing faintly as though itching to grab tools without knowing why.

"Show me."

Link didn't argue. He moved slowly, deliberately — pulling the Heartcoil from his satchel with the care of someone handling a living thing. The room reacted instantly. Or seemed to.

Pipes groaned softly overhead. The filament lamp flickered once, sputtering like a candle. Mara's apprentice — unnoticed before, working quietly in the far corner — stopped, breath held, as though even his small adjustments risked breaking the tension.

Mara's lips parted slightly. Not awe — assessment.

"This speaks," she whispered, as her eyes tracked the faint glow seeping from the cracks in the coil.

As they worked, the space grew tighter. Every motion became a negotiation. Link's fingers brushed Mara's occasionally as they passed tools. Cutter shifted in the background, his bulk creating a pocket of warmth that pressed against Link's spine. Mara's apprentice began humming faintly — a nervous, repetitive tune — before catching himself and falling silent. Only steam whispered then, dripping slowly down cracked conduits and hissing into the heat.

The coil began to pulse — faint, subtle. The light danced across Mara's cheekbones, turning sweat into liquid fire, catching in the tiny imperfections on her soot-smudged glasses. She leaned in unconsciously, breath shallow. Link felt his own quicken.

"Resonance," Mara murmured. "Not power. Voice."

Outside, beyond thick walls, something struck metal — a deep THOOM that rippled through the chamber in subtle vibration. Neither of them flinched. The city itself was breathing. It always was.

Cutter spoke quietly at last, his voice carrying more weight than volume.

"This isn't just rebellion now."

Link swallowed, feeling the coil warm between his palms. His thumb brushed faintly against the casing — and for the briefest moment, the coil thrummed louder. Like it agreed.

Or like it was waiting.

Chapter 19
The Weight of Sparks

E ve sat upright with difficulty, shifting inch by inch until her back pressed firmly against the warm stone. Each movement felt exaggerated, every tug of fabric and flex of her muscles amplified by the oppressive closeness of the foundry air. The texture of the wall behind her was rough and flaked against her shoulders, dusting her collar with grit. She didn't brush it away. The discomfort grounded her.

Outside her small hollow, Free Steam's heartbeat continued unabated.

Metal rang like distant bells. Hammers struck iron with methodical rhythm—some slow and purposeful, others erratic as apprentices missed and readjusted. Steam hissed in bursts through strained joints and valves that coughed with age, filling the corridors with a constant undertone. It wasn't white noise. It breathed, like the lungs of the old city exhaling in intervals of fatigue.

Eve's ears picked up layered conversations drifting down from the busier cat-walks. Voices overlapped, woven through with the hiss of welding torches and the clatter of bolts spilling from overturned buckets. Laughter flickered here and there, brittle but present—relief forced between shifts of exhaustion. Nearby, someone cursed softly in frustration, voice tight with strain. The foundry didn't stop. It murmured always, like restless sleepers shifting through endless dreams.

She exhaled slowly, her breath briefly joining the steam in the air. It rolled upward in a thin, ghostlike tendril before dissipating into the heavier smog swirling near the ceiling. Her lips parted again, this time as she reached down, fingers clumsy with weariness, and peeled the bandage back slightly from her thigh. The cloth peeled away wetly, the faint tearing sound lost in the forge's distant growls.

Eve winced. The wound was angry and red, the heat radiating outward in waves she could feel against her palm. She didn't speak. Words wasted energy. Instead, her jaw flexed tightly as she wrapped the cloth again, the motion deliberate and slightly trembling. When she knotted the strip, the coarse fabric bit into her fingertips, scraping them raw. She welcomed the sting.

With a grunt, she pressed forward. Her good hand gripped the edge of her bedroll and pulled until she was upright, shoulders tight and rounded forward as she steadied herself. The air clung to her skin now, humid and heavy, and her hair matted against the sides of her face where sweat gathered. She tucked a loose strand behind her ear with a careless swipe of her wrist, her nails raking lightly along her temple.

Outside her chamber, the sounds deepened.

Boots struck grates in steady cadence as workers changed shifts. She heard the subtle shuffle of tired bodies brushing against one another, shoulder to shoulder in the narrow passages. Murmured exchanges passed in low tones—workers trading toolkits, issuing short warnings in clipped speech. "Pressure's up near the Redline." "Don't let the vent seal slip again." "Double torque that frame." Warnings, advice, and exhaustion all blurred together.

Eve hobbled forward, leaning heavily against the curved wall. Her knuckles grazed the soot-smeared surface, leaving faint smudges as she passed. In the distance, a pressure valve released, its sharp screech cutting briefly through the background hum. Sparks rained in arcs as someone misaligned a saw blade on sheet metal—angry voices followed, blending into the forge's ceaseless choir.

Her steps were uneven but steady enough. Each footfall sent faint splashes into puddles hidden beneath the grime-layered floor. The water carried heat, and the droplets clung to her boots, soaking in slowly and weighing her down further. Still, she pressed on.

As she reached the central walkway, more subtle signs of life filled her senses. A young girl with sleeves rolled up to her elbows wiped sweat from her forehead with the back of her wrist, leaving a streak of soot across her brow. Beside her, a man hunched over a crate of spare rivets, his broad shoulders rising and falling as he muttered counts softly beneath his breath. A group nearby debated fervently about coolant placement—hands gesturing sharply, the tension hanging thick but familiar. Disagreements didn't halt work here—they shaped it.

Tension rippled deeper below.

On the hangar floor, a technician tripped near a loaded crane track. A crash rang out as a box of bearings spilled across the plating. Link shouted from across the floor — not at the tech, but to warn another crew in the path of the rolling load. The bearings scattered into shadows.

"That crane's off pattern," someone growled. "It keeps drifting."

"So rewire the damn stabilizer," another snapped.

"It's already rewired. Twice. You want to climb in there and touch the coil yourself?"

Eve paused, watching a brief flare of heated argument between the two crews before Mara stepped in, issuing sharp instructions and gesturing toward the scaffolding.

The moment simmered, then broke apart. Work resumed.

But even from up high, Eve could see the pressure building. Not in machines. In people.

Eve paused at the railing overlooking the assembly hangar. A hot gust from below brushed past her face, carrying scents both acrid and strangely warm—molten metal cooling in troughs, oil burning faintly on machine joints, and the unmistakable tang of soldered copper hanging thick and bitter in the back of her throat.

She gripped the railing harder, her fingers curling tight as she steadied herself. Below, Link's voice rose faintly—sharper, faster. She couldn't hear the words, but his gestures said enough. Palms open one moment, stabbing forward with pointed fingers the next. Tension radiated through his movements, a quiet fury he wasn't bothering to hide.

Mara's stance mirrored his frustration, her arms crossed so tightly her shoulders hiked toward her ears. Cutter paced nearby, head low, dragging a hand through his beard. Every few seconds, he stopped to tap the side of a nearby crawler shell with his knuckles—a hollow, metallic tonk that echoed through the hall like a metronome of restless thought.

Eve let her eyes drift shut briefly, breathing through her nose. The heat of the foundry pressed inward, dense and cloying. When she opened her eyes again, they burned faintly from the sting of rising forge smoke curling lazily overhead in ribbons of dull gray and orange.

She shifted her weight again, thigh muscles twitching involuntarily as nerves fired too early. She grimaced and reached down, fingertips brushing lightly against the bandages to ease the sudden cramp. Her hand lingered there, thumb tracing idle circles on the cloth.

Nearby, whispers crept through the haze. Workers gathered on break spoke in soft tones, eyes darting toward the hangar floor. "That coil's different." "Saw it hum near the old rig, swear on it." "Could change everything—or kill us faster." The words were barely audible beneath the clangor, but they carried weight nonetheless, seeding uncertainty even amid resolve.

Eve's eyes narrowed slightly. Her chest rose and fell with measured care, breath shallow as though unwilling to disturb the fragile balance hanging in the air.

The scarred woman from earlier emerged from a side passage carrying another tin cup of broth, shoulders squared and steady. She paused briefly near Eve, the heat from the broth rolling outward in gentle waves as she handed it over without speaking. Their fingers brushed briefly—rough and calloused—before parting.

Eve took the cup and held it close, the warmth bleeding into her palms. She drank slowly, eyes fixed downward now toward Link, Mara, and Cutter. She watched every nuance—Link's foot tapping with subconscious urgency, Mara's gloved hands gripping the table edge, Cutter's thick arms folded and unmoving as his jaw shifted in silent deliberation.

The coil between them glowed faintly, its pulse synchronized with the heartbeat of the foundry. The flickering orange cast by forge fires mixed with its subtle blue shimmer, creating ghostlight that danced across their faces like whispered promises.

As Eve finished the broth, distant alarms rang softly in the deep. Not urgent—yet. Just a shift change or pressure warning somewhere beyond the halls. Still, the faint resonance echoed through pipes and grates like veins carrying news through the body of a slumbering beast.

In that moment, Eve whispered again—but this time, the words fell flatter. Heavier. Almost a plea.

"Don't break."

She set the empty cup down slowly, metal clicking softly against the railing.

Above her, unnoticed, shadows shifted among the girders. Boots scuffed softly on mesh flooring. A faint whirr of hydraulics whispered like breath. Eyes—one human, one mechanical—remained fixed on the Heartcoil.

And beyond them all, Eastland groaned softly in its sleep, unaware or uncaring of the sparks slowly gathering strength within its veins.

Chapter 20
Sparks in the Tunnels

T he tension in Free Steam's camp wasn't just palpable—it had seeped into the walls, the pipes, the very breath of the place. In the central workshop bay, the air hung heavy with moisture and smoke, wrapping around every surface like a living thing. Steam curled up from cracked valves, drifting lazily through shafts of pale yellow lamplight that cut through the gloom in angled beams. Dust and soot danced like spectral ash motes caught mid-fall, clinging to workbenches and the shoulders of silent onlookers.

Link stood at the center of it all, framed by shadows and the muted glow of the Heartcoil prototype suspended above. Rusted chains groaned softly as the device swayed almost imperceptibly, creaking in time with the hiss of unseen pressure vents along the walls. Sparks arced across the exposed copper wrappings with idle menace, casting stuttering flashes across Link's tense face.

Mara crouched nearby, her fingers wrapped tightly around a rust-slick wrench. She adjusted a coupling, the motion deliberate and slow as steam hissed against her gloves. Each turn of her wrist was accompanied by faint metallic groans—like the old crawler frame didn't appreciate being woken from its slumber. She blew out a breath through pursed lips, the exhale instantly visible in the cool, stagnant air as a soft plume.

Around them, the gathered rebels formed a rough semicircle, packed tight—close enough that shoulders brushed and the rustle of layered coats and scrap-woven clothing blended into a soft, constant hush. Boots shifted, leather creaked, and now and then a throat cleared awkwardly. Some leaned forward, elbows on knees, jaws tight. Others whispered quietly to each other, their voices thread-thin and wary, threading through the wider tension like weaving needles.

"You promised us working weaponry, not another smoke box!" Dren's voice cut through the murmuring like a blade against steel. His stance was wide, fists clenched tight enough that his knuckles whitened under grime. He wasn't just angry—he was scared. Fear smelled like sweat and hot metal. Link caught the subtle tremor in the man's leg as he leaned forward slightly, challenging without crossing a line he knew Cutter wouldn't tolerate.

A ripple spread through the crowd. Heads tilted. Low muttering picked up—too low to discern, but filled with hard edges. In the far back, a woman with short-cropped hair muttered under her breath, drawing invisible lines in the air with an oil-streaked finger as though tallying losses only she understood.

Walder didn't raise his voice. He didn't need to. When he spoke, the subtle undertone in his words pulled focus like gravity. His fingers drummed twice on his forearm, the only sign of unease. "We didn't promise miracles. We promised a chance."

"Miracles don't hold barricades," came a voice from the left side—sharp, bitter.

"Neither does waiting to die," Eve answered before Link could, limping into view, her entrance sudden but commanding. She carried herself like tempered steel—weathered, but unbroken. Each step brought the faintest crunch from loose gravel underfoot. Steam curled against her legs, swirling like fingers trying to tug her back.

Her eyes scanned the bay quickly, her breath visibly hitching as she took in the scene. Workers paused mid-hammer strike, leaning subtly forward in anticipation. Someone in the rafters coughed twice and then fell silent.

"Recon's back," Eve continued, voice carrying despite its hoarseness. "Guild movement east—light patrol, slow-moving. Might be an opening."

Her words, casual as they were, detonated softly through the bay. Conversations broke into whispers. Someone cursed quietly in disbelief. Others straightened slightly, hands unconsciously drifting toward weapons hanging from their belts or strapped to their backs. The subtle shuffle of dozens of boots repositioning sent faint echoes through the chamber.

Walder's fingers tightened slightly against his crossed arms, the leather of his coat creaking faintly. "Supply route?" he asked, voice pitched low enough to demand silence from the others.

"Could be," Eve replied evenly. Her eyes met Link's briefly across the distance—a flicker of silent understanding passing between them like a spark between coils.

Link could feel the shift in the room like static charge building against his skin. The air grew warmer with the collective heat of bodies pressing inward. Mara turned to him subtly, the wrench resting across her palms now as though weighing more than metal. Cutter leaned slightly forward from where he stood near a set of makeshift stairs, his fingers tapping slowly against his thigh in a rhythm that suggested readiness, not impatience.

Dren wasn't done. "And who's taking the risk? Who walks into a Guild kill box hoping the steam gods feel generous today?"

That cracked the surface.

Another voice: "We've lost two patrols this month. If we keep bleeding bodies on 'maybes'..."

"You want to sit on your hands until they torch the rest of Eastland?" someone snapped back. "We're out of time."

The murmurs fractured. Angles sharpened. A worker near the front half-stood, then sat again, hand on his blade's hilt. The space between people became brittle, voices overlapping.

Cutter took one slow step forward.

The room froze.

"Enough," he said.

Just the one word. Even the pipes seemed to go still for a breath.

"I want in," Link said suddenly. His own voice surprised him—low, steady, cutting through the muttered calculations like a blade drawn clean.

Eve raised her brows faintly but said nothing. Cutter's mouth curled into a faint, crooked grin, his teeth faintly visible in the forge glow. He shifted, boot scraping softly on the floor as he moved closer.

"You sure?" Cutter asked, voice rich with quiet amusement and approval in equal measure.

Link flexed his fingers once before answering, his thumb brushing instinctively against the edge of a fresh scar along his palm. The Heartcoil hummed above him—just once, soft and low, as if acknowledging his words before they even left his mouth.

"Most qualified," he replied. "And if this thing comes, it needs someone who understands when to pull its reins."

The forge behind them flared briefly—someone stirring coals, sending sparks spiraling upward in lazy arcs. It illuminated the backs of the gathered crowd, casting flickering shadows up the scarred walls. No one spoke in those few seconds. Even breathing seemed quieter.

Walder gave a tight nod. Mara tapped twice on the converter schematic beside her and then motioned toward the crawler at the far end of the bay. Cutter followed her gesture with a glance but said nothing—his approval was wordless, given in the angle of his shoulders and the way his hands finally relaxed at his sides.

"If this works," Mara said softly as she stepped closer to Link, her breath ghosting faintly in the cold air, "it won't just power a crawler."

"It will prove we can break their chains," Cutter finished for her, voice low and hungry.

Eve shifted beside Link, her coat brushing against his arm as she leaned in slightly. The warmth of her body pressed faintly against his side—unspoken solidarity. She whispered, only loud enough for him to hear.

"Then let's make them afraid."

All around them, the foundry pressed tighter. The walls seemed to lean inward, the gathered rebels pulling the crucible's glow into themselves like kindling waiting for a match.

And overhead, the Heartcoil sang quietly to itself. Not loud. Not eager.

But awake.

And the whispers threading through the crowd—barely more than breath—spoke of tomorrow. Spoke of striking back. Spoke of war.

Far away, in the cold guts of a ruined command gallery deeper in Eastland's understructure, Roland stood alone.

The remains of one of his personal guard automatons lay twisted at his feet—its helm shattered, limbs torn free by plasma scoring and brute force. He didn't speak. He didn't move. Just stared at it.

Ash and blood stained the floor.

He knelt slowly, one gloved hand brushing the edge of the frame's chest plate, where the Guild crest had once been. The metal was scorched beyond recognition.

He didn't curse. He didn't scream. He simply rose, turned his back to the ruin, and walked away.

Not like a man defeated.

Like a boy who no longer knew what he was walking toward.

Chapter 21
Ash Streets Falter

The mist tasted of metal tonight. Not clean, not sharp—cloying, as if every breath drew rust into the lungs. It hugged the tram lines of southern Eastland like a second skin, slithering low and slow, pooling in gutters and broken windows where the wind no longer reached. The air felt thick, not just with moisture, but with weight—like inhaling the memory of a dead city. It clung to the throat, leaving an aftertaste of old iron and colder days.

The streets narrowed the deeper they went. Building bones shouldered inward on either side, cracked facades propped up by ribs of scaffolding and bent rebar. The walls pressed in claustrophobically, whispering faintly with each shift of the wind—murmurs of the past carried in the hollow creak of corroded beams and fraying wire nets that swayed overhead.

Somewhere far above, hidden behind the gray, something knocked softly—a loose sign or broken pulley chain tapping against brick like skeletal fingers drumming in impatience.

Eve crouched in the gloom, the broken husk of a vending kiosk shielding her from sight. She pressed a gloved hand against the cracked surface, steadying herself, her other hand resting lightly on the hilt of her blade. Her knees ached faintly, cold biting through her layered trousers into old bruises. Her breath came slow and shallow, each exhale briefly visible before being swallowed by the fog.

Ahead, two Guild patrolmen ghosted past. They moved with clockwork grace, the hiss of breath regulators cutting sharp against the night. Shoulder-mounted lanterns cut clean lines through the murk, twin cones of pale light that flickered softly as they pivoted from side to side like watchful eyes. The beams passed inches from where Eve crouched, casting fractured shadows that danced across her face.

She did not move. Not even to breathe.

The patrolmen spoke briefly—coded exchanges, hollow behind mask filters, words reduced to sterile orders.

"Sector sweep complete." "No contact. Proceeding."

Boots clanked against slick stone in perfect rhythm, and the fog rolled back to reclaim their passing.

Eve counted silently.

One. Two. Three.

She moved.

Her limbs stretched tight as she unfurled from her crouch like a bow being loosed. She slipped across the lane, each footfall measured, knees bent slightly to distribute weight. Water splashed softly under her boots, the ripples darting outward like fleeing fish before fading into stillness. She kept low, head forward, fingers grazing walls and rusted pipe edges for balance. Every motion spoke of practiced speed checked by caution.

Link was already ahead—half-shadowed beside a drainage tunnel rimmed with broken pipework and old wiring that hung loose like torn veins. He worked quickly but precisely, mouth set in a hard line, jaw flexing with each adjustment of the worn tool in his hand. His shoulders shifted minutely with every rotation, the tension visible even in the subtle tightening of his back muscles beneath his soot-dappled coat.

Sweat clung to his temples, trailing in thin lines through smudges of soot and grime. The cloth-wrapped Heartcoil sat nearby, emitting a soft hum that buzzed faintly against the metal around it. The wires attached to it vibrated subtly, twitching now and then—as far as Link could tell—like nerves reacting to phantom touch.

"You're late," Link muttered, not looking up. His voice came tight, half-focused, half-chiding.

"You're welcome," Eve shot back, sliding down beside him with a muted grunt. Her gloved fingers brushed the cracked stone wall briefly before settling on her blade again. She scanned the rooftops with quick, darting eyes. No glints. No silhouettes. For now.

"Two patrols rerouted. One decoy fire. Cutter's creating noise on the other side. We have maybe ten minutes," she continued in a low tone. Her lips barely moved. Her breath steamed faintly before vanishing again.

Link offered a terse nod, fingers continuing to tighten clamps with sharp, deliberate motions. His hands worked steadily, but tension radiated off him. Veins stood out subtly along his wrists, and the skin on his knuckles had split slightly from exposure and strain.

A distant metallic groan rolled through the tunnel network—the sound of shifting architecture or wind grinding loose sheet metal together far overhead. Both tensed instinctively. Eve's free hand closed tighter on her blade, her shoulder pressing harder into the wall. Link paused his work, lips thinning, listening.

When nothing followed, they relaxed. Slightly.

"Trust Walder's coordinates?" Eve asked after a beat, watching the fog thicken across the far end of the street.

Link's hands didn't stop. He twisted a valve one final time before answering, his words dry and low. "I trust he hates failure more than death."

Eve allowed a quiet, humorless snort, brushing dust from the tip of her boot with her other foot. She shifted slightly to ease the dull ache in her injured leg, hiding the wince that flickered through her face.

A sharp hiss erupted nearby from a cracked vent shaft. The burst of sound echoed down the passage like a distant scream. Eve's hand shot instinctively to her weapon. Link froze mid-motion, muscles locking tight. Their bodies stilled in unison—breath caught, ears strained.

The moment passed. They exhaled softly, shoulders lowering fractionally.

They entered the tunnel.

Inside, the atmosphere thickened to oppressive levels. Damp heat enveloped them, the air heavy with moisture that clung to skin and made each breath feel syrupy. Thin tendrils of steam curled lazily from fractured pipes, brushing against cheeks and necks like insistent, unwelcome fingers. Every drip of water from above hit with sharp, rhythmic ticks—like a clock counting down.

Mara and Cutter stood ahead beneath a flickering light source barely strong enough to push back the gloom. Cutter's fingers tapped constantly against the metal railing beside him, nerves worn bare despite his relaxed posture. Mara stood slightly hunched, adjusting a tangle of wires, lips pressed thin, eyes narrowed in annoyance and concern.

"Thought you got sliced," Cutter offered when they approached, but the humor didn't reach his tight shoulders.

"Delayed," Eve replied, brushing stray hair from her face. Her fingers, still stiff, tugged her collar tighter to block the rising warmth and humidity that pressed against them.

"Panel's hot. Capacitor's unstable," Mara stated bluntly, voice tight with frustration.

"We do this now," Link said simply, moving without hesitation.

He approached the Heartcoil reverently, unwrapping it with care. The glow within deepened instantly, casting faint golden halos against the condensation-flecked walls. As he hooked in clamps and tightened wiring, his hands trembled faintly—not from fear, but sheer exertion and stress.

Eve stayed nearby. Her hand never strayed far from her knife. She pressed her weight against a rusted pillar, foot tapping softly. Every so often her eyes flicked sideways—toward the shadows deeper in the substation where movement could be hidden.

"Voltage climbing," Cutter called softly, staring at the dials with a predator's intensity. Mara muttered calculations under her breath, chewing the inside of her cheek, glancing between readouts.

The tension pulled taut, like a bowstring at full draw.

"Do it," Eve commanded. Her voice sliced through the tension, breaking hesitation.

Link flipped the relay.

The world screamed.

White-blue arcs burst outward like grasping fingers, lightning coiling across the ceiling as though desperate to claw free. Heat punched outward, throwing dampness into violent steam that blurred vision and burned bare skin. Cutter flinched, instinctively shielding his face. Mara threw herself sideways, narrowly avoiding a discharge as cables overhead sparked dangerously.

Eve braced herself, biting back a shout. Her hair blew wildly in the sudden storm, loose strands slapping across her face. She tasted metal and ozone on her tongue, her ears ringing faintly from the surge.

Link remained still.

Teeth clenched, arms locked, every tendon in his neck visible as he forced the override lever down against howling resistance. For a moment, it seemed as though he might snap in half from the strain.

Then — release.

The arcs dissipated. Steam sighed back into place. The coil's glow dimmed to a steady heartbeat—at least, that's how it seemed to Link, watching it with eyes still wide from the surge.

Silence pressed in briefly. Breathless. Waiting.

"It held," Eve said softly, her voice dry but alive with disbelief.

"It held," Link echoed, voice raw.

Mara let out a ragged laugh, sinking to her knees, wiping grime from her eyes with shaking hands. Cutter slapped the rail twice in quiet approval, nodding firmly to himself.

Eve didn't celebrate. Not yet. She only exhaled slowly, brushing damp strands from her forehead as she watched Link lower his arms. His hands trembled faintly as the adrenaline bled away.

A voice shouted from the shadows — rough, young, panicked. "We've got one! Caught a straggler—Guild armor!"

Several rebels rushed forward dragging a stunned, soot-covered figure. The prisoner stumbled, barely conscious, a half-shattered mask still clinging to one side of his face. His hands were bound in scrap cord, his coat scorched, the Guild sigil charred but still visible.

A young fighter raised his sidearm. "Say the word. We finish it now."

Eve stepped in front of him before the sentence finished. Her hand didn't move to her blade. She didn't raise her voice. She simply stared.

"No."

The word landed like steel.

The young fighter hesitated, confused. "But he—"

"If you kill him while he's defenseless, you make him right about us."

Silence.

Eve's gaze never broke. "Take him to Marrow. Strip his armor. Feed him. And if he lifts a hand to hurt anyone again, I'll do it myself."

The fighter lowered his weapon. Slowly. Then nodded.

The others pulled the prisoner away. No one cheered. No one clapped.

But they looked at Eve.

Differently.

Outside the substation, distant voices murmured. Somewhere through cracked walls, workers in Free Steam's outer yards passed rumors in hushed tones. A child's laughter rang out briefly before being shushed. Tools clattered. Wheels creaked. Farther still, the Guild's patrols clicked and hissed in clockwork rhythm, unaware.

Eastland groaned faintly in its sleep.

But beneath that, something deeper stirred.

The city wasn't breathing tonight.

It was listening.

Chapter 22
Gilded Thorns

Roland Valtor sat beneath the gilded arches of the Guild's Eastern War Pavilion, watching the drizzle streak across the glass ceiling above. He had been sitting there far longer than the wine in his hand warranted. The room had grown still, time marked only by the slow dance of droplets threading down carved channels overhead. The arches curled like ribs of a mechanical beast, gilded veins catching soft lamplight that hummed faintly with residual steam. Through that glass canopy, the city pressed close but silent, cloaked in iron skies. No stars dared pierce Eastland's veil anymore—only the glow of signal towers and smog-burnished moonlight broke the dark. Beyond the glass, sulfur clouds stirred. The city wheezed quietly, as if struggling to breathe beneath its own weight.

He let the rain distract him longer than usual. He did not like where his mind wandered when left unguarded. Rain fell in careful, symmetrical patterns—funneled by channels carved in the likeness of winged lions and screaming angels. The beasts looked down in frozen fury, mouths agape in eternal condemnation. Gilded and polished, yes — but hollow. He had often wondered if they judged.

The acoustics were perfect. Every drop landed with a practiced hush. Controlled. Refined. Silence, Roland had learned, was cultivated. Manufactured. It did not exist in the wild. Here, even the weather obeyed. For now.

He twirled a silver ring around his finger — twice, three times — before setting his wine glass down. Old habit. When he was younger, he did it to soothe his nerves. Now he did it without thinking. The ring bore the Valtor sigil, its once-sharp etchings softened from years of idle rotation. A lion devouring flame.

He understood that hunger now, better than when the ring first slid onto his hand.

The vintage was expensive. Dull. Like everything lately. Even as the liquid clung stubbornly to the crystal, it whispered of obligation. Not pleasure. He drank because it was expected — not because he craved it.

Outside, the steam gardens hissed in precise intervals. Orchids bloomed on command, petals opening and closing according to the will of hidden regulators and moisture sensors. Luxury required oversight. Life here was curated. Caretakers, faceless in slate-gray uniforms, moved like ghosts along manicured paths. Each snip of their shears echoed faintly, disciplined and restrained. Not even nature was allowed unruliness. Roses bled only when commanded. Each thorn was sharpened to perfection. Roland knew — he had tested them, long ago. The faint scar at his thumb remained. A lesson, like so many in his life, written in quiet pain.

Inside, the air was too still. The Pavilion did not permit clutter or warmth. Everything was aligned to the principles of presentation and authority. Servitors lined the perimeter, unmoving. Their blank faces reflected the lamplight. They stood vigil without fatigue, without complaint. They did not question. He envied them, sometimes.

A string quartet played softly from the adjoining atrium. Something classical. Something predictable. Notes drifted like polite conversation at a funeral — elegant, empty. The musicians played without passion. They had been selected to do so.

He had spent the last two weeks in cycles of empty gestures. Council meetings with perfumed diplomats who smiled too readily. Efficiency reports that danced around inconvenient truths. Galas where nobles congratulated themselves while feigning concern for the Eastern Sectors.

And always, behind every exchange — whispers. Free Steam. Heartcoil. Disrupted shipments. Sector Nine sightings. The names lingered, more persistent than rumors had any right to be.

He offered reassurances. He told them what they wanted to hear. But each time, when the curtains closed and the gilded wine glasses emptied, he was left with the same quiet rage: Someone is stealing the spotlight.

A servant approached, head bowed. The man's movements were measured, but not confident. His gloved hands trembled faintly as he extended a sealed dossier. Roland noted it. He always noted weakness. Fear was natural. Weakness was unacceptable.

The dossier felt warm from the servant's touch. It faded quickly in his grip. Information, after all, held no sentiment.

Another raid. Another convoy lost. Each loss stung less as data. Yet, each victory for Free Steam bled deeper into Eastland's psyche. That was what angered him most — they weren't winning with guns. They were winning with attention.

He flipped through images. Burned wrecks. Toppled automatons. Graffiti in bold, haphazard strokes that reeked of rebellion. HEARTCOIL WORKS. FIRE BENEATH THE STONE.

And faces. Blurry. Distorted by surveillance fog. But recognizable.

Link. The boy with soot scars, every line of his posture screaming insolence. Eve. Hard-eyed. Unbowed. She stood with arms folded like a war goddess born in refuse.

Roland's stomach knotted — not with fear, but with something worse. Recognition.

His father had dismissed Heartcoil. An engineering anomaly. A curiosity. A myth. So had Roland, once. It was easier.

Now? It disrupted his supply lines. Undermined his image. Excited the masses. Worse — it romanticized rebellion.

Even here, in the Pavilion's curated silence, nobles whispered about innovation and change. Hope spread faster than orders.

He rose, crossing to the mirror-paneled wall. Boots echoed on polished marble. Each step was crisp, calculated — a rehearsed statement in movement. His reflection stared back. Perfect posture. Tailored silk. The face of order and inevitability. He despised it tonight.

Annoyance simmered deep in his chest. He hadn't bled for Eastland. He hadn't buried comrades or earned scars. He hadn't needed to.

But now, rats in crawlspaces dared to steal his thunder. They dared to believe themselves protagonists.

"They'll remember the name Valtor," he whispered. The glass absorbed the words, offering nothing in return. "But not yours. Never yours."

He turned sharply and left, the echo of his stride chasing him down corridors gilded in obedience.

In the Citadel vault, the Gilded Fang slumbered beneath heavy canvas. Even asleep, it radiated menace.

The air here tasted different — iron and oil, untouched by the sweet filters of the Pavilion. Few were permitted entry. Fewer still had reason to come.

Roland studied the automaton as if revisiting a forgotten scripture. It was built to kill and impress — a blend of artistry and execution.

Gold plating gleamed faintly in the low light, but beneath it, the true skeleton waited — triple-forged alloy and whisper-hydraulics. It was not delicate. It was not gentle. It was precisely what the world below needed to remember.

He approached slowly, reverently. The automaton had been silent too long. Dormancy bred irrelevance.

"Have it cleaned. Repaint the crest." Appearance mattered. Symbols spoke where orders could not.

Iskra — the engineer — nodded. She did not argue. She understood. Her staff emerged quietly, draped in workshop robes. They did not meet his eyes.

"It hasn't been synced in over a year. The command latency—" "Fix it."

She hesitated, then yielded. No one argued twice with a Valtor.

Roland circled the Fang, gloved fingers trailing along its plated thigh. Ownership was not spoken. It was demonstrated.

"I want it ready by tomorrow." "Sir, there's risk if the telemetry—" "No excuses."

The vault fell silent. Machines obeyed where people hesitated. He savored that.

He climbed into the cockpit. The cradle welcomed him with the familiar pressure of snug straps and rigid anchors. Tight. Unforgiving. Necessary.

Power did not comfort. It restrained.

Sensors awoke, drinking him in. His breath. His pulse. The twitch of his pupils. He let them take him. Machines asked no questions.

The Fang's core flared amber. Recognition pulsed through its frame, through his spine. It knew him. Unlike people, machines remembered loyalty.

For the first time all day, Roland relaxed.

Later, alone in his chambers, rain punished the glass. The world beyond blurred and fractured — a broken mirror too far away to mend.

He poured wine, but did not drink. The ritual had meaning even in abstinence.

He thought of Link. Of Eve. Of crawlspaces turned into stages. Of soot-covered engineers daring to speak of heroes and futures.

He hated them. Hated how vividly they lived in his mind.

Eve, especially. The way she stood. Not desperate — deliberate. She did not fear him. Not yet.

He crushed the glass in his palm. The pain was sharp. Grounding. Honest.

Blood joined wine on marble. They pooled without prejudice.

He would find them. He would erase them.

Not because it was required. Because they dared.

Principle, to a Valtor, was sacred. Defiance was blasphemy. And he would drag Heartcoil's champions into the square—not just to silence them, but to remind the world what happens when false idols try to steal fire from gods.

And soon, every street and every whisper would know what blasphemy cost.

129

Chapter 23
Embers of Control

L ord Valtor had stopped sleeping through the night. He still woke early, as always. The old habit of command. But now, the hours before dawn were haunted. Not by dreams, but by the weight of decisions made and futures unraveling.

Tonight had been worse. Three hours in the warroom. Two more reading reports. One spent staring at the map of Eastland, his eyes tracing the red-labeled districts like an old soldier counting scars. None of it reassured him.

He sat alone in his study now, not in his usual chair but at the edge of the cold hearth, sleeves rolled to the elbow, a sealed bottle of tincture untouched at his side. Across the chamber, the mirror showed him a face more drawn than he cared to admit—lined deep around the eyes, jaw taut with strain. The pressure behind his eyes pulsed faintly. He blinked once. Again. The mirror did not.

I'm aging into the monument they want to carve, he thought. And monuments don't bleed.

His reflection didn't blink.

A knock at the door.

He didn't answer. Not right away. He closed the journal in his lap—a private log, ciphered, its pages littered with sketches of mechanical diagrams and phrases too guarded to be poetry, too personal to be orders.

"Enter," he said at last.

The door hissed open. Kass stepped in—his adjutant, loyal, unshaken. For now.

"Report from the Central Foundry line, sir."

Valtor took it without looking. "Any new defectors?"

Kass shifted. "Three apprentices. Fourth-tier. Took equipment with them."

Valtor nodded slowly. "Send word to their families. Reassign their kin to vent-clearing in the Deep Quarters. No funerals."

Kass hesitated. "Understood."

He left without another word.

Valtor moved to the tall window of his study, overlooking the city core. The mist was thinner here, where heat rose from the stacked furnaces below. But even here, ash collected on the sills like dust on a forgotten relic.

His hand drifted to the back of the chair, gripping hard.

Link. Eve. The Heartcoil.

He didn't need names to see the shape of the threat. It wasn't sabotage. It wasn't even rebellion.

It was proof. That power could exist outside the Guild. That order wasn't divinely granted to the chosen, but forged—painfully, sacrificially—by the desperate.

He'd known men like that before. Had buried them.

But this generation? They didn't die. They adapted. They whispered. They built. And their silence grew teeth.

His fingers ached. He realized he'd been clenching the edge of the desk. A tremor passed through one hand. He flexed it twice, trying not to look at the shake.

And Roland?

Valtor's face darkened.

The boy hadn't reported in two days. His last correspondence was full of triumphant drivel—how his Gilded Fang automaton had frightened rebels into retreat, how nobles were praising his daring. But Valtor had seen the footage. The "rebels" were children. Scared. Starving. And Roland had flaunted his conquest like a stage actor curtain-bowing after a farce.

His son. Not steel. Not even bronze.

Still, the name bought loyalty in the higher circles. So long as Roland played the icon, he had value. But that value thinned with every true rebellion that rose beneath the Guild's boot.

Valtor walked to a wall panel and unlocked it with a biometric tap. Inside, hanging on thick velvet, were relics of a different age:

A shattered coil blade from the Eastern Collapse. A leather-bound treaty, signed in ink and blood. A broken insignia pin—the original symbol of the Guild, before the flames. And at the center, the cloak of the last commander to lead the Iron Procession.

Valtor ran a hand over the cloth. It was heavier than memory.

"Prepare it," he said aloud, to no one. "This time, they will see."

In the lower sectors of Free Steam's holdout, Link stood before the Ghost-frame.

The chamber was dim—barely lit by a few swaying filament lanterns over-head—but the silhouette was unmistakable. It loomed in the half-dark, still scorched from the last engagement, still standing.

But not untouched.

Link's eyes narrowed. He took a step forward, running a gloved hand along the flank. The plating was... wrong. Welds he didn't recognize. A panel he'd sealed days ago now reinforced with vented brackets and burn shielding. Someone had added an auxiliary junction beneath the right shoulder. The housing bore fresh marks—scorch-tested, riveted. Functional. Precise. Necessary. And not his.

He circled to the back. New coolant lines. Heat sinks. Scrapped components from a crawler frame had been fitted to the spine. And not by trial—by design. Someone had prepared for failure. Someone had assumed he wouldn't return in time.

His hand dropped.

"Who touched it?"

Silence.

Mara stepped out from the shadowed edge of the bay, oil streaked across one cheek, expression unreadable. "We did."

Link didn't turn.

"It needed to survive," she added. "So we made sure it would."

He stared at the Ghostframe. The plating caught the light just enough to gleam like skin under sweat. It didn't move. It didn't breathe.

But something about it felt... aware. Expectant. Like it had been waiting for his return.

Link swallowed hard, jaw tight. "Next time, ask."

Mara didn't flinch. "Next time, we might not have the time."

A beat passed before Cutter's boots echoed on the metal floor. "It survived," he said gruffly. "So maybe they were right."

Link turned. "That's not the question. It's not about survival anymore. It's about what we become while we're doing it."

Mara crossed her arms. "You built something that can change everything. Power like that doesn't sit idle. It moves—through wires, or through people."

Walder stepped out from the stairwell, arms folded. "They've started whispering—about making more. Crawler cores. Perimeter defenses. We could reroute energy from the smelters."

"The Heartcoil isn't a forge stamp," Link said. His voice was lower now. Tight. "You can't just reproduce it. It's not a model. It's... alignment. It's resonance."

He paused then, eyes still on the Ghostframe, the pulse of its core reflected faintly in his gaze. "If you get the resonance wrong... it doesn't just fail. It becomes something else. Something you can't control."

Cutter looked toward the Ghostframe. "Then maybe we need to learn how. If one spark can change everything, maybe it's time we light the whole damn skyline."

Link didn't respond at first. He looked up at the machine—his machine—and saw how little of it was still his. How quickly it had become theirs.

"Just remember," he said finally, "fire spreads fastest through cities already burned."

The warning wasn't a rejection. It was the price.

Four days later, the Iron Procession began.

Chapter 24
Cracks in the Alloy

The ceiling of the warehouse groaned under a morning fog so thick it clung like oil, dampening sound and crawling across exposed skin with a clammy chill that seeped into sleeves and under collars. Steam hissed from every corner pipe, rising in whorls that bent the light of the hanging lamps into feverish halos, drifting like restless ghosts through the rafters. Each curl of vapor shifted with the slightest movement, trailing behind Link and Eve as if reluctant to let them pass. Shadows quivered across the walls, warping as the fog stirred and folded through the beams above. Somewhere far off, a hammer fell against metal—once, twice—like a forge calling the day to begin. The air smelled of rust, scorched cloth, and stale lubricant—thick enough to taste.

Link wiped condensation from his goggles, the weight of another sleepless night dragging behind his eyes. A faint twitch pulsed beneath one eye, and his jaw tightened reflexively—small betrayals of exhaustion etched into his face. Hunger scraped at his ribs, but he barely noticed anymore. Time stretched thin between coil pulses and broken gear teeth. Somewhere nearby, a valve misfired with a hollow thunk, echoing like a distant heartbeat. Somewhere deeper still, beneath the clamor, the floor carried a quiet hum—low, thrumming—like something buried and breathing.

The Ghostframe stood before him like a shadow caught mid-stride. Steam bled from its joints, its plates dark with weld-scars and scavenged rivets. Sparks crackled faintly where an exposed wire met condensation. The latest Heartcoil sat locked deep in its chest—palm-sized still, but throbbing with a low, resonant hum. Blue light seeped from its core, flickering with each diagnostic pulse like the machine was breathing in time with him. A faint vibration rippled through the floor beneath it, sending tremors through scattered rivets left on a nearby tray. Occasionally, its inner coils made a noise not unlike a breath held too long—then released.

It had moved. Walked. Turned. But something was still wrong.

"Feedback's too sharp on the second pivot," he muttered, crouching under the left leg.

The Ghostframe's stabilizers twitched, throwing off balance in the rear knee assembly. Link grimaced, tightening the coupling beneath the rotating collar. Sparks hissed from the contact point, and he jerked his hand back, cursing under his breath. The burn left a faint smell of scorched skin beneath the copper tang of the machine. Beneath the heat, he thought he felt something—pressure?—like the machine noticed.

He hadn't felt his fingertips in days. He laid his palm briefly against the Ghost-frame's thigh plating—just for balance, he told himself. But the contact lingered. Beneath the metal, the Heartcoil's pulse hummed once, almost in answer. Link closed his eyes. For a moment, he imagined the machine breathing with him—flesh and alloy, fatigue shared.

Eve sat nearby on a rusted crate, still dressed in her field coat from the patrol hours earlier. Her gloved fingers curled tightly around the mug, unmoving, as if bracing against something unseen. Every so often, one thumb twitched against the ceramic—subtle, but rhythmic—like a metronome ticking off the seconds until something cracked. She held a mug of boiled mushroom broth in gloved hands but hadn't drunk any. Her posture was rigid, boots muddy, hair damp with sweat and mist. Her eyes weren't focused on anything—just the haze around the Ghostframe, where the steam met the flickering torchlight. Drops of moisture collected at the tip of her nose, refracting light in tiny, trembling orbs. The shadows in the mist danced just wrong enough to stir old memory.

"You ever think it's... too much?" she asked. Her voice was hoarse, worn down to the steel undercoat. "Like the coil wants more than we can give."

Link didn't answer right away. He adjusted the servo tensioner again and stood slowly, joints cracking as he rose. Grease streaked across his sleeve, then smeared across his forehead as he wiped at the sweat clinging there. His breath steamed white in the chilled air, curling upward and vanishing into the warehouse gloom.

"It doesn't want anything," he said. "It just is."

Eve tilted her head. "Feels like it wants. Like it listens. Like we're not building a machine. We're waking something."

Somewhere far below, the old pipes groaned. Or answered.

Before Link could reply, a distant clang echoed outside. Raised voices drifted in through the cracked ceiling vents—Free Steam mechanics arguing about part allocations. One name repeated in the air like a curse: Link.

The door slammed open.

Cutter strode in, coat flaring behind him, mud still drying on his boots. Walder followed, flanked by two Free Steam techs hauling a half-dismantled actuator cradle between them. Their faces were tight with frustration, eyes rimmed with soot and sleeplessness. One of them dragged the cradle's end, metal scraping in protest across the concrete floor.

"You gonna tell me why the crawler nearly crushed two scouts this morning?" Cutter snapped. His coat was unfastened, revealing the brace wrapped around his ribs. His voice cracked like steel under stress. A distant klaxon chirped once, briefly, then went silent.

Link blinked, his eyes flicking briefly to the floor before meeting Cutter's again. His shoulders tightened, the muscles bunching slightly under his shirt. "It wasn't the coil. It was the rig. The crawler frame isn't syncing to the new control feedback. The old valve relays can't handle it."

"So your miracle core works," Walder said quietly, "but not for anything bigger than your Ghostframe."

"Yet," Link said. The word tasted like rust.

Walder's brow furrowed. "We salvaged a pressure-mapped actuator from the east rail. Could help balance the pivot sync. But if this thing backfires again, the rebels will turn on you. Some already want the coil scrapped. They say it's cursed. One tech refused to even enter the hangar last night, claiming the Ghostframe whispered when no one was near. Another left tools scattered mid-shift and hasn't come back. They're scared—not of failure, but of something they can't name, something they think we woke up by mistake."

Cutter ran a hand over his scalp. "We don't have 'yet.' We need machines in the field yesterday. The Guild's closing the tunnels west. And we can't hold the foundry line forever."

Link wiped a layer of grime from his cheek. "I can build the bridge. But I need time. I need cleaner gear mesh. Better power bleed filters. Half these parts are held together with rust and faith."

"Time burns," Walder muttered.

A long silence followed. Steam curled between them. Somewhere high above, an old banner shifted with a creaking sigh as air pressure fluctuated. Eve stood and passed her untouched mug to Cutter. The ceramic clinked faintly against his brace.

"You can scream later," she said. "For now, let him work."

Cutter stared at her, then downed the broth in one gulp and walked out. Walder lingered a moment longer, then nodded to one of the techs to set down the actuator cradle and followed.

They worked into dusk.

Link's hands moved without rest, dismantling old servo gyros, testing load-bearing joints, measuring magnetic sync tolerances. The warehouse filled with the clang of tools and the hiss of torch welds. Free Steam techs came and went, some helping, some just watching—curious, suspicious, desperate. Murmured speculation threaded between them like smoke: fragments of overheard blame, whispered warnings, the scrape of boots and the rattle of dropped tools. Somewhere near the back, someone muttered Link's name again, just loud enough to be heard but not owned. Shadows stretched long across the floor, warping under the flicker of arc lamps and open flame—like the city itself was drawing in a breath, bracing for a storm not yet arrived. Each wavering silhouette twisted with a quiet warning, hinting at fractures deeper than steel. The rhythmic beat of someone hammering out a bracket in the adjacent hall pulsed like a second heartbeat.

An older mechanic named Grell offered a hand with the actuator mount. He said little, but when he did, it was precise. He had a daughter in the shelter block. He didn't say her name. He only asked if the Ghostframe would be able to shield a crawler column.

Link promised nothing.

Another engineer, a wiry girl named Brin, argued heatedly with Eve about fuel allotment. Brin insisted the Ghostframe was a waste of precious coal—a luxury project born from someone who didn't know what it was like to watch their sector freeze during a fuel shortage. Her voice cracked not just with frustration, but with the bitterness of ration lines and empty stoves, of promises broken by those who still had tools and shelter. That it was a vanity project. That if it failed again, they'd all pay.

Eve didn't raise her voice. She only stared at the woman, her eyes narrowed—not angry, not pleading, but fixed with a weight that felt ancient. Her jaw was set tight, muscles clenching once, and her nostrils flared with the ghost of some distant restraint. Brin looked into those eyes and saw something waiting—something that did not bend. She faltered, blinked, and walked away.

Outside, the mist darkened. Steam curled tighter around the warehouse like a hand closing. Beyond the fogged windows, shadowed figures moved in silence—shapes slipping between lamp posts and scaffold frames, just out of focus. From deeper in the industrial maze, the rumble of distant machinery stirred, a low groan rising like a warning from the belly of the city. Distant horns sounded twice—short, clipped, warnings without details. Near the loading docks, wind caught a frayed length of canvas hanging from a rusted pulley, setting it flapping in slow, syncopated rhythm.

Inside, Link crawled under the Ghostframe again, tightening bolts by torchlight. Every clang echoed through his spine, his jaw locked against the vibration. His breath came in shallow huffs. Every joint in his body ached.

He didn't notice Eve had returned until a familiar parcel hit the floor beside him. He blinked, startled, then let out a breath he hadn't realized he was holding. Gratitude stirred somewhere beneath the fatigue—a quiet, wordless relief that someone still saw him, still remembered to care. Wrapped ration bread. Flat, dense, still warm.

"Eat," she said.

He did.

And in that moment, he wasn't building a revolution. He was just trying to stay upright.

The Heartcoil pulsed once—stronger this time. The floor beneath him buzzed. The pulse echoed in his molars.

He exhaled.

Neither of them spoke. They didn't have to.

And in the far corners of the city, steam curled around broken towers, and something vast and silent began to shift in response. It was not metaphor. Deep in the abandoned arteries of Eastland—beneath steel, beneath soot—sensors blinked to life. One clicked softly. Another pulsed. Then silence again. The air there held no breath, but it remembered breath. The old machinery stirred, no longer forgotten, and somewhere in the dark, a mechanism began to count. It had no name, no shrine, no scripture. But it remembered the shape of fire, and the rhythm of change. And now, it listened.

Chapter 25
Ash Marches

The Iron March was never announced. It simply began. Fog draped over Eastland's skeletal skyline, thick as gauze soaked in oil. It clung to twisted girders and collapsed walkways, rolling through broken archways and dripping gutters like smoke from a dying god. The city's soundscape, normally harsh and metallic, softened—muted. Distant clangs of falling scrap became muffled thuds. Steam vents exhaled slow, breath-like pulses. Rebar groaned softly beneath invisible strain. It was as if the city itself had taken a breath it could no longer hold.

Then came the march. A thudding, measured beat. Metal boots against cracked stone. Iron-shod feet stepping in perfect cadence down a forgotten boulevard. The sound rose not like music but like judgment—raw, deliberate, terrible. Fog swirled in rhythm, displaced by the vibration of armored weight against stone.

A column of Guild troops. Automata led them—massive bipedal walkers with smoke bleeding from their shoulder vents. Their sun-gear sigils spun slowly in their chests, half-buried in carbon scoring and battle tarnish. Each step sent faint vibrations through puddles along the guttered road, water trembling in rhythm with the machine pulse. Lantern-eyes scanned the ruins, shafts of pale light slicing the fog into broken beams. Steam vented with every few steps, curling skyward and illuminating drifting flecks of ash.

Behind them came infantry in reinforced boilerplate armor, trudging forward with the grace of siege engines. Gas masks cloaked every face, the rubber hissing faintly with each breath. Tubes swayed behind them like leeches in the mist. Their rifles clicked now and then, checked and reset by gloved fingers without pause.

Boots struck the stone with a cadence too precise to be human. The pressure in their jaws, the slight tremor in the visors—beneath those masks, some were sweating.

Shadows moved in alleys, shutters creaked open and closed. A pair of workers pressed against a collapsed tram rail and stared silently at the marchers—neither running nor calling out. A child's hand reached through a broken window, then vanished just as quickly.

And at the head, standing tall upon a crawler-chariot flanked by dual cannon arms, was Lord Valtor. He wore no helmet. His black-and-gold command coat gleamed wet with condensation, its medal-cluttered breastplate stiff as iron parchment. His jaw was set like a forged edge. One gloved hand rested calmly on a steel grip, the other closed over his knee, unmoving. Smoke wafted across the deck of the crawler, coiling around his shoulders like a waiting storm. His eyes didn't blink. His cheek twitched once—only once.

The Iron Procession. Not since the First Collapse had it marched through Eastland. And now, it moved not to reclaim. But to punish.

Hours earlier...

The Free Steam warehouse had not yet cooled from the last weld arcs when the warning bells rang—two sharp pulses, then silence. Guild scouts northeast. Too close to the water siphons.

Cutter's command cut through the rising noise. Four squads deployed in under five minutes. Link and Eve were not among them. Cutter didn't need inventors on the front. Not yet.

But Link watched from the rooftop.

Below, runners shouted over hissing pipes. Boots slapped across catwalks. The Ghostframe, draped in a soot-dark tarp, pulsed faintly underneath—the coil's hum steady as a drumbeat too deep to hear. The air shimmered with residual heat, and faint sparks still glowed in the seams of recently sealed armor plating.

The warehouse groaned as metal shifted under new tension. Banners along the rafters stirred faintly despite the still air. Outside, the clatter of a dropped wrench rang too loud and too fast. Someone whispered a prayer from beneath a half-welded engine bay.

It felt wrong. Like pressure gathering behind a faulty pressure valve. Not panic—not yet. But the kind of tension a machine feels before a coupling bursts.

"Something's different," Eve murmured beside him, crouched low with one hand braced against a rust-worn vent. Fog curled past her glove, brushing against her sleeve like breath. Her brow furrowed deeply, lips pressed tight. Her eyes flicked left, then down, scanning for exits as much as threats.

Link didn't look at her. His mouth tightened. "They don't move like this unless they want to be seen."

"Or to scatter us." Her hand trembled briefly, then stilled against her knee.

The clangs came again—too rhythmic for scavengers. Too heavy for foot patrols. The sound bloomed in the mist, thick and certain, like iron drums buried beneath the street. The rooftop's rusted railing vibrated faintly beneath Link's fingertips. He adjusted his grip, knuckles whitening for a second before relaxing.

The beat of iron feet.

Eve's breath hitched. Her nostrils flared. "The Iron Procession."

Stories echoed in that name. Everyone knew them. No one had seen it.

Link leaned forward. Heat shimmered in the mist. Shapes swam in the fog—at first uncertain, then undeniable. His jaw clenched. A bead of sweat ran down his temple despite the cold.

They weren't just marching. They were occupying.

"They're not scouting," he whispered. "They're declaring."

They ducked lower as the fog shifted—not with wind, but with heat and density. It curled in slow spirals, then with sharper pulses, each wave stronger than the last. From deeper in the city came faint echoes—metal collapsing, a pressure valve screaming open, boots slipping on iron mesh. The city's breath caught.

And then: a gleam. Sun-gear helix. A second. A dozen.

Eve tensed. "They'll cut power again. Like the day Mara—" She cut herself off. A beat of silence passed.

Then Link said, low, "We won't give them that chance."

Eve exhaled slowly, one gloved hand brushing the edge of her belt where Mara's old insignia pin was still clipped—bent, half-burned, but carried every day since the fallback. She didn't speak of it. Just tapped it once, lightly, like checking for its weight.

Before Eve could respond, a faint voice crackled through the makeshift radio receiver clipped to her belt.

"Warehouse echo-nine—be advised. Word from Cutter's forward scouts... there's talk of a sympathizer. Someone's been relaying entry points. Might explain their route."

Eve's stomach sank. "Say again?"

The voice hissed with static. "Could be nothing. Could be planted fear. But Cutter wants eyes on everyone. Especially engineers who had contact with the new coil rig."

Link's jaw flexed. "They think it's internal?"

"Enough to seed doubt," Eve murmured. She didn't take her eyes off the haze below. "That's all they need."

A silence fell. Not the stillness of quiet. The silence of knowing.

The city groaned beneath them. And then the first shell hit the outer line.

Chapter 26
The Edge of Iron:
When Silence Breaks

Link had heard the stories—passed in whispers, old soldiers claiming they could feel the Iron March coming in their bones. No horns. No warnings. Just the rhythm of inevitability rolling through the fog. He crouched low on the rooftop, breath held, watching Eastland vanish beneath curtains of steam and silence. Fog clung to the city like a burial shroud, muting even the clang of a dropped tool. The streets felt strangled. And beneath his gloves, the metal railing began to tremble.

Then came the march. Not just sound—it was pressure, rising through stone. A vibration that crawled up his arms and settled in his chest like a second heartbeat. Heavy. Unrelenting. Closer.

Down below, something moved. Shapes in formation. Lantern eyes. Sun-gear sigils. Pistons breathing steam.

"That's not a sweep," he murmured.

Eve crouched beside him, her eyes narrowed. "They want to be seen. Want us to break before they fire."

And still the march came.

The Iron Procession.

The rooftop trembled beneath the weight of it. And Link, for just a moment, understood what it meant to be in the path of history. Fog draped Eastland's skeletal skyline, thick as gauze soaked in oil. It blurred edges and swallowed sound, dampening every clang and echo until even footsteps felt muted. The mist made distances lie—near and far folding into one murky veil. It bled down towers and caught on broken spires, muffling sound and turning every street into a dead echo chamber. The city felt strangled. Air clung to skin. Pressure built behind the stillness.

Then came the march. The sound didn't just echo—it changed the air itself. It rolled low through the mist, sending ripples through steam and stirring loose grit from shattered stone. Somewhere far off, metal groaned in answer, like the ruins themselves remembered fear.

A thudding, measured beat. Metal boots crushing cracked stone. Iron-shod feet stepping in perfect cadence down a forgotten boulevard. No banners. No horns. Just sound—raw, deliberate, inevitable. Like a sentence being carried out.

Automata led the column. Massive bipedal walkers vented steam with each stride. Lantern eyes scanned in smooth sweeps, casting pale cones of light through the mist. Their sigils of the sun-gear spun lazily on their chests, tarnished but unyielding. Pistons hissed. Gears turned with a deep, bone-shaking groan.

Behind them came the infantry—ranked soldiers in reinforced boilerplate. Gas masks covered their faces, tubes trailing from canisters that pulsed faintly with pressure. Fog clung to their armor and hissed softly beneath their boots with each step. Condensation gathered on their masks, beading and dripping as they marched. Their breathing echoed behind the rubber, harsh and regular. Rifles clutched to chests, checked every few steps with mechanical precision.

And at the head of this procession, towering over the advance in his crawler-chariot, sat Lord Valtor. He wore no helmet. His command coat, black trimmed with tarnished gold, hung stiff with starch. Medals lined his breast, glittering dully beneath the mist. One hand rested on his knee, the other on the railing. His jaw was tight, his expression unreadable. A monarch of silence and fury.

The Iron Procession. Not seen in Eastland since the First Collapse. And now it came not to reclaim. But to erase.

Hours earlier... The Free Steam warehouse still reeked of hot metal. The scent of scorched copper and coal oil hadn't yet faded when the bells rang—two sharp pulses, then silence. Guild scouts. Too close.

Cutter moved immediately. Four squads dispatched. No hesitation. Link and Eve were held back.

From the rooftop, Link watched. Runners moved like blood through arteries, delivering orders. Engineers scrambled to protect equipment.

A young girl—no older than ten—huddled in the shadows near the back wall, bundled in an oversized coat patched with copper wire and canvas. She clutched a tin cup too tightly, eyes fixed on the tarp-covered Ghostframe. Her mother, crouched beside her, whispered something meant to soothe, but the girl's eyes didn't leave the machine. Not with fear. With belief. Like it might stand up and keep the monsters out.

Link saw them only for a second before a runner passed between. But it stuck. That look. That quiet hope. It made his hands shake harder. The Ghostframe sat beneath its tarp, humming faintly. Fog coiled around its base, and the rising warmth beneath the canvas distorted the folds with a heat shimmer. Dim Heartcoil light pulsed through the fabric in waves, casting ghostly patterns across the ceiling like a heartbeat, or so it seemed to Link—like tension coiled within a sleeping beast. Its presence hung over the room like a loaded weapon. Some avoided looking at it too long, whispering when they passed. Others watched it with guarded hope, as if it might roar to life and save them before the first shell fell.

Later, as the Ghostframe stepped into the fog, Link saw that same girl from the shadows again—just a glimpse through the parted wall, clinging to her mother's coat and watching with wide, unblinking eyes. The machine had moved. The promise had answered.

"Something's off," Eve muttered. She crouched beside Link, eyes narrowed. Her breath fogged faintly.

He nodded. "This isn't a sweep."

"They want to be seen. Want us to panic."

Then they heard it. Not from below, but from beyond. A low thud. Then another. Steady. Heavy. Rhythmic.

Eve's eyes widened. "That sound... it's real."

"The Iron Procession," Link whispered.

Mist thickened as shapes began to emerge. Armor. Pistons. Flags of the sun-gear standard. They weren't advancing to search. They were advancing to crush.

The rooftop trembled beneath the weight of inevitability, a deep vibration that climbed through Link's boots and settled into his bones like a warning from the stone itself.

At dawn, the first shell struck.

Not an explosion. A hiss. Green mist rolled across the trench line. Chemical. Corrosive. Designed not to kill, but to break ranks.

Cutter's squads fell back. Not chaos. Controlled retreat. But tension rippled through every motion.

Inside the command alcove, Walder hovered over a salvaged table scrawled with fallback routes. Steam curled around the edges of the room.

"Should we move the Heartcoil?" one of the younger engineers asked, voice tight with apprehension.

"No," Link answered, calm but unyielding.

Heads turned.

The tarp had been peeled back halfway. The Ghostframe crouched in the far corner, inert but imposing. Its eye-sockets were dark, its chest plate rising and falling in time with the slow thrum of the Heartcoil embedded inside—blue light flickering beneath seams like breath held in tension.

"If we move it now, we lose the only edge they fear."

Brin crossed her arms, tension in her voice. "They'll level the block. Flatten the rig with crawler artillery."

Link didn't blink. "Then let them try. The Ghostframe's not just a machine. It's a question they can't answer."

Cutter stepped forward, wiping soot across his cheek with the back of his glove. "Then we bleed them. Inch by inch."

Walder folded his arms, brow furrowed as he studied the map. "We buy time. Force hesitation. Make them wonder if the ground under them is stable."

Outside, the march slowed.

Valtor stood on the prow of his crawler, fog parting around him. The ash in the air settled onto his shoulders like snow. A telegram sat tight in his coat—Free Steam was organizing. Unacceptable.

Valtor's gloved hand rose, fingers steady, palm tilted just slightly.

The automata halted mid-stride. Their pistons locked in place. A low hiss of steam sighed from their chests as gears recalibrated, rotating back into readiness with the precision of killing clocks.

Then—forward.

Steam vented in a single unified blast, sending a curtain of white rolling through the ranks. Pressure plates struck the stone beneath them with the weight of verdicts. Boots stomped. Rivets clicked. Iron roared—not loud, but deep, like thunder trapped underground.

And then—through the mist, a shadow moved.

Not clearly. But enough.

A silhouette materialized—taller than a man, hunched slightly forward, broad across the shoulders, with a pulse of faint blue shining like breath beneath armor plates.

The Ghostframe.

Its glow rippled faintly through the fog. Not bright. Not aggressive. But defiant. The kind of light that said: "You missed your chance."

Valtor didn't flinch, but his jaw tightened. His gaze fixed on the shape, and for a fleeting second, something flickered behind his eyes—not fear, but the simmering burn of obsession. The kind that haunted men too proud to admit they felt it.

It wasn't just a machine. It was defiance made visible. A heresy of design. An affront to everything the Guild had crushed beneath its doctrine.

And that insulted him more than any rebel blade.

Within the trench line, Link snapped a final harness in place, metal clasps biting home with a dull click. Left shoulder stabilizers had been rewired twice already—any real pressure might tear the joint. The arm might not survive more than a single sustained clash. His breath fogged faintly inside the collar of his rig suit.

Eve stood beside him, sliding charge cores into a reinforced satchel. Her fingers moved quickly, but her jaw was set, eyes scanning the fog beyond the barricade. Cutter barked orders just behind them, his voice cutting through the low murmur of readiness. Sparks flew where engineers still welded last-minute supports into place, and the air reeked of grease and ozone.

Walder approached with a repeater rig slung over his shoulder, heavy and well-worn. He passed it off with both hands. "Heavy shot," he said. "Make it count."

A scout's whistle pierced the haze. Close.

The enemy had arrived.

Roland's silhouette shifted deeper in the mist, adjusting his gauntlets with theatrical flair—a practiced motion born less of vanity and more of a man clinging to the echo of relevance, desperate to perform the role he believes history still owes him as he mounted his Seraph frame—grinning like a man stepping onto a stage.

In the trenchworks, the Ghostframe stirred beneath its bindings. A soft thrum radiated through its limbs.

Eve stepped forward, eyes sharp, and sealed the cockpit hatch with a solid clang. Steam vented from the rig's joints as Link climbed in, movements practiced, deliberate.

She placed a hand on the frame's side, voice low but unwavering. "Time to be remembered."

Inside, Link exhaled through his nose, jaw tight. He paused for just a moment, gloved fingers tightening around the control yokes. Around him, the cockpit hummed with latent energy. The light from the Heartcoil shimmered across the interface glass, casting faint pulses against his cheeks like a heartbeat urging him forward. A bead of sweat slid down his temple, unshaken by fear—only weight. "Let's make them regret coming."

The Ghostframe pulsed—once, deep—and stepped forward into the fog. Steam hissed from its ankles as its foot met the ground with a hollow, echoing clank—each step a hammerfall in the silence. Each footfall echoed like the promise of resistance—not willful, but resolute, forged by the hands that built it.

Chapter 27
Where Steel Breaks

The Ghostframe's first stride into the ruins felt like dragging history itself forward—a rumbling defiance that split the silence like a faultline. Steam hissed from ruptured pipes as the ground trembled beneath its weight, a low quake that rattled shattered windows and dislodged chunks of masonry from nearby facades. The fog recoiled from its path in slow, writhing currents, peeling back to expose the looming silhouette in motion. Old banners above twisted in the displaced air, iron joints echoing like distant bells as the past stepped forward to meet the war now unfolding. Even the air seemed to pause—sound tightening, pressure shifting—as if the ruins themselves held their breath in anticipation.

The heavy pistons groaned, gears locking and releasing in fluid precision, as Link guided the machine down the fractured main avenue. Eve sat tight in the gunner's seat, fingers curled around the rigged controls. The Heartcoil pulsed beneath them, steady and hungry.

Smoke clung to every jagged edge of the ruins. Steam curled up from shattered vents like ghosts too tired to rise. The light from scattered forge-fires flickered against broken glass and fractured iron, casting long, twitching shadows across the scarred street. A soft hiss of pressure echoed with each step of the Ghostframe, followed by a muted clank of impact as its feet hit the ground.

Behind them, fog rolled in thick coils, reacting subtly to the weight of the Ghostframe's motion. Each thunderous footfall disturbed the mist in pulses, stirring the air like ripples across the surface of a blackened lake. High above, broken tram rails creaked faintly in the distance, swaying on ancient, rusted cables.

"Visual on advancing hostiles," Eve said, voice tight. The optics flickered through layers of heat distortion. Automata—at least five—moved methodically between the collapsed tram towers, followed by Guild infantry in staggered formations.

Link gritted his teeth. For a moment, he saw the image of Eve crumpled behind cover during the last raid, smoke and screams blurring into chaos. His jaw tensed harder. "Line up the rail launcher. We'll make them step careful."

The Ghostframe's right arm shifted, servos whining as Eve guided the barrel toward the advancing iron tide. From the misted windows, distant silhouettes moved like shadows on puppet strings, angular and precise.

She exhaled sharply. "Firing."

The railshot cracked like thunder, tearing through the fog in a shockwave that made the air ripple and the Ghostframe lurch slightly in recoil. The mist parted violently, peeled back by the force, as the shot struck the lead automaton center mass. The impact sent the enemy machine staggering, its chest plating crumpling inward with a scream of warped metal. It fell sideways, limbs twitching as steam vented violently from its broken spine.

"That got their attention," Eve muttered.

It had. The other automata spread out instantly, adjusting tactics. Infantry ducked into cover, rifles raised. The battle shifted from looming threat to active engagement in a breath. Sparks rained from ricocheted fire as stray rounds glanced off twisted debris and slag walls.

"Here they come," Link warned.

Rounds struck the Ghostframe, pinging off the reinforced hull. Link felt the impacts in his teeth, vibrations thrumming through the cockpit. Not enough to stop them. Not yet.

"Left side—Seraph frame incoming!" Eve barked.

Link twisted the Ghostframe's torso, shifting weight to meet the challenge. Through the haze, Roland's Seraph machine emerged, graceful and gleaming. It moved with aristocratic precision, sliding between ruined columns and firing twin pulse-cannons in measured bursts.

"This is it," Link said under his breath. "He's here."

The Seraph's rounds slammed into their left shoulder plating, denting but not breaching. Eve snapped back with a railshot, but Roland's machine darted sideways—far faster than the heavier Ghostframe could follow.

"He's quick," Eve growled.

"Too quick," Link agreed. He adjusted throttle flow, pushing the Heart-coil harder. The Ghostframe groaned, but responded. Pressure climbed, steam hissed through reinforced joints, and the frame's plates flexed with effort.

Roland's voice echoed through the soundscape—arrogant, theatrical. Not a comms link, but shouted from an amplifier. "You're a nuisance. Time to snuff out fairy tales."

Link ignored him, focusing. "Cut right. Angle him between that tower base and the rubble. We'll box him."

Eve shifted their path. Roland pursued, eager.

That was the mistake.

As the Seraph swept wide, Link rotated hard, swinging the Ghostframe's heavy arm around and catching Roland's machine mid-dash. The impact was brutal—metal shrieked as the Seraph slammed into the ruined tower. Shards of stone and steel fell in a cascade.

Eve fired point-blank. The railshot tore through the Seraph's leg actuator. Roland cursed as his machine stumbled.

"Now!" Link pushed forward.

The Ghostframe lunged, shoulder-checking the Seraph and sending it crashing into the ground. Roland's automata flailed, pinned beneath tons of iron fury.

"End him!" Eve shouted.

But Link hesitated—just a heartbeat. Roland was still inside that cockpit. And in that moment, Link saw not a memory, but the truth behind the armor—a privileged boy raised far from the fire, now playing at war with lives that weren't his. The thought struck like a jolt of clarity. Just enough to slow him.

That heartbeat cost them.

A sharp alarm blared. Target lock.

From beyond the melee, Guild crawler cannons opened fire.

The ground erupted. Shockwaves hurled debris and fire across the battlefield. The Ghostframe staggered, its grip on Roland's Seraph breaking as shrapnel pounded their armor.

"Pull back!" Eve yelled.

Link didn't argue. He reversed thrusters and bounded backward as Roland's crippled machine limped away, vanishing into smoke.

More automata were closing in—steel silhouettes emerging from the fog in disciplined waves, gears clanking and steam venting with every step. Pulse-cannons fired in sweeping arcs. Rubble exploded to their left, narrowly missing the Ghostframe's leg actuator. Link gritted his teeth, recalibrating balance. Eve shouted over the din, "They're surrounding us!" Link pulled hard on the controls, wrenching the frame backward as suppressive fire rained around them. This wasn't a fight to win. Not here. Not yet.

"Fall back to Sector 7!" came the cry from a runner dashing past—face masked, cloak scorched.

Link twisted the Ghostframe, shielding Eve as they retreated through the crumbling avenues. The street twisted beneath them, rubble catching their footfalls and casting long shadows in the morning light. Windows shattered as artillery boomed behind them, raining glass and ash across their wake. The mist swallowed the distance, offering no mercy.

Behind them, the Iron Procession advanced again—slower now, but relentless. Lantern-eyes flared through the haze. Chemical firelight burned on metal edges. The sound of gears grinding against soot-choked joints rolled forward like a funeral hymn.

As they reached the fallback line, Link glanced once toward the ruins where Roland had disappeared. His knuckles tightened around the control levers, breath fogging inside the visor. Flames still licked at broken stone. Steam belched from cracked conduits. The air pulsed with distant cannon rhythm. His heartbeat thudded in his ears, echoing the Ghostframe's deeper churn. Roland had vanished into smoke, but Link could still feel the weight of him—somewhere out there, smug, untouched. That would change. The next time they met, it wouldn't be armor that decided the victor—it would be resolve. Grit. Fire.

Next time, he thought grimly, eyes narrowing. Next time, I'll drag him from that gilded shell myself—and show him what the rest of us bled to build.

The Heartcoil's pulse slowed as they disengaged—but it still burned, steady and alive, promising that this wasn't the end.

Not even close.

Chapter 28
Shattered Advance

The retreat did not feel like survival. It felt like surrender—like stepping backward into shadow while fire still burned behind your eyes. Link's stomach clenched as the Ghostframe took its final, limping steps, each one rattling through his bones with the weight of failure. He wanted to scream. Or hit something. Or rewind time by one heartbeat and not let Roland escape.

The Ghostframe limped heavily into the fallback zone, its left leg actuator shrieking with every step, the sound scraping against the bones of the street like a rusted blade. Smoke hissed from a dozen breaches along its joints, and coolant bled in faint mist from the exposed venting ribs along its lower torso. The reinforced hide of the machine bore the scars of its baptism—plasma burns streaked in warped lines across its flank, deep rakes from crawler cannon shrapnel, and a spiderweb crack etched into the cockpit's forward plate where the enemy's final volley had landed too close.

Inside, Link let out a breath he hadn't realized he'd been holding. It came in sharp, shallow bursts, fogging the inner visor. He powered the Heartcoil down to standby, and with a low hum and soft flickering of the core's light, the machine exhaled with him—systems settling, tension unwinding into a mechanical lull. Eve moved beside him in the gunner's seat, her gloved hands slow and deliberate as she unclipped her harness. Her shoulders sagged just slightly, like armor sliding off. She didn't speak. Neither did he. Silence had weight after combat—an invisible armor that had to be peeled away in layers.

Outside, the trenches were alive. Free Steam personnel raced along mud-slick pathways between half-buried scaffolds and pulleys rigged from pipe scrap. Engineers hauled crates of munitions over shoulder poles. Medics stitched wounds beneath lanterns that guttered in the wind. The ground trembled intermittently with distant shellfire, a reminder that peace had only fled to the edge of the line. The chill clung to the bones, sinking past layers of grease and fabric, and the mist curled low around ankles like grasping fingers.

Walder met them at the platform's edge. His face was pale beneath layers of soot, his jaw tight as copper wire. Sweat clung to the back of his neck where his collar was frayed open. "You gave them a bloody nose," he said, not quite congratulating. His eyes flicked up to the Ghostframe, now hunched like a war-worn sentinel. "But they're still marching."

Link stepped down from the rungs and winced as he hit the ground. His boots sank slightly into the mud, and a sharp breath hissed between his teeth. "We slowed them. That's all."

Cutter strode over, wiping his neck with a grease-streaked rag, his coat slung over one shoulder like a banner left in the dirt. His voice cut low and sharp. "Slowed ain't stopped. They'll be pressing again by dawn. Roland's down, but not out." His gaze locked onto Link. "You got close. Too close to let him walk away."

Link looked away, jaw flexing. "I hesitated."

Eve dropped from the platform beside him, her boots splashing faintly in a shallow puddle that shimmered with coolant and rain. Her eyes met Cutter's, steady and flint-hard. "You made the right call," she said, firm. "We don't execute pilots unless we have to."

Cutter didn't flinch. "Mercy's nice. But Roland ain't the type to repay it."

No one disagreed. The silence didn't need to. The war would judge who was right.

Hours Later The trenches had dimmed. The world pressed low under smoke-thick skies. Link stood beside the Ghostframe in the cooling dusk, one hand resting against the machine's battered flank. His fingers traced the cracked weld lines, the gouges where enemy fire had kissed too deep. Beneath the frame's armored ribs, warmth still radiated faintly from the Heartcoil. It pulsed like a living thing—slower now, but no less potent. The casing around it was scorched and blackened in places, still bearing streaks of coolant that had boiled off during overload. A crack ran through one of the copper stabilizer rings, spidered and jagged.

This was not a prototype anymore. It was no longer a thing built just to test theories or survive sparring drills. Link could feel it now—etched into every scrape of metal, every residual hum through his boots, every delayed breath that synced with the quiet lull of the Heartcoil's core. The Ghostframe had crossed a threshold. It wasn't alive—but it remembered in the way machines did. Its restraint in battle, its response to his hesitation—these weren't choices. They were the echo of his input, his fear, his will reflected back in steel.

It was a weapon. And weapons didn't forget.

Somewhere in the ruins beyond, automata stalked the edges. Their metallic footsteps echoed faintly across abandoned masonry. Patrols. Maybe scouts. Link didn't care. He wasn't afraid. Not tonight. What filled him now wasn't fear.

It was fury.

His shoulders squared. Fingers curled unconsciously at his sides, knuckles blanching as the tension he'd buried during the retreat surfaced again.

"We need more than power," he muttered to himself, pacing the repair gantry. "We need control. Responsiveness."

He turned, brows furrowed, lips drawn taut with the taste of iron and frustration. Sparks fluttered from a half-sealed panel where cooling coils still hissed weakly. The metal beneath his boots felt like a living conduit, vibrating with memory.

Behind him, a voice gravelled through the dusk. "You're thinking fast-resolve control systems, aren't you?"

Link turned to find Walder leaning against a support brace, arms folded.

"Manual loop's too slow," Link said. "The pilot needs seamless feedback. Like muscle. Like instinct. Not command, but reaction."

Walder chewed on that. "That's dangerous thinking. You're talking reflex mapping. Neural latency thresholds. If you miss even one feedback delay…"

"I'm talking about surviving," Link snapped. "Roland's Seraph frame isn't better because it's stronger. It's better because it moves like him."

Walder approached the platform, stepping around a cooling vent with the ease of habit. He clapped Link on the shoulder—heavy, measured. "When you're ready, I'll help lay the groundwork. Can't promise you won't get cooked. But I'll try not to leave scorch marks."

Link managed a faint smile. "Story of my life."

Later That Night The Free Steam command tent felt more like a furnace than a war room. Sweat beaded on every brow, clinging to grease-smeared skin. The air was thick with the scent of burning oil, scorched metal, and old canvas soaked in breath and urgency. The crackle of steam vents outside punctuated the tense murmurs within. Tools clattered on makeshift tables, and the low rasp of whispered arguments curled around the room like smoke. It wasn't quiet. It was suppressed—heat and desperation pressing in from all sides. The table at the center was bowed with maps, schematics, hastily scribbled field logs. Around it stood Cutter, Eve, Mara, Walder, and two dozen others—tired, dirty, alive.

"They'll press again by midday," Cutter began. "And we can't keep taking the brunt head-on."

"We won't," Eve replied. "The Ghostframe changes the terms. Link's got something cooking, and I'm betting on it."

Mara gave her a skeptical look. "Even if he fixes the reflex sync, it won't stop Valtor. That Procession's a hammer looking for a skull."

Link stepped forward, tapping a section of the map. "Then we don't give them a skull. We give them a trap."

His finger landed on a faded district—The Old Gasworks. Subsurface tunnels. Gas ruptures. Cracked foundation lines. A graveyard waiting to collapse.

"We bait their automata forward," he said. "Then bring the ground down beneath them."

The council stared at the map. Then at him. Walder gave a low whistle. "Brutal."

Eve's grin came slow and sharp. "I like it."

Cutter rolled his shoulders, tension dropping. "It's bold. It's ugly. It might work."

The meeting broke with urgency—orders to relay, scouts to brief. Only Link and Eve remained behind in the fading torchlight.

She didn't move at first, just stood beside him, quiet in the glow, her arms folded but not defensive. A flicker of something unreadable passed over her face—relief, maybe, or the ragged tail of fear she hadn't let show during the meeting. She hadn't slept. None of them had. But it was etched deeper in her posture now.

Link turned to her, his brow still furrowed from the strain of command, but his voice was soft. "You alright?"

Eve gave a small nod, then tilted her head toward him, her eyes catching the torchlight just enough to shimmer. "I hate waiting," she said.

He offered a faint, crooked smile. "Then it's a good thing we're bad at it."

She bumped his shoulder gently with hers. Just enough contact to stay grounded.

They didn't say more. But they didn't step apart either.

She leaned close, shoulder brushing his.

"Still thinking too much."

He stared at the flickering edge of the map. "Still breathing."

Beyond the trenches, thunder rippled—not from the sky, but from distant engines and gears.

The Iron Procession was not done. And neither were they.

Chapter 29
The Furnace Below

Morning in Eastland came as an accusation, not a reprieve.

Light didn't break cleanly. It seeped through the choking clouds of ash and steam, casting the ruins in pallid, corpse-colored hues. The air smelled of scorched metal and old, wet brick. Even silence here carried a weight, like something listening. The only thing that truly stirred was the Iron Procession—still advancing, slow and merciless, toward Free Steam's crumbling refuge. Its march was felt more than heard, a dull, distant tremor beneath their feet.

But Link and the others were already moving.

The tunnel entrance yawned before them like a throat prepared to swallow hope. Accessed through a shattered storm drain, the path descended quickly into ancient maintenance shafts that predated even the Guild's oldest maps. Rusted rail tracks split down the center of the corridor like an exposed spine. Condensation dripped from above in irregular beats, echoing in the metal dark.

"This used to feed the central furnaces," Walder explained quietly, pulling his scarf tighter against the chemical stink. "Before the Collapse, anyway. Half the district was powered from down here."

"Perfect place to hide and strike," Eve muttered, checking her coil-lance. "Or to die and never be found."

Link followed without hesitation, but something in his chest coiled tight — not fear, exactly, but a dread forged in the shape of memory. His jaw clenched as he adjusted the strap on his shoulder, dragging a satchel packed with diagnostic coils, spare capacitors, and the Ghostframe's hastily patched remote core. This wasn't the full unit—the main Heartcoil remained locked in the rig. But this smaller pack, hastily retrofitted, could still trigger a controlled discharge if calibrated right. The weight of it wasn't just mechanical — it felt like responsibility in iron form. He didn't speak, but in the dim tunnel glow, his eyes burned with a silent resolve: if this didn't work, there would be no second chance. They couldn't bring the full machine through these tunnels—not yet. This strike was purely on foot.

But if the plan worked, it would change the war.

The descent was miserable.

Link barely felt his legs after the first mile. Not from fatigue — but from the gnawing pressure that built behind his sternum, the slow grind of memories clawing up through the dark. Every step through that subterranean maw reminded him of places he had fled, of screams in narrow spaces, of shadows that moved wrong. He pushed those ghosts aside with gritted teeth, but they whispered still.

Heat clung to the walls like something alive. Even so deep underground, steam hissed from ruptured pipes, creating narrow passageways slick with condensed grime. Every step felt like wading through old breath. The air tasted metallic and sour, sweat pooling in their collars before dripping to the floor. Somewhere above, the faint rhythmic hum of the Procession's engines never ceased, vibrating faintly in the soles of their boots like a distant war drum.

They moved single file. Cutter led, flanked by two demolition engineers carrying heavy-payload charges. Mara and Brin watched their rear. Link and Eve remained in the center, quietly discussing fallback trigger codes. There were no radios down here—only pre-set charges and runners waiting topside. Timing was the only voice they had.

"Roland won't fall for another ambush," Eve whispered. "If this works, we bury half their iron in one shot."

"Won't kill them all," Link said. "But enough to make them hesitate."

Eve's mouth tightened. "We need hesitation."

Link gave her a glance, then looked away. He couldn't admit how much he wanted it to hurt—how badly he wanted them to feel loss. Not because it was right. But because it was human.

By midday, they reached the lower staging point.

A cathedral of rust and shadow. Enormous boilers stood cold and dead, their sides scored with age and stained with ash. Catwalks twisted overhead like ribs from a long-forgotten beast. The flicker of torchlight danced off stagnant pools on the floor, throwing distorted reflections across the walls. Drips echoed like footsteps in places no one stood. Through cracks in the ceiling high above, the low whine of automata servos drifted like static from a broken speaker.

"They're right above us," Walder muttered, voice almost reverent.

Cutter didn't wait. He and the engineers rigged charges along the rusting braces. Brin and Mara placed shock triggers near pressure seams, their footsteps echoing faintly against old iron.

Link and Eve crouched near the Ghostframe's remote coil pack. Link's hands worked quickly, calibrating volt discharge and stabilization arrays, the light from the control panel casting pale glows across their faces.

"If I mistime this," he murmured, "we collapse before we're clear."

"Then don't mistime it," Eve said, half a smirk lifting the edge of her mouth. Her presence grounded him, steady as steel.

But when she turned away, her fingers lingered on the charge pack just a second longer. Not doubt. Just a quiet prayer that they'd walk out together.

By late afternoon, all was set. Fighters cleared the fallback tunnels. Only Cutter, Walder, Eve, and Link remained.

Above, the Iron Procession passed directly overhead—heavily laden automata, war crawlers, and Roland's Seraph moving in perfect, arrogant rhythm. Dust rained like ashfall. Steam curled down through the cracks like breath from sleeping giants, warm and sour with fuel.

"Now or never," Cutter said.

Link keyed the remote Heartcoil array.

Vibration began first. A low, growling hum that built through their bones. The walls groaned.

Then came the crack—metal shearing from concrete.

Then collapse.

The floor above buckled with a shuddering scream.

Guild forces plunged downward—hulking automata, crawler tanks, and infantry alike vanishing in a rain of steel and dust. Roland's Seraph leapt too late—one leg caught in twisting rebar. He fell with the rest, crashing in a spray of sparks.

Steam roared outward as if the world exhaled. A heat wave washed over them, carrying the stink of oil, blood, and ruptured hydraulics. Concrete screamed as it gave way. The noise was deafening.

Link shielded Eve as debris hammered the floor around them. Dust and soot blasted outward, drowning the chamber in a storm of falling ash and pulverized steel. For a breathless moment, the world was only sound and force.

Then—stillness.

The Procession's vanguard was gone.

"We did it," Eve whispered. Her voice shook, half with awe, half disbelief.

"Not all of them," Link said. "But enough."

Cutter peered into the crater, sweat shining on his soot-streaked face. "That'll make them bleed. Maybe even rethink."

Link didn't speak. His eyes had caught movement—something half-buried, twitching in the dust-choked ruin. For a moment, a pulse of heat climbed his spine. Not fear. Not entirely. A sick twist of guilt. He'd seen that shape before—too many times in his dreams. The Seraph wasn't just alive. Its cracked lens pulsed faintly—just a sensor, Link knew. But still it felt like a stare. Like it remembered him.

He clenched his jaw. No more hesitation. Not again.

There, amid the wreckage—Roland's Seraph. Crushed, but not dead.

Link returned its gaze. A flicker of heat crawled beneath his collar—frustration, fear, something deeper.

"Next time," he said under his breath, voice low with a heat that surprised even him, "you stay buried."

His fists tightened at his sides. A flash of guilt rippled through him—not just for the destruction, but for the part of him that had wanted this. That still wanted more.

He didn't flinch from the Seraph's flickering eye. He wanted it to see him. To remember. So that next time, when steel met steel again—there would be no doubt, no pause. Only fire.

Then he turned, followed Eve into the tunnels, and left the Iron Procession in ruins.

But even ruins could crawl.

Chapter 30
Wounded Steel

T he city did not mourn the fallen iron. It swallowed it, as it had swallowed everything.

But Roland did not fall.

Beneath twisted girders and broken automata limbs, deep in the hollow wreckage left by Free Steam's trap, the Seraph stirred.

Power sputtered through its cracked chestplate. The once-elegant machine, gilded and ornate, was now smeared in rust and filth, half-sunken into a grave of its own making. Sparks danced weakly across exposed conduits. One arm was gone, severed mid-bicep. The head hung askew, its decorative crest shattered.

Inside, Roland seethed.

He tasted blood in his mouth—a warm, metallic tang that mingled with the bitterness rising in his gut. His jaw throbbed where he'd slammed into his harness during the collapse. But he was alive—and more importantly, his pride was not yet dead.

Through the fractured viewscreen, he could see what was left of his once-flawless formation. Guild automata littered the ruin. Infantry corpses blended into the rubble, masked faces staring up blankly at the heavens they would never curse again.

Roland gripped the control yolk with shaking hands.

He could already imagine his father's voice—not raised, never that—just quiet and cutting. "You had every advantage," it would say. "And still, you lost."

The shame was worse than the pain. Not because he feared his father's judgment, but because it confirmed what he had always suspected: that Roland was still, in his father's eyes, the ornamental son. Gilded like the Seraph. Impressive. Hollow.

He closed his eyes for a heartbeat. What would Father say if he saw me now? he wondered bitterly. Not a word of comfort. Just silence thick with disappointment. It burned more than the shrapnel still lodged in his side.

"Unacceptable," he hissed. "This was supposed to be... definitive."

He triggered the Seraph's secondary systems manually, forcing the ruined warframe to move. Servos screamed. The machine lurched sideways, dragging itself free of debris with painful slowness. Roland's teeth ground together as the machine bucked under his commands.

His mind burned hotter than the steam coils surging beneath the Seraph's scorched boilerplate—rage boiling behind his eyes, shame clawing at the edges of his thoughts. For a brief, traitorous second, he wondered if it was his fault. Then he crushed the thought like a spark under iron.

Free Steam. Link. Eve. Scum. Vermin that refused to die when ordered.

Images burned in his memory — Link's Ghostframe rising defiant, Eve's eyes cold and sharp with resolve.

He should have crushed them. Crushed them like insects beneath his boot.

And yet—he hadn't. His Seraph, designed for spectacle as much as power, had faltered. Not because of his skills—no, never that—but because of their desperation and cruelty. Their trap. Their cheating.

The machine groaned as it stood fully upright. Sparks danced across its ravaged form, but Roland smiled bitterly. The frame still moved. And so did he.

"You think you've won," he muttered as he initiated emergency recall protocols. A signal flared in the distance—Guild recovery units, already mobilizing.

"You think this is a victory?"

His voice lowered, twisted with venom.

"I will show you victory. I will show you the cost of humiliating me."

He slumped back into his seat, breathing heavily as the Seraph began its slow, pained march back toward Guild-controlled lines. Every step was an echo of his humiliation, jarring his bruised ribs and scraping raw against his ego. Every clank and hiss of strained hydraulics echoed through the twisted hull like a sneer from the machine itself—grinding, rhythmic, and merciless. The acrid scent of scorched oil filled the cockpit, seeping into Roland's clothes and lungs, as if the Seraph wanted him to carry the stench of failure back with him. He welcomed it. Let it burn. Let it mark him.

Outside, smoke curled up from the wreckage like shame made visible. The wind moaned through shattered girders. Somewhere below his boots, steel groaned like a dying beast. The sounds pierced deeper than shrapnel, each one a reminder: You failed. You faltered.

But shame could be a forge.

The Guild recovery units arrived before dusk. Their crawler sentries unfolded from their armored hulls with methodical grace, hissing steam and grinding plates echoing across the rubble. White-coated engineers in soot-streaked aprons approached the wreck with solemn efficiency. They offered no sympathy—only protocol.

"Lieutenant Roland," one said, saluting with two fingers as he peered up at the mangled cockpit. "Extraction team. Orders to retrieve the frame and report to Valtor."

That name almost undid him.

Roland didn't answer. He stared at the man as though through fog.

Valtor. His father. His disappointment made manifest. He imagined the report already reaching headquarters—his failure inked cleanly into official logs, dissected and filed before he even arrived.

"Prepare for crane lift," another engineer called out. Chains clanked. Hooks groaned. The Seraph was being dismantled piece by piece, its limbs secured, joints locked, pride stripped away with every mechanical gesture.

Roland remained in the cockpit, silent as they worked around him.

Is this what you see when you think of me, Father? A shattered frame. A gilded ornament turned obsolete. A waste.

He clenched the yolk again—not to move, but to feel something solid. His fingertips trembled.

As the Seraph's shell rose on metal hooks, Roland finally stepped free of it. He didn't speak to the engineers. He didn't look back.

This was not over.

As the wreckage fell away behind him, Roland's mind raced—not with doubt, but with ideas.

He had contacts. Allies among the Guild artisans who envied Link's inventiveness. Private machinists who built forbidden things in the shadows of sanctioned factories. Nobles with appetites for cruelty and gold, who saw automata as symbols of absolute control.

He would make the Seraph more.

No—he would make himself more.

When next they faced him, Link and Eve would not find the pampered noble playing at war.

They would find the man Eastland's rot had carved from silk and vanity. They would find a weapon dressed in pride, sharpened by humiliation, its edges honed not just in anger but in the slow erosion of everything he once thought made him untouchable. A man reshaped by failure, no longer cloaked in silk but armored in resolve, skin stung by steam and shame, walking not in memory of what he was—but in defiance of it.

And somewhere in the back of his mind, faint and painful, came the thought: If Father sees me like this... maybe then... maybe finally...

The wind shifted. Hot air off the wreckage curled around him — acrid and suffocating. Each step behind the convoy sent a tremor through his bruised ribs.

Still can't hold it, can you?

It was the echo of Valtor's judgment, so deeply etched it didn't need words anymore. Not loud. Not cruel. Just... undeniable.

He gritted his teeth, throat tightening.

This time, it wasn't a saber slipping from his grip. It was a whole war.

And still — still — part of him burned with the same question he'd never outgrown: Would you see me now? Would you finally see me?

Roland smiled thinly as smoke curled from his ruined machine.

"Next time," he whispered, eyes burning with vindictive fire, "I make the rules."

And he walked alone behind the convoy, dragging his fury and ambition behind him like a blade across the bones of the dead.

This time, there would be no asking to be seen. Only the demand.

Chapter 31
Fragile Allies

The tension in Free Steam's makeshift war council could have been cut with a dull blade.

Link stood at the center of the crowded chamber, shoulders tense as eyes drilled into him from all sides. His hands itched to move, to build, to fix something—anything other than stand here and wait for judgment. Mara leaned back against the cracked pillar near the entrance, arms crossed tight, jaw set, like she was holding back the urge to pace. Walder shuffled through maps and reports spread haphazardly across a rust-stained table, pretending calm. Cutter, bruised and bandaged from the tunnel collapse, paced like a caged animal, every step echoing frustration.

And Eve — silent, sharp-eyed, watching it all unfold without yet choosing a side.

"What you did bought us breathing room, Link," Mara said at last, her tone laced with both reluctant admiration and a trace of unease—approval, perhaps, but also a warning of consequences yet to come. Her voice was measured but strained, like she'd rehearsed it on the way in. "No question about that. But collapsing a district? Dropping half the Procession into a pit? You think the Guild's going to just lick its wounds?"

"They'll retaliate," Cutter growled, cutting through the rising murmurs. "Hard. They always do. They'll come down on us with both boots and every automata they've still got standing."

"They'll come anyway," Link countered, voice steady but raw. He glanced around the circle, not looking for agreement—just acknowledgment. "That's the part everyone keeps forgetting. There was no avoiding this. We didn't invite war. They did."

Walder cleared his throat carefully. "Still. We need allies, not just chaos. There are tribes outside the city, isolated worker collectives—if we don't win them now, we'll be alone when the next hammer falls."

The debate fractured further. Some wanted to consolidate power inside Eastland and fortify what little they controlled. Others, like Mara, argued to spread Free Steam's message outward—to gather more support from the starving, desperate masses in the wastes. A few proposed contact with dormant districts once thought loyal to the Guild, hoping to spark quiet uprisings. None of them spoke with certainty. None of them knew if they'd survive the week.

Link's patience frayed.

"The Heartcoil changed everything," he said. Not loudly, but with the kind of conviction that silenced the room. "It makes resistance viable, not suicidal. We can't hide underground forever, patching holes while they dictate how many of us starve each winter."

Eve finally spoke, her voice soft but cutting. The kind of voice that didn't need volume to leave a mark.

"He's right. The moment we buried that Procession, we became something more than scavengers and rebels. We became the future. Whether they want us to be or not."

A heavy silence settled. Some looked away. Some simply held still. No one breathed easily.

It was Walder who broke it with reluctant agreement. "Fine. Then it's decided. We prepare for the worst. But if we're going to step up, we do it with eyes wide open."

"Agreed," Mara added, though she looked less convinced. Her fingers tapped the map unconsciously, tracing no path in particular.

Cutter just grunted. "I had to pull two recruits from the training hall yesterday," he added, voice low. "One froze when the automata powered up. The other ran. We can't afford either."

He looked to Link — not blaming, but pressing. "If these machines fail under pressure again, it won't be just metal that breaks."

Link nodded grimly. He could feel it—something shifting beneath the surface, a thread tightening. The meeting broke apart soon after, but the fracture lines remained visible on every face.

As the others filtered out, Walder lingered behind. He stood staring at the table for a moment longer, hand resting on the edge as if afraid to let go.

"Tell me we won't become them," he said softly, his voice carrying the tremor of someone who had seen too many promises rot into power. Link felt the words settle in his chest like solder—hot, heavy, bonding with doubts he hadn't yet named. not looking at Link. "Tell me we won't trade one tyrant's boot for another."

Link met his gaze, but said nothing. There was no reassurance left to give.

Walder nodded to himself and left the chamber. He didn't blame them. Hope was heavier than despair.

Later, in the quiet of the engineering hold, Link sat beside the Ghostframe. Its frame was partially stripped now, undergoing a rebuild after the tunnel assault. He ran a hand across the exposed Heartcoil chamber, feeling the faint warmth still radiating from the core. The chamber had scorched slightly near the stabilizer ring—he'd need to realign the converter array before the next field test. He made a mental note, then another. Always more work.

He slid beneath the Ghostframe's ribbed undercarriage, torch in one hand, a set of field-calibrated dampeners in the other. The stabilizer bolts had warped from the last surge — he could see the scoring along the coil bracket. A quick twist of the spanner, a hiss of pressure as one valve bled heat from the core. He muttered under his breath, checking the arc clamps along the rail housing. Two were loose. Again.

Sparks spat as he adjusted the locking ring, fingers burning through the gloves. The rig fought back — not sentient, not aware, just unforgiving. He winced and wiped his hand across his coat. Smelled like burned oil and copper.

Beside the stripped frame, a second rig sat idle—one of the converted crawler units they'd tried to retrofit with a smaller coil. The housing still bore stress scoring from its last failed test.

"I'm thinking of trying a four-point dispersion route next," Link said aloud. "Spread the heat before it bottlenecks. Might buy us two extra minutes at full output."

Eve's eyes flicked to the secondary frame. "And if it doesn't?"

"It cracks," Link said flatly. "Like the others."

"But it might not," she replied.

He shrugged. "That's what testing is."

Eve crossed her arms, gaze fixed on the Ghostframe's inner chassis. "And if it fails again in the field? With people inside it?"

Link didn't look at her. "Then I carry that. Not them."

He stared at the frame as he said it, knowing full well what it meant. Fear could inspire, but if it broke under pressure—if it shattered with someone inside—then it wasn't hope anymore. It was betrayal. Responsibility wasn't a symbol. It was weight, and he had chosen to bear it so no one else had to.

Her expression tightened, but she let it go. For now.

"This thing makes them believe," Eve's voice broke the quiet, and Link looked up.

He didn't answer at first. Just stared at the coil, still warm from the last test.

"Had a kid stop me two days ago," he said. "Fourteen, maybe. Called the Ghostframe 'the god-engine.' Link hadn't known whether to laugh or worry—it was just a kid's word, but something in it made his stomach turn. Was it awe? Or burden? Said if we could build that, maybe we could win. Just walked off after. Didn't wait for a reply."

She stood in the doorway, arms loose at her sides, no weapons. Just watching him with that half-curious, half-wary expression she wore when she saw past his bravado.

"Maybe," Link admitted. "Or maybe it just makes them desperate."

Eve tilted her head, jaw tight. "Then we'd better make sure desperation doesn't look like madness. Or martyrdom."

Eve came closer, settling beside him. For a long moment, neither spoke. The only sound was the occasional hiss of pressure in the distance and the faint hum of the Ghostframe's dormant circuits.

Then she said quietly, "Desperate people change the world. Not the ones content to wait."

Link smiled faintly. Not hopeful, not entirely bitter. Just... weary.

"They're scared of us now," he murmured, tapping the Ghostframe's exposed conduits. "Scared of what we represent."

Eve rested her head lightly against his shoulder. "Good. Let them be scared for once."

Link didn't reply, but something shifted behind his eyes. He thought of that fear—the same weight the Guild had wielded for decades. It was power, yes. But power demanded caution. To be feared was not the same as to be just. And if they misused it, they'd become exactly what they'd sworn to defy.

Outside the engineering bay, the sound of drills and distant automata movement echoed through the halls. Steam hissed from pressure vents high in the ceiling. A blowtorch flared in the distance, casting stuttering light across the walls. Somewhere down the corridor, a mechanic swore — followed by the clatter of dropped tools. Torchlight flickered across riveted bulkheads. Tools clanged. Orders barked. Free Steam was shifting gears, preparing for war without illusions.

And for the first time in years, Link did not feel entirely alone in the weight he carried.

Together, they sat in silence as the city above whispered promises of coming blood.

Chapter 32
Emerging Fires

N ight hung heavy over Eastland, yet no one slept. Wind tunneled through broken pipeways overhead, rattling loose scaffolds like distant percussion. In the refuge tunnels, beneath a city waiting to crack, Free Steam prepared.

In the refuge tunnels, beneath a city waiting to crack, Free Steam prepared.

Link stood in the command chamber—such as it was—staring at a hand-sketched map of the central districts. The table it lay on had once been a rail signal console, its edges rusted, dials long dead, now covered in oilcloth and layered intel sheets held down with bolts. Oil stains and ash smeared the lines, but the intent was clear. Cutter and Walder argued quietly near the far side of the table. Cutter's voice was clipped, hands moving as if shaping battle lines in the air. Walder's tone was cooler, but his eyes flicked toward the door more than once—already thinking ahead to who they might lose. Mara, leaning against the stone wall, flicked a coin between her fingers. Tension clung to them all like the ever-present soot. No one raised their voice. The silence wasn't calm—it was taut, like a rope straining before the snap. A low generator hum vibrated faintly beneath their boots, and the air stank of iron and nervous sweat.

Outside, the Ghostframe loomed in silhouette. Its form had changed subtly—no longer the patchwork of scavenged steel it had once been. Reinforced joints braced the legs with smoother plating, and its chest housing now bore a flush-mounted coil port wrapped in thermal shielding. Welding sparks flashed intermittently as tech crews made last-minute adjustments, their shadows cast huge across the tunnel walls. Freshly repaired, armor reinforced, and its heartcoil humming in a deeper, steadier pulse than ever before, the machine stood taller now—leaner, more efficient. A spinal fin of venting plates had been added down its back, still unpainted and catching the weld-light like a serrated blade. It wasn't just a machine anymore. It was a symbol. One the Guild could no longer afford to ignore.

"They've begun closing the gates," Mara reported grimly. "Guild patrols are tightening all outer approaches. Valtor's shifting to a siege."

"He thinks he can starve us out," Cutter spat.

Link tapped the map softly. "He might be right. We're running low. Ammo, food, time... we can't outlast him underground forever."

"So, we hit back before he finishes squeezing," Eve said simply, stepping into the light.

All eyes turned to her. For a heartbeat, the room held its breath. She carried herself with quiet confidence now—shoulders squared, eyes clear. Not just speaking. Leading. Not reckless, not naive—tempered steel forged by survival and purpose.

"We raid," she continued, nodding toward a series of marked supply routes. "Before they seal them completely. If we hit them fast, take their fuel and food stocks, we keep breathing and hit their morale."

Walder frowned. "And if we fail?"

"Then we die slower," Eve said flatly.

The room fell silent. Even Cutter couldn't argue.

Link glanced at her, pride mixing uneasily with fear. He'd once protected her. Now, she no longer needed it. That was its own kind of ache. She'd grown sharper. Harder. So had they all. But every time they rose, the Guild rose harder.

Still, there was no choice.

"Alright," Link decided. "We raid. Prep the Ghostframe and the crawler squads. We'll hit in force, but fast. Before they know we're coming."

Mara nodded. Cutter cracked his knuckles. Walder sighed but gave his reluctant blessing.

The meeting broke. Plans whispered, weapons readied. Worn boots shuffled across concrete, steam valves hissed overhead, and loaders groaned as crates of munitions were rolled toward staging corridors. By midnight, Free Steam's warriors moved like shadows reborn.

Hours later, Link found himself alone atop the entrance ramp, watching the city's heart flicker faintly in the distance.

Eve joined him quietly. She handed him a flask—thin broth, lukewarm but welcome. Somewhere below, a pressure-release hiss vented from the coil rooms, punctuated by the faint rhythmic knock of someone calibrating a jointed frame.

"They're scared," she said softly, meaning both Free Steam and their enemies.

Link took a slow sip. The broth steadied his hands, but not the knot in his chest. "They should be. So am I."

She smiled faintly, not mocking. Just human.

"Scared means alive," Eve said. "Means you're still in the fight."

The two stood in silence, shoulder to shoulder, watching as distant flames marked where Guild forces burned rebellious districts in punishment. Somewhere out there, Valtor watched too. And Roland.

But unlike them, Link and Eve knew what real fire was.

Not hatred.

Not control.

But defiance.

The night shuddered with distant gunfire. The raid would begin soon.

Link adjusted his coat, eyes narrowing. He didn't feel like a symbol. He felt like a man who had run out of places to hide. "No turning back anymore, is there?"

Eve shook her head. "No. Only forward now."

As they descended into the tunnels to lead their people, Eastland itself seemed to hold its breath. Shadows stretched long across the stone, flickering under the glow of flame-fed lanterns and crackling coils.

The first true fires of rebellion were about to burn.

Chapter 33
Sparks in the Veins

The tunnels came alive in muted motion. Torchlight flickered against sweating walls, casting stuttering shadows across rust-worn beams and exposed steam lines.

Free Steam's warriors filed through narrow, uneven corridors, boots silent on cracked stone and rusted catwalks. The air was thick with anticipation, and the low, rhythmic hiss of pressure release valves echoed through the lower levels like a heartbeat. Automata pilots walked with faces drawn tight, their breath visible in the cold damp air. Some wore scavenged armor fused with padded plating, each step calculated. Old scavenger bands now wore patches and armbands marked with the thorned gear symbol, signifying their shared oath—no longer just survivors, but soldiers.

Above them, the Ghostframe marched.

Link rode high in the armored cockpit, his hands steady on the controls. The cockpit was housed in the upper torso of the Ghostframe, accessible only from a hatch at the rear spine. Once inside, the hatch sealed behind him with a hiss of pressure clamps, enclosing him in a chamber of steel ribs and exposed conduits. The space around him was tight, barely wider than his shoulders. Bolted steel braces framed the seat, and overhead piping dripped condensation from the tunnel's humidity. The control levers vibrated subtly with each footfall, and the scent of warm copper, scorched lubricant, and aged leather filled the cabin. A narrow slit viewport showed the world in compressed angles, and every alert light blinked just a little too dim from overuse. Panels flickered around him, casting amber light across his jawline. He barely noticed the sweat at his brow or the faint vibration in the frame—it was part of him now. The machine's movements were fluid now, refined beyond its early days. Eve rode with him, crouched beside the communication arrays, eyes scanning the night ahead through narrowed slits.

Before they breached daylight, Link took one last glance across the panel. Heat gauges hovered high but stable. Surge indicators pulsed in rhythm. His thumb brushed the release lever twice—ritual, not habit.

Eve didn't look at him. "We're committed now," she said softly. Her voice carried no fear, but there was weight in it—the kind of resolve shaped by too many close calls and too few second chances.

He nodded. No jokes. No bravado. Just the hum of the Ghostframe beneath them.

The mission was simple in theory.

Hit the Guild's primary fuel and logistics depot on the eastern fringe. Disable their crawlers. Seize enough fuel, food, and spare automata parts to buy Free Steam weeks of breathing room.

Simple on paper.

But nothing in Eastland was simple anymore.

"Eyes up," Eve murmured through the private channel. Her tone wasn't urgent, but it tightened Link's grip nonetheless.

The strike force emerged from the tunnels in staggered waves. Mara's unit took the northern breach, Cutter's the south. Link and the Ghostframe led the spear directly toward the depot's heart.

What they found wasn't encouraging.

Guild sentries were everywhere. Their breath ghosted in the cold air, steam-powered exosuits clanking slightly at the joints as they rotated through fixed routines. Automata patrols clanked slowly in programmed patterns. Spotlights stabbed through the night, sweeping in mechanical arcs. Steam vents hissed from fortified barricades like slow, steady breath, masking the scent of oil and char.

"They're ready," Cutter hissed over comms.

"Not ready enough," Link replied, and gave the signal.

Chaos followed.

The Ghostframe surged forward, heavy feet smashing through barricades with the screech of tearing steel. The tunnel shook with every impact. Cutter's shock troops followed, coil rifles spitting arcs of heat and shrapnel that lit the air with stuttering blue fire.

Free Steam didn't hold back. They couldn't afford to.

The battle became frantic and close-quarters fast. Sparks flew as metal struck metal, coil rounds ricocheted off hull plating, and screams cut through the cacophony like jagged wire. Mara's unit slipped through side alleys, setting charges and pulling sentries into deadly ambushes. Cutter's heavier units used makeshift armor and mounted coil cannons to hammer the Guild's fortified positions. One squad breached a side tower under heavy fire, dragging out two wounded before the upper platform collapsed behind them. Cutter led from the front—his voice raw over comms, barking orders through smoke and grit.

The Ghostframe drew the most fire.

Guild automata closed ranks, forming firing lines and pummeling Link's machine with steam cannons and harpoon launchers. Link adjusted on the fly, diverting power from auxiliary systems to shield arrays, using the Ghostframe's reinforced arms to block incoming shots.

The Heartcoil pulsed in his chest.

Every movement came with danger now. He could feel the strain on the Ghostframe—metal flexing, joints creaking under sustained pressure. They hadn't yet solved the core efficiency problem. The Heartcoil could only give so much before demanding more from everything connected to it.

And it would take everything tonight.

Eve's voice cut through the chaos. "Crawlers to the east, disengaging. They're pulling supplies!"

"No," Link said flatly, turning the Ghostframe hard.

He stormed through shattered walls and burning barricades, smashing aside Guild infantry like insects. At the depot's eastern yard, two crawler transports churned to life, engines belching smoke as they prepared to flee.

Link didn't think. Rage wasn't what moved him—only clarity, sharpened to a point by exhaustion, pressure, and the knowledge that if he hesitated, they'd lose everything.

He pushed the Heartcoil further.

The Ghostframe roared as excess energy bled from every seam. Its limbs moved faster than before—reckless, almost violent in their precision. The machine slammed into the first crawler, driving reinforced claws into its engine housing and ripping it apart in a shower of molten metal and flame.

The second crawler fired back wildly. Steam mortars detonated against the Ghostframe's side, rupturing armor and sending warning lights screaming inside Link's cockpit.

He pushed anyway.

Eve's face flashed in his peripheral monitor. "Link, that's too much—" Her voice was tight with concern, not panic. She knew him well enough now to recognize the look in his eyes—one he'd worn in the tunnels after the first collapse, the one that said: *I'll break before I back down.*

"Not enough yet," he gritted back. Pain laced his grip, and every motion of the Ghostframe translated into a deeper throb behind his eyes. He didn't care. Not now.

With a brutal overhead swing, the Ghostframe caved in the second crawler's turret and tore open its fuel lines. Flames erupted as fuel met exposed power cores.

The depot burned. Crates of volatile fuel erupted one after another, casting heatwaves that shimmered over the Ghostframe's scorched hull. The smell of burning metal, oil, and cloth mingled in thick, throat-stinging clouds.

Guild forces broke almost immediately. Without supplies and heavy transport, their lines buckled. Mara's team swept in to mop up. She moved like a phantom through the smoldering depot, directing strike groups to seize fuel casks and disable wounded automata. One of her lieutenants flagged a hidden gear locker—old Guild tech, still functional. Mara ordered its salvage with a single nod, never breaking stride. Cutter's squads drove the survivors into retreat. And Link stood amidst the ruins in the Ghostframe, watching as the night sky above Eastland turned orange.

Victory.

But costly.

Inside the cockpit, the Heartcoil's hum had shifted.

Not steady now. Not smooth. It pulsed erratically, strained to the breaking point. A thermal vent warning blinked red beside the heat coil stabilizer graph. Power draw from auxiliary systems had spiked during the final charge, and the converter array's integrity read below 60%.

Eve climbed into the cockpit beside Link as the battle died around them. She ducked through the rear hatch and braced herself against the wall, boots clanking as she settled next to his seat. The stench of scorched insulation lingered thick in the enclosed space. Her eyes fell to the flickering readouts.

"That wasn't sustainable," she said quietly.

"No," Link admitted, slumping back in his seat, sweat stinging his eyes. "But we survived." His voice was quiet. Tired. Not triumphant—just relieved to still be breathing.

"For now," Eve whispered, but her gaze remained on the Heartcoil's soft, irregular pulse.

Outside, Free Steam celebrated amid burning crawler wrecks and scattered debris. Children and elders would sleep warmer this week. The stolen fuel meant heat, the food meant days without ration fights, and the parts—those meant fewer dying frames holding up collapsing shelters. Smoke curled into the sky in tight black columns, backlit by the glow of still-burning barricades. Somewhere in the distance, a voice cried out in victory, echoed by a dozen more.

But even in triumph, Link could feel it. Beneath the celebration and firelight, something cold had settled behind his ribs. A question that hadn't yet found the courage to speak.

The machine was warning them.

Nothing burned forever.

Chapter 34
Aftermath and Resolve

Morning dragged through Eastland like smoke through broken teeth. The light was gray, thin, filtered through soot still hanging in the air. Metal groaned in the rafters above, and ash drifted down like snow over the wreckage.

The fires still burned. A layer of oily soot clung to every surface, and the air tasted like scorched copper and wet ash. Hot iron glowed beneath collapsed beams, and soot-blackened bricks wept thin streams of condensation from the night's chill. Not as roaring infernos anymore, but as stubborn embers chewing through the wreckage of the Guild's eastern depot. Black smoke drifted through broken towers and empty streets, a grim banner of Free Steam's first real victory.

But victory, Link knew, came cheap in words and costly in blood and bone.

He stood outside the Ghostframe, arms crossed as Cutter's squads hauled debris and counted the dead. The machine still hummed faintly, Heartcoil pulsing erratically as engineers carefully disconnected its overloaded systems for repairs. One of them muttered under her breath to Eve nearby, not knowing Link could hear: "Maybe one more push like that. After that? It's scrap." Link's jaw tightened every time he saw the jagged tears in the Ghostframe's armor.

They had pushed it too far. Nearby, two bodies lay under gray tarps, unmoving and unspoken for. A young woman knelt beside one of them, hands clenched in silence, her face streaked with ash and grief. Link looked away—but only for a moment. He made himself look again. The weight of it settled behind his ribs, a quiet grief he couldn't name, only carry.

Eve approached quietly, two mugs of weak tea in her hands. She handed one to Link without speaking, and together they watched Mara and Walder argue over supply counts a few yards away.

"They're saying we won," Eve said softly.

Link sipped the tea and grimaced. It tasted like boiled rust, steeped in fatigue. The cup radiated faint warmth against his cracked knuckles, but it did nothing to ease the knot in his chest. "They want to believe we won."

"Didn't we?"

"We took a depot. Burned a few crawlers. That's not winning. That's surviving." He glanced sideways, eyes shadowed. "Valtor's still out there. Roland too. And now they'll come harder than before."

Eve didn't argue. She knew. They all did. But in her eyes, there was still a flicker of something steady—not hope, exactly, but resolve born of hard-won clarity.

Still, there was no going back.

Cutter stomped over, face grimy and knuckles bloodied, one sleeve torn from hauling wreckage. The faint hiss of pressure leaks and the distant clatter of retooling frames echoed down the corridor behind him. His boots were crusted with ash and something darker. "Council's calling for a full assembly tonight. They want to decide next moves before morale slips again."

"Good," Link said immediately. "We need to set expectations. Before anyone thinks we've already won this war."

"Some already do," Cutter warned darkly. "They're drunk on the victory. Talk of pushing into upper districts started before dawn."

Link felt a stab of anger. Not at the hope — but at how fragile and dangerous it was. He'd seen it break before, and when it broke, it took people with it. False hope killed faster than despair.

"I'll speak," he said firmly.

That evening, the chamber they used as Free Steam's heart was packed shoulder to shoulder. Lanterns hissed and guttered in wall brackets. Somewhere beyond the chamber walls, the rhythmic thud of automata joints echoed like distant drums. The chamber smelled of old oil, solder, and the damp stone of the tunnels. Shadows stretched wide on the walls, each flickering with the breath of those gathered inside. Some in the crowd leaned forward eagerly. Others crossed their arms, doubtful. A few carried visible wounds, bandaged and fresh. Faces grim, faces eager, faces scarred and desperate. Link's gaze caught a mechanic still in welding leathers, grease streaked across his face; a mother clutching her child's hand, both of them thin and wide-eyed; an old woman using a broken cane, who had made the climb anyway. These weren't just fighters. They were everything left. Link stood before them not as a leader chosen, but as the only one who wouldn't step back. His coat was still scorched at the hem, and his voice—though sharp—carried the rasp of exhaustion earned in fire.

He let them cheer. Let them cry victory.

Then he quieted them. For a moment, he hesitated—just long enough for uncertainty to flicker across his eyes. Would they hear him? Would they follow? Or would they turn the first chance they got, chasing ghosts of victory instead of enduring the long war ahead?

"This was a step," Link said plainly, voice cutting through the crowded room like a blade. "A hard-earned one. You fought like hell to take this ground — and I won't let that be wasted by rushing into another fight blind."

A murmur rippled through the crowd. Some supportive. Some impatient.

"Valtor won't crumble because we smashed a depot," Link continued. "Roland won't step aside because we outmaneuvered his patrols. They will come. They will adapt. And if we don't do the same, if we think victory is already here—"

He let the silence hang heavy. He saw Mara nod once. Cutter didn't move. A boy in the back lowered his eyes.

"They will destroy us."

That sobered them.

"We rebuild. Smarter. Stronger. The Heartcoil gave us a fighting chance, but we need more than that. We hold the depot for now—strip it, reinforce what we can. But we don't grow roots in burned ground. We use what's left to move forward. We need alliances. Engineers. Builders. Fighters. Everyone."

Eve stepped up beside him then, not needing words to show solidarity. Mara nodded from the front, and even Walder, reluctant as ever, looked grimly resolved.

When Link finished, there was no wild cheering. No blind optimism.

But there was something better.

Acceptance.

They understood the long road ahead. And in that moment, Link saw something in them he hadn't dared hope for: not fire, not fury—but endurance. Only that would carry them through what came next.

Later, when the crowd dispersed, Link stood alone at the edge of the council hall, boots silent on scorched stone. The walls still held the heat of gathered bodies, and the acrid sting of oil smoke hadn't yet cleared from the air. He stared at a cracked wall where old Guild banners had once hung, the outline of their anchors still embedded in the masonry like phantom chains.

He imagined Valtor doing the same somewhere above, eyes cold, calculating his next cruelty. Roland's smug expression surfaced too—irritated, maybe even shaken, but never uncertain. They watched not because they feared Free Steam yet... but because they knew it couldn't be ignored anymore.

Good.

They were watching. They were afraid. Or angry. Or both.

That meant Free Steam wasn't just a nuisance anymore. They were becoming what the Guild had never feared until now—unified, tested, and unwilling to die quietly.

They were a threat.

Link clenched his fists and whispered under his breath. For a heartbeat, he thought of the two bodies under the tarp. Of the girl still kneeling. Of all the ones who didn't hear this speech, who wouldn't see what came next. It wasn't a boast. Just a promise:

"Not enough yet. But we're getting there."

Chapter 35
Blood in the Streets

Eastland woke screaming. Steam sirens wailed from torn ducts, echoing off steel-clad towers as the first shells hit home. Fires bloomed like artificial dawn across the skyline.

Before dawn could paint even the grayest smudge across the smog-heavy sky, Valtor's forces struck.

Heavy crawlers clad in soot-black armor rolled through the lower districts. Guild automata moved like executioners through alleys still warm from Free Steam's victory fires. No announcement. No mercy. Orders whispered down from on high — Valtor's iron resolve made manifest.

Cut the arteries. Bleed them dry.

Link was jolted from sleep by the shriek of steam mortars and the crash of collapsing iron. For a breathless moment, he didn't move—just lay there, heart pounding, the ghost of ash still in his throat from the day before. He'd barely closed his eyes. His coat still smelled like burnt oil. In the silence between blasts, he thought he heard crying—but it might have been memory. Eve was already up, strapping her coat and belt on in practiced haste.

"They're here," she said simply.

They burst from the tunnel barracks into chaos. The ground shook with distant detonations. Acrid smoke laced with burnt cloth drifted through the corridors. A wounded boy limped past, clutching a bent coil rifle, blood in his teeth and nowhere else to go. Cutter's squads were rallying near the outer barricades. Walder bellowed for engineers to pull wounded into secondary shelters. Mara was already gone—leading a team to hold the north bridge.

The fallback tunnels sloped sharply west, toward the ruined tramway station and the central barricade node near Sector Three. Eve and Link passed through a crumbled checkpoint, veering behind a slag heap where medics crouched beside steam-fed pressure tanks.

The Ghostframe roared to life seconds later. As Link brought it online, pressure gauges flickered in warning and fluid valves groaned with strain. He swung the frame out of the tunnel mouth and into the burning street, shielding evacuees from a collapsing overpass before driving a shoulder through the flank of a Guild automaton. Sparks cascaded over the hull as the Ghostframe twisted, pivoted, and rammed—never elegant, but relentless. The cockpit bucked with each impact, the world narrowing to a grid of motion, heat, and noise.

Link climbed into the cockpit, pulse pounding as the machine shuddered beneath him. The entry hatch groaned as it sealed. Inside, the air was thick with the scent of scorched insulation and copper. Warning lights blinked on half-power. Heat bled through the floor plating. One of the stabilizer vents had melted shut during the last fight—it hissed now, faintly, in protest. Damage from the last raid hadn't been fully repaired. Armor plates rattled loose as he powered up the Heartcoil, but it was enough.

It had to be.

The Ghostframe crouched behind the central tram hub, using an overturned crawler husk as partial cover. Eve's squad fought just north of the plaza, visible in glimpses through alley gaps. Her rifle fire flared bright against encroaching shapes, her movements crisp, tactical.

The clash was brutal and immediate. Civilians scattered through the crossfire — a butcher dragging a child behind a steam cart, a nurse shielding wounded beneath a collapsed tram arch. Screams folded into the metal din as Free Steam's fighters struggled to shield their own while firing blind through smoke and debris. Every corner flared with muzzle bursts and steam flares. Broken storefronts bled glass onto cobblestones. Automata screamed metal on metal as gears seized and limbs tore free. Guild shocktroopers in heavy steam-plate fired volley after volley into Free Steam's barricades. Automata clashed in the cramped city streets, their massive limbs tearing through shopfronts and rooftops like parchment. The plaza near Crankwell Square—once a salvage market—was now a cratered ruin, its familiar gear-statue reduced to twisted slag.

For hours, the line held.

Then, cracks.

"They're cutting power to the outer pumps!" Eve's voice crackled through the relay box—distorted, frayed by steam and interference.

Without water pressure, fire suppression and steam reservoirs feeding half their automata would fail. Valtor had learned. He wasn't just hammering them anymore — he was dissecting them.

"We fall back to sector three!" Link ordered. He had no illusions — the pumps were bait. Valtor wanted them reactive, retreating. But Link needed him confident. Needed him to think the trap had worked.

"Draw them deeper!"

Somewhere behind him, Eve hauled a fallen gunner toward the fallback gate, dragging her by one arm while firing blindly with the other. Her coat was torn at the shoulder, blood smeared across her cheek, but she never stopped moving. As she dragged the wounded clear, Eve glanced north—toward where Mara's signal should've returned. Nothing. Her jaw tightened, but she didn't speak. Didn't need to.

The retreat was bloody. Cutter lost half his squad covering the withdrawal. When they regrouped, he didn't speak. He just sat against a bulkhead, one boot stained dark, staring at the wall until Walder tossed him a new rifle and moved on. Mara's team never came back. At first, there was silence—no signal through the copper-thread relay line, just a hiss of steam and dead silence. Then, a fireball on the horizon. Cutter whispered her name once, low and ragged, before ordering the fallback.

Later, Link passed the wreckage—twisted girders, blackened steel, a half-melted armband caught on a rebar hook. Beside it, half-buried in the ash, lay a soldering tool — one Mara never went without. The grip was scorched, the casing cracked, but her initials were still etched into the side. Link reached for it, then stopped. Just looked. Then moved on. He didn't stop. He couldn't. But something in him folded inward, hard and quiet. His hand trembled once on the throttle. He gritted his teeth and steadied it before anyone could see, but the ache beneath his ribs remained. Eve met his eyes as he dismounted beside the fallback tunnel. Neither said her name. They didn't have to. The silence between them carried it.

By nightfall, Free Steam was driven deep into their final redoubts. The city fell into choking silence, interrupted only by the groan of settling wreckage. Smoke hung in the tunnels like low fog. Walls trembled from distant fighting. Engineers worked by lantern light, dragging cables and wounded in equal measure. Link stood atop the Ghostframe, armor scorched and cracked, his boots slipping in oil that wasn't all machine-born. He watched the black banners of Valtor's personal guard unfurl over the eastern ward like funeral veils stretched from tower to tower.

"We can't hold forever," Eve whispered. Exhaustion clung to her voice.

"No," Link said, eyes hardening. "But tonight wasn't about holding."

Eve frowned. "Then what?"

"Making him overreach." Link's eyes tracked the distant crawl of a second wave moving too fast, too heavy. "He committed everything to crush us here. If we survive tonight, he'll have to pay for it somewhere else."

Neither of them moved. The only sound was the hiss of cooling metal and distant screams echoing through the lower shafts.

Chapter 36
Roland Ascendant

F ar above the chaos, in the crystalline halls of the Guild's elite, Roland smiled. The floors were polished obsidian veined with gold, the air faintly perfumed with incense and ozone from the mirror towers. Steam valves hissed quietly behind marbled walls, releasing measured puffs that smelled faintly of lavender oil and heated brass—luxury maintained by invisible pressure.

He reclined lazily in his private solar, sunlight from magnified mirror-towers glinting across his gold-threaded jacket. In his hands, a glass of imported wine — likely the last vintage left untorched in Eastland.

Below, death. Above, triumph. Hours had passed since the banners of Valtor's personal guard unfurled over the eastern ward. The second wave had gone in with full force—and still, the Ghost moved.

"Father plays too conservatively," he mused aloud. The only other presence in the room — a pale, silent automata servant — said nothing. It stood motionless by the door, its smooth faceplate catching the firelight like a mask. Roland glanced at it once, satisfied that even silence here was obedient.

Roland rose, brushing invisible dust from his coat with the same precision he used to dispatch underlings. His steps clicked sharply across the polished floor as he moved toward the large, arched window. The city burned below. Firelight shimmered off the glass surfaces of the upper towers, painting the white marble in blood-orange hues. Smoke spiraled upward like grasping hands, curling around the gilded spires of the high halls. He had grown up in those towers—bathed in steam and silk, fed from golden dishes while others toiled below. To him, Eastland wasn't a city. It was inheritance. It was legacy. And now rebels dragged their soot-stained banners through what had once been his nursery streets. Crawlers rolled through rebel quarters. Automata crushed barricades beneath gilded boots.

But Roland's eyes were not on the destruction.

They were on the Ghostframe. Still standing. Still limping. A smear of soot and defiance that refused to bow. It wasn't just a machine. It was everything he wasn't: raw, admired, alive. He turned away before his rage cracked the glass.

"It still moves," he muttered, voice tight. "That machine. That pilot... Link, they call him. Father only cares because of the device. He doesn't see the man."

His face twisted — part scorn, part hunger.

"They think they're heroes. Champions of dirt and rust. They don't realize this city belongs to me. Always has. Father would never risk this. That's why they follow me now. The others—those sniveling nobles and polished-tongue strategists—they laughed once. Whispered that he was ornamental. They wouldn't be laughing when they saw what he commanded."

Behind closed doors, Roland's obsession had festered. Not with strategy. Not with duty.

With humiliation. But more than that—jealousy. Not for power. For attention. For the first time in his life, Valtor had spoken a name not his. Not in command halls. Not in scorn. In curiosity. In interest. 'The pilot of that machine,' he'd said once, after reviewing reports. 'He may be worth watching.' Roland had pretended not to hear. But it had rooted itself like a rusted bolt behind his ribs.

Every victory by Free Steam was a slap to his ego. He wore his resentment like a pressed cuff—always visible if you knew what to look for. He remembered one image too clearly — a Free Steam banner unfurled over the north watchtower, blotting out the gilded sun-emblem he'd ordered installed. He remembered the rumors: that Link had once spared a squad that surrendered — that people respected him. That they whispered his name now instead. A personal wound.

No more.

He gestured sharply. Before summoning his captain, he turned to the armor stand tucked into the corner. He ran one finger along the collar of his gilded overcoat, where ceremonial plating had been newly sewn in—more for effect than defense. From a drawer, he withdrew a matching shoulder clasp and pinned it into place himself. The weight felt good. Purposeful. His private security captain — a man with a deep scar across one cheek and hands that trembled when they thought they weren't being watched — appeared immediately.

"Prepare the Gilded Fang," Roland ordered. The elite squad—his custom-built automata, adorned in burnished gold and scarlet crests—was more ceremonial than practical, but that no longer mattered. They were beautiful. They were his. Father had always forbidden their deployment—called them gaudy, untested, dangerous. But tonight, no permission would be sought.

In the courtyard below the solar, he watched as engineers polished their burnished plates to mirror sheen, fastening ornamental steam-vents that hissed with theatrical bursts. One unit bore a sculpted crest of his own profile across its chestplate; another had blades etched with gold filigree, useless in combat but magnificent in ceremony. Roland lingered at the glass, studying each form with an artist's pride and a tyrant's hunger. Behind them, the tiered ledges of the Guild's command bastion overlooked the industrial districts. Beyond that: the rubble-lined trench corridors Free Steam had retreated into.

"My lord?"

"My personal automata squad. We march before dawn. I will see this rebellion crushed. Personally."

The captain hesitated. Roland stepped closer, watching the slight twitch in the man's eyelid. He liked that. The fear. Roland's smile grew sharp.

"Or perhaps you doubt me too?"

"No, my lord," the man stammered, bowing quickly.

Roland's smile widened as he turned back to the burning city. If he lost, they wouldn't imprison him. They'd bury him beneath silk, lock him in ceremony, and erase him from consequence. Failure didn't end in exile. It ended in irrelevance.

When the door clicked shut behind the captain, Roland exhaled slowly—then turned toward the tall mirror beside the hearth. His reflection stared back: perfect posture, sculpted hair, unflinching eyes. But they looked through him. He reached toward the glass and paused, fingertips brushing the surface as if he expected it to ripple.

"Link," he whispered—not in scorn, but something colder. Quieter. "He sees you. Not me."

For the briefest moment, a tremor of doubt brushed the edges of his thoughts—what if the Ghost didn't fall? What if it grew stronger?

He crushed the thought like an insect beneath polished heel. But the words still echoed — not his own, but Valtor's, thrown casually at a council table weeks ago: 'You're not a soldier, Roland. You're decoration.'

He'd laughed with the others then. Smiled through clenched teeth. But that sentence had festered like rot beneath polished brass.

The glass in the window distorted the flames, twisting the streets below into a vision of writhing ruin. The trench line outside the eastern barricade formed a jagged crescent, one corner brushing against the outer causeway and the other tapering into the furnace district's slag path. It was a kill zone — and tomorrow, he would walk straight into it.

It pleased him.

"Soon, they'll kneel. And when they do, I'll make them watch as I pull their Ghost apart, bolt by bolt."

Chapter 37
Last Bastion

The night that followed was the longest Eastland had known since the Ash Wars. They had crawled through fire. Smoke clung to their clothes. Oil and blood smeared the walls they leaned against. The taste of ash still coated their tongues, bitter and hot like grief turned physical. The retreat from Sector Three was chaos—steam lines bursting, crawlers crushed in narrow alleys, wounded dragged beneath torn awnings while the sky thundered from the Guild's siege guns. When they reached the Iron Hall, it was barely more than a carcass — its high arches sagged under collapsed beams, the air heavy with metal dust and soot. The great central furnace sat cracked and dormant, its belly cold for the first time in generations. Statues of old manufactors stood like headless saints, their plaques blackened by fire. The hall echoed with every breath, as if reluctant to shelter the broken who now claimed it.

Link gathered what remained of Free Steam in the crumbling ruins of the Iron Hall — an ancient manufactorum long since converted into their fallback redoubt. The hall had once been a shrine to industry, but now it bore the smell of ash and rusted blood. Great cranes hung overhead, motionless, while broken banners of long-dead Guild houses drooped from cracked pillars. Eve stood beside him, her face drawn and bruised. Cutter leaned heavily against the wall, his arm wrapped in a bloody bandage, eyes distant. Walder and the engineers worked quietly nearby, salvaging what they could—coils, rivets, stripped wire from shattered crawlers. He wasn't a fighter, but they owed every spark of motion to his team now. Without them, even desperation would seize and die.

Silence hung thick. No hammer strikes. No hiss of steam. Only the creak of cooling metal and the occasional cough, like ghosts refusing to rest. Then—footsteps. A young scout stepped through the side arch, out of breath, eyes wide.

"The lower markets are gone," he rasped. "Guild patrols sweep twice a day. No resistance left above the canal line." The room absorbed the news like a bruise. Someone sobbed quietly near a pile of torn blankets. A child clutched an empty ration tin. Cutter muttered Mara's name once, under his breath, then shook his head like trying to erase it.

No speeches now. No roaring declarations.

Just survival.

"We can't win," someone whispered from the crowd.

Link stepped forward. His boots echoed faintly against the cracked iron floor. For a moment, he looked like he might falter. Then he found Eve beside him and stood straighter.

Someone else rose — bitter-eyed, voice sharp. "So we crawl again? Until when? Until they crush us underground?"

Link looked at them, not with anger, but something colder. "Until they forget what safety feels like. Until fear sits in every one of their steam-choked halls. We stop fighting like they do. We make them fight like us."

"No," he said, voice rough but steady. "Not like this. Not face to face with Valtor's armies or Roland's gilded knights."

He gestured toward the wounded and weary.

"But that's not what Free Steam was ever about. Not crushing them head-on. We're builders. Tinkerers. Scavengers. Survivors. And we still have what they don't understand — maps of the old infrastructure, access points they thought were myths, tunnels older than their towers. Two days' rations. Maybe three. Less if the pumps fail. But we've stretched less into miracles before."

Murmurs spread through the chamber like wind stirring ashes — cautious, brittle. A few eyes lifted. Most stayed down, watching their hands, the floor, the firelight flickering against broken pillars. An old machinist stepped forward. "I still remember the tunnels. Show me what to seal." Another voice followed: "My daughter can run messages. Fast. She's small enough to slip by."

206

"We fight smart. We disappear into the cracks again. We strike where they expect safety. We remind them this city isn't theirs just because they hold the towers. There are still corridors they haven't locked. Tunnel routes they don't understand. Supply paths that belong to us. We hold the blueprint. They hold the shell."

Eve nodded, stepping in. She didn't raise her voice, but the words carried. One of her sleeves was torn, blood crusted down one side. She hadn't slept. Her fingers trembled when she gestured toward the west exit—but her voice didn't.

"We know these streets better than they ever will," she said. "We'll turn their might into dead weight. She wasn't just with him. She was beside him. Ready to lead, to bleed, to vanish and strike if he fell. Brin died rerouting power through the canal grid, alone. So others could escape. Her hands are still on this fight, even if she isn't."

Later, she would pass Link in the hall and pause, just long enough to brush her hand across his shoulder. No words. Just weight. Trust.

"We'll bleed them in alleys. Starve them of fuel. Turn every automata they rely on into a liability."

Link let the plan sink in. Cutter grunted from the wall, nodding once. "About time we stopped trying to match them blow for blow." He didn't smile. But he didn't walk away either.

He hadn't slept. Hadn't eaten. Part of him wanted to disappear into the dark corners of the Iron Hall and let someone else rise. But they looked to him. And he could not—would not—look away.

"Let them come," Link thought. "The Ghost is watching. And so are we." This wasn't retreat. It wasn't surrender. One by one, callused hands reached for tools, coils, makeshift blades. No orders. Just movement. A forge-hand dragged a length of pipe like a warbanner. A child sharpened a scrap of steel against a broken gear. The uprising had no uniform, only intent.

It was insurgency.

And Free Steam would thrive there. Not in glory, but in grit. In soot and silence and patience sharpened to a blade.

Even as dawn broke cold and gray, and Valtor's banners crested over the outer wards, Link's eyes burned bright with quiet, dangerous resolve.

"Let them think they've won," he murmured.

The Ghostframe stood silent behind him — repaired overnight with every scrap they had left. A salvaged plate from an old mining rig covered its flank. One arm joint groaned when it moved, and its exposed power lines had been wound in copper braiding like surgical stitching. It didn't shimmer with power. It hummed like memory — heavy, patient, and watching. But it stood tall. Waiting. Not flawless. Not mighty.

But ready.

The next chapter of rebellion would begin in the ruins, beneath melted banners and rusted cranes, in the hollowed bones of a city that remembered how to fight back.

The last time Eastland burned, it buried the old world. This time, it would ignite something new.

And this time, they'd burn the Guild from the inside out.

Chapter 38
Iron in Their Veins

———⟨◈⟩———

T he mist returned with the dawn.

Thin and sharp this time, like knives hidden in the folds of morning. It clung low over the shattered tram rails and spilled through the cracked teeth of broken walls, whispering through Eastland as though it too sensed the change.

Not the kind of change banners sang of, nor the kind that built statues.

The quiet, bloody kind.

The kind that came after the last speeches faded and the bones beneath the city remembered only hunger.

Eve crouched low on the roof of a half-collapsed tenement, eyes narrowed against the shifting fog. Her breath came slow and even, ghosting from her mouth in thin streams that vanished as quickly as they formed.

Below, the Guild's Procession marched.

Steel-clad boots stomped in unison, moving like parts in an engine too large to comprehend. The automata — gleaming with fresh brass polish and painted crimson lines — hissed steam as they trailed the soldiers. Their glass eyes glowed faintly — dead ornaments atop machines that saw through slits in their torsos, not skulls. The heads turned anyway, like masks trained to mimic intent.

And yet...

No one fired.

No rebels sprang from the shadows.

No traps sprang loose.

The Procession moved in silence save for the grind of gears and the bark of orders. At its head, a standard-bearer marched with a black-and-gold pennant emblazoned with the Guild's triple flame — one for dominion, one for purity, one for silence. It fluttered like a threat above the fog, a false sun in a city that no longer bowed to its light.

Eve's fingers tightened on the coil-rifle slung across her lap. She could feel her heart trying to sprint even as the rest of her stayed still.

"Hold," came Link's voice quietly through the steam-crackled receiver pressed to her ear. "Wait for the cut point."

She didn't answer. No need. He knew she heard.

They all did.

Across Eastland's dying bones, Free Steam lay in wait.

Juna was positioned with her rifle team three streets over, hidden in a blown-out tram station. Tamsin and the mechanics rode low in the drainage tunnels, ready to collapse entire blocks with coil-cut charges. Ren—coughing still, ribs bound so tight he couldn't stand straight—manned the ghost beacon. He'd light the flare when the Procession passed the chokepoint. The receiver trembled in his hand from the force of his cough. Eve had told him not to volunteer. He'd just smiled, blood on his teeth. If this worked, he wouldn't need a second chance.

And Link...

Link stood at the old ironwater tower, its rust-stained ribs jutting high into the gray mist. He was halfway up a maintenance scaffold, cables snaking around him and a faded Guild inspection sigil flaking from the wall behind. The vantage point gave him eyes on the entire northern thoroughfare — a perfect perch for what was coming. His eyes swept the ruined horizon with quiet calculation.

The Heartcoil pulsed faintly in the makeshift rig they'd mounted to a repurposed steam-vent turret. It wasn't a proper weapon. Nothing in Eastland was anymore.

But when it discharged, when the pressure built and the converter ring split — it would slice through steel and flesh alike.

That was the idea, anyway.

The plan wasn't elegant.

It wasn't clean.

But it was built from rage and scrap and sleepless nights spent wiring hope into rusted bones.

And sometimes that was enough.

Eve's receiver crackled softly.

"Signal up," Ren's voice rasped. A second later, his beacon tower shook violently — bricks crumbling as a mortar blast struck the far edge. The line cut to static. No one had time to check if he was still breathing. Ren's flare had risen like a match struck in the dark — not bright, not long. But it was enough to start the fire.

Eve shifted. Her knees ached from crouching so long, but she didn't rise yet.

Below, the Guild soldiers were beginning to look uneasy. The streets were too quiet. The mist too thick. The silence too heavy.

They knew something was wrong.

But not wrong enough.

Not yet. She thought of Mara. Of the way the barricade fire had looked against her back. Of the silence afterward. Then she let it go. There was no room for mourning in the moment before a kill. This wasn't vengeance. It was reclamation. One shot at a time.

She thought, too, of Vessa — the engineer who'd taught half the younger crews to rig power couplings by torchlight, who vanished behind the Crankwell gates before the fallback. No body. No confirmation. But a spare set of goggles had been found, cracked but clean, placed on the control desk where the final failsafe was armed. It was enough. Vessa, like so many others, would be part of the fire now.

Eve exhaled slowly and whispered into the steam-crackled receiver.

"Trigger."

The city screamed.

Not human voices — but stone and steam and buried grief all cracking loose at once.

Tamsin's charges blew first — a cascading wave that collapsed a row of decayed manufactories into the Procession's flank. Dust and rust and shattered steel rained down, splitting the formation and severing lines of sight.

Then came Juna's rifle fire — sharp and exact, each shot cracking open helmet visors and piercing exposed hydraulics. She took a glancing hit to her side; sparks burst from her armor and she tumbled behind a broken pillar, gasping — but she waved her team forward even as blood trickled down her ribs. Automata fell hard, limbs sparking, steam gouting from severed lines.

And finally —

Link pulled the Heartcoil's release.

The turret's modified vent core roared to life, brighter than the sunrise had dared to that day. The Heartcoil at its center screamed — a high, vibrating wail that sounded almost like denial. The charge stuttered for half a second, its coils whining too long, too loud — then it caught. It had never been built to kill. But it learned. It was a relic pressed into rage. The pulse lashed out in a searing arc, catching the Procession's rear line and cutting clean through automata and soldiers alike. A Guild officer — tall, broad, his rank stripes painted in burnished crimson — tried to rally the front line. He made it three steps before a rifle round caught him in the throat and dropped him beside the fallen banner. The triple-flame banner lay in the dirt now, soaked in ash — no dominion, no purity, no silence.

Where it touched, metal warped and bodies blackened into charred silhouettes.

Eve was already moving.

Sliding down the cracked drainpipe, boots hitting the ground running.

Her rifle barked once, twice — dropping two stragglers trying to regroup. Around her, rebel fighters poured from hiding places: from sewer mouths, shattered window frames, even from under floorboards long buried in ash.

They didn't shout. Somewhere, from a broken loft window above the wreckage, a pair of wide eyes watched. A young scavenger — no more than ten — saw the Guild's Procession shatter. Saw the red lines split and scatter. Someone shouted for medics. Another waved smoke to signal fallback. But no one cheered.

Not yet. And the child vanished into the smoke, running to tell someone what the silence had finally given way to.

No war cries.

No declarations of revolution.

Only the grim, methodical work of taking back what had been stolen.

By the time the Procession broke fully, half their number dead and the rest scattering into side streets, Eve found Link standing amid the wreckage, steam curling around him like ghosts unwilling to leave. He stood like the last piece of an old machine — barely holding, but vital. A faint crack in the Heartcoil housing pulsed near his wrist. The machine had screamed — and now it bled, slowly.

He held the Heartcoil rig loosely in his hands, eyes distant.

She approached quietly, voice low.

"That it?"

He looked at her — really looked this time — and his lips twitched in something that wasn't quite a smile.

"No," Link said softly. "That was just the message."

Eve's brow furrowed.

"And the answer?"

He lifted his eyes toward the northern sky, where the Guild's main holdfast still loomed beyond the mist, untouched.

"That comes next. The mist didn't lift. It just thinned — enough to see the fire behind it.

Chapter 39
Crown of Smoke

◦—◦◆◦—◦

*V*altor *watched.*

Morning broke over Eastland with the clarity of glass — sharp, bright, and ready to shatter. From his vantage point in the control chamber, Valtor observed the city like a man reading the final page of a book he did not write. Valtor had not sanctioned the duel.

Roland had made the announcement himself — public, theatrical, without clearance. A play for pride dressed as strategy. Typical.

And now it was too late to recall him.

The duel had already begun — or rather, the performance that dared to call itself one.

Ash still drifted in the higher wards, but the Procession was gone. The Guild's banners no longer hung from the railways. And for the first time in weeks, no steam whined across the rooftops.

That silence was shattered by the golden roar of the Gilded Fang — a sound too refined to be war, too loud to be anything else. The ground trembled beneath its weight.

Roland's personal automaton descended the northern ramp with theatrical slowness, flanked by a pair of painted guards and a flag-bearer holding the Guild's triple-flame standard. Sunlight caught the etched panels of the automaton's flanks — ceremonial armor polished to a mirror sheen, inscribed with lineage, authority, and inherited pride.

At its head, Roland stood in the open pilot frame, jacket fluttering, one hand on the rail, the other clutching a gold-plated loudspeaker.

"Link!" he called, voice magnified and smug. "Let's not prolong what we both know is inevitable. I've come to deliver terms."

No answer.

Around the plaza, Free Steam fighters remained hidden in the broken buildings and alley mouths, rifles quiet.

The Ghostframe crouched silent in the rubble, hidden beneath scaffolded stone and ash. Inside its cramped torso cockpit, Link waited — eyes steady, hands resting on the controls like they were part of him.

Outside, his voice echoed from the hull's speaker slit.

"I'm here, Roland."

The head turned slowly. The machine rose.

Link did not step into the plaza.

He brought the Ghostframe with him.

Roland blinked.

"This your surrender?" he asked, voice echoing.

Link stopped in the center of the square. "No," he said. "Just didn't want to stain my boots stepping over your body."

Murmurs passed through the ruins. A few Free Steam scouts smirked. One of Roland's guards tensed.

Roland straightened.

"So that's how it is," he muttered. Then louder: "Fine. I'll grant you spectacle instead of dignity."

The Gilded Fang hissed and stepped forward. Link stood still as the massive automaton circled.

The rubble behind Roland shifted. A low whine bled into the air — the sound of coils waking, of something ancient and angry drawing breath.

The Ghostframe rose, its form unfolding from a scaffolded ruin like a beast reassembling itself from ash. Its limbs gleamed with fresh welds and the faint pulse of a new Heartcoil core, fitted just hours ago by rebel engineers — names Valtor didn't know, but results he could no longer ignore. At its heart, Link sat within the torso cockpit — already inside, already waiting.

Roland didn't see it until the Ghostframe lunged.

A blur. A strike. The Fang reeled sideways, one of its golden arm plates torn free.

The fight was on.

The Gilded Fang barreled forward, faster than expected. Roland was reckless, but the automaton obeyed him with disturbing precision. Its clawed limb smashed through a support pillar, sending stone shrapnel cascading toward the Ghostframe. The Ghostframe ducked low, narrowly missing the strike. Steam vented from its side as it swung a hammering elbow into the Fang's midsection — metal shrieked against reinforced plating.

They traded blow after blow. One of the Ghostframe's shoulder guards was peeled half loose. A vent line ruptured along the Fang's hip. The Ghostframe pivoted into a wide arc, limbs grinding as it swung low toward the legs — but the Fang met the motion with a brutal counter-kick, and both machines tumbled across scorched flagstones.

The Ghostframe skidded, trailing vent steam and sparks as it slammed into broken stone. Valtor noted the loss of momentum, the imbalance in posture — signs of strain through the machine's external systems.

He righted it just in time to intercept a downward slash — and then drove forward with everything the Heartcoil had to offer.

Sparks ignited in a ring where the two titans collided. The sound split the air.

And slowly, the Ghostframe began to push the Fang back.

Steam vented in screaming jets as the two machines collided — blade against blunted claw, polished edge against scavenged steel. The plaza shook with every impact. Spectators scattered. Shapes moved at the edges of Valtor's monitors — rebels pulling others to safety, hiding behind rubble, too afraid to intervene. One of them dragged the wounded away — a woman with grit and silence in her movements. Valtor noted her precision, her composure. Trained? Or simply desperate?

Roland screamed from his cockpit, hurling insults as much as attacks. "You think you can unmake centuries! You think that thing makes you noble? You're nothing, Link! Nothing!"

In the control chamber, Valtor's brow twitched. He heard the desperation in his son's voice — not authority, not strategy. Just ego unraveling under heat and pressure.

"You never learned restraint," he said quietly. "Only spectacle.""

Link said nothing. The Ghostframe pressed harder.

One strike tore through the Fang's knee housing. Another cracked the left chestplate. Roland panicked. He kicked the emergency pressure valve, venting a burst of steam from the rear boilers that hurled the Gilded Fang into the air. From above, he fired a volley of spike-bolts — needle-thin shards that punched into stone like driven nails.

The Ghostframe spun, its upgraded Heartcoil humming dangerously now, heat shimmering from its joints. Valtor's eyes narrowed as the Ghostframe staggered, steam pressure blooming dangerously from its limb joints. The strain was visible — no stabilizers left, no safeties engaged. He could see the pilot was pushing the Heartcoil past design limits.

Link feinted low, dragging the Ghostframe into a crouch beneath a hammering overhead strike. The Fang followed — too fast, too committed.

Valtor narrowed his eyes.

"Predictable," he muttered.

Link's machine surged upward, steam vents bursting wide as he twisted the momentum into a rising arc. The reinforced claw punched clean through the Fang's chestguard and tore skyward.

The Fang's ceremonial helm — shaped like a lion, gilded and hollow — was ripped clean off. His crown was hollow. And now, it was gone.

Inside, the true cockpit shuddered.

Roland was exposed, sweating, bleeding from his nose.

The Guild sigil across his chestplate sputtered, its glow pulsing weakly before guttering out entirely — not from a fault in wiring, but from a command upstream, cold and final.

And then, the call came.

Valtor turned slightly to one of the aides behind him. "Strip him of rank. Now. Let them hear it before the Fang hits the ground."

A nod. Fingers moved across copper-run relay panels. The order was transmitted.

Moments later, the plaza relay horn rumbled to life — a pressure-fed chamber wired through copper lines and brass valves.

"Unit 07 — Roland. You are hereby relieved. The Flame no longer recognizes your rank."

The voice was flat. Rehearsed. Like cutting a wire.

Roland's face froze.

From his vantage, Valtor saw it clearly — not through a screen, but through the smoke-thinned air and magnification lenses. His son's expression was raw. Not rage. Not defiance.

Fear.

Genuine, hollowing fear.

"No... no, you can't—"

Static.

Then silence.

The Gilded Fang twitched once, steam joints buckling — then collapsed onto one knee. Its steam core vented sideways in a final hiss. Sparks danced across the exposed joints. Armor peeled like wet bark. One leg gave out entirely, and the rest of the machine slumped in a heap of twisted gold and silence.

He tried to scream something — a name, a curse, a plea — but it was swallowed by the wind. What remained of Roland's legacy drifted upward — not in banners, but in smoke.

Link stepped back. The Ghostframe turned its head slightly, as if even it found pity in the gesture.

Roland dropped to his knees inside the open cockpit, gripping the edge like it might somehow keep him from falling any further.

Somewhere beyond the plaza, a deeper rumble began to rise.

And in a control chamber lit only by boilerlight, Valtor watched.

His arms were folded, jaw locked in still fury. The glow of the monitors flickered across his face, casting his features in rust and shadow.

Below the grated floor, the engineers worked in rigid silence. Every tool stroke echoed. Every movement was measured. Behind them, towering over the workshop, loomed the Colossus — chained to steel pylons, its arms the size of tram cars, its frame pulsing faintly with dormant fury.

Valtor did not pace. He did not shout.

He simply stared.

Watched as Roland's machine collapsed.

Watched as the rebellion dared to stand.

Aide voices whispered updates behind him, but he didn't respond.

At last, he spoke — low, as if speaking to the machine more than the men around him.

"Children should not be trusted with legacies."

The room stilled. Even the engineers hesitated.

Valtor stepped toward the control dais, placing one gloved hand on the ignition switch.

"Prepare the Colossus," he said.

Then, to no one and everyone:

"Let them see what remains when the old flame dies."

He pressed the trigger.

And the great machine began to wake.

Chapter 40
The Beast Beneath

———◈———

E ve pulled herself from the rubble.

Ash clung to her lashes, her coat, her skin. The square was a ruin of steam-scored stone and twisted iron. She coughed once, then again, tasting copper and grit. All around her, the wreckage of battle settled — but the square was far from still. Free Steam fighters moved in scattered bands, dragging the wounded, pulling weapons from wrecks. Two cobbled-together automata — rust-stitched and steam-vented — were already repositioning near the plaza gates under shouted orders from Cutter. They weren't pretty, but they walked. Engineers rearmed them with salvaged plating and strapped-on coil cannons.

The duel might have ended, but chaos had not. If anything, it was only beginning. Gunfire crackled from side alleys. Screams rose from the second-tier platforms as Guild infantry pushed inward. One of Free Steam's patched automata let out a coughing burst of pressure and fired a coil round into the fray — more defiance than precision. A second automaton turned to shield a medic dragging a body clear of the kill zone. The defenders were moving, shouting, scrambling to form a wall before the Ghostframe. Not out of command — out of instinct.

The Ghostframe stood at the plaza's center, silent now. Motionless.

It looked almost reverent — one arm lowered, its reinforced claw slack at its side. Steam drifted upward in lazy ribbons from cracked seams along its back. The Heartcoil's core casing glowed faintly through the pressure vents. Not bright. Not gone. But not right either.

Eve's boots crunched over broken tile as she moved toward it. Others stirred behind her — Walder dragging a wounded scout, Cutter shouting orders to pull the fallback line into cover — but their voices were muffled. Dim. Like the city itself had dropped into the breath between heartbeats.

She reached the Ghostframe's side and climbed, fingers numb as she found the footholds still warm from battle. Her legs shook — not from exertion, but from fear she refused to name. Each movement upward felt heavier than the last. Her mind fought to stay focused — not to think of how quiet Link had gone, how the last time she'd seen him like this had been in the aftermath of a failed raid. Back then, he'd woken up cursing and smirking, blood on his sleeve and a bad joke on his lips. She needed him to do the same now.

Inside, Link hadn't moved.

He was slumped in the harness, eyes closed. Pale. Breathing, but barely.

Eve knelt beside the cockpit. For a long moment, she just watched his chest rise and fall. The control levers were scorched. One of the copper-ringed gauges had split. A red smear trailed from his temple into his hairline, half hidden by soot.

"Idiot," she whispered. It came out as a tremble. "Brave, stubborn idiot." She remembered the way he once said, 'I don't get to quit. Not until it means something.' And damn him, he meant it.

She reached out and touched the Heartcoil's edge. Heat pulsed against her fingers — not enough to burn, but enough to remind her this thing still lived. Still pulsed.

Still asked for more.

A low sound reached her ears — distant, rhythmic, deep.

She turned.

And the ground answered.

A single, massive footfall.

The city trembled. Dust leapt from the rooftops. Pipes groaned beneath the streets.

Cutter's voice cut across the square — not panic, but urgency. "Fall back from the arches! Get the line reset!" Walder crouched low behind a shattered wall, one hand pressed to his side where blood soaked into cloth. His other hand still gripped a wrench, jaw clenched as he scanned for his next repair route.

To the east, a squad of Guild loyalists emerged from smoke. They moved cautiously at first, forming staggered firing lines along the plaza's ridge. A steam whistle cut through the chaos — short, sharp, unmistakable.

Orders.

Guild banners unfurled above the southern towers. Officers shouted in tight cadence, steam flags signaling target sectors. Riflemen took positions atop rubble mounds while shock troops advanced in overlapping ranks, steam packs venting like war drums. They weren't hesitating anymore. They were converging on the plaza's heart — and Link's still form.

And amid the wreckage, a lone figure crawled from the broken chest of the Fang. Roland. His coat was scorched, gold trim tattered, one eye swollen shut. He staggered, coughing steam, looking not toward the rebels — but upward, as if he already knew what was coming.

And amid the wreckage, a lone figure crawled from the broken chest of the Fang. Roland. His coat was scorched, gold trim tattered, one eye swollen shut. He staggered, coughing steam, looking not toward the rebels — but upward, as if he already knew what was coming. Then another footfall — louder. Closer.

Eve scrambled down the Ghostframe, landing hard.

Across the far edge of the plaza, shadows peeled apart.

And the Colossus stepped into view.

It was not a machine built for war.

It was built to end it.

Taller than any automaton ever fielded, it moved like a walking furnace — plated in blackened alloy, each step venting pressure through reinforced knee-valves. Its arms dragged coil-linked engine mauls. Its chest bore the full sigil of the Guild — glowing, unbroken.

Eve stared, heart hammering. Her legs locked in place. Somewhere behind her, someone screamed. Another voice shouted to retreat. But Eve couldn't move. All she could think was that Link was still in that cockpit — and if she ran, no one else would bring him back. Her breath hitched, but her eyes wouldn't look away.

"Link," she said — and turned back to the Ghostframe. "You need to wake up now."

He didn't.

Eve's expression hardened. "Fine. Have it your way."

She slapped him — not cruelly, but sharply, across the cheek. The sound cracked inside the cramped cockpit.

"Come on, Link. You don't get to die. Not yet."

No movement.

Below, the screams changed. Not just fear — panic. The kind that came when the first line broke.

The Colossus raised one arm.

And brought it down on the first line of defenders.

Two of Free Steam's patchwork automata moved to intercept — brave, rust-choked things with barely-aligned limbs. The Colossus didn't stop. It swatted one aside like scrap, tearing its frame into molten ruin. The second tried to fire — too slow. It was crushed underfoot.

A nearby wall of defenders collapsed as debris and superheated pressure rolled through the street.

Eve shielded her face, staggering back from the shockwave.

And so did the silence.

Chapter 41
The Last Coil

Darkness hummed. Not silence — not stillness — but a pressure that buzzed behind his eyes like the memory of impact.

Link's breath caught. His ribs screamed. His thoughts scattered.

Then: heat. Familiar, pulsing.

He blinked.

His body screamed under him — ribs tight, shoulder grinding, something sharp lodged behind his knee. The urge to pass out again hit hard, but the sound of steam and screaming kept him tethered to the present.

The world swam back into view — copper-lit and smoke-warped, the edges of the cockpit barely visible through streaked glass and warped seams. Steam hissed somewhere behind his head. The smell of scorched metal and old blood clung to his tongue.

Movement. Eve's voice, distant.

"Link."

He turned toward the sound — sluggish, blurry.

She was crouched beside him again, her face drawn tight with worry and firelight. Her hand hovered over the control harness like she wasn't sure if she should shake him again or hold on longer.

"You're back," she said.

Her voice was steady, but her eyes weren't. They shimmered with the strain of too many close calls. He saw something there — not relief, not yet — just hope holding its breath.

He coughed once, managed a rasp. "Didn't leave."

Then it hit — the memory, the weight. Roland's fall. The surge. The Heartcoil screaming as he pushed it too far.

And now —

He looked past Eve toward the open frame.

Smoke.

Screams.

Pressure detonating in rhythmic blasts.

The Colossus.

He sucked in a breath, forced his hands to move. The controls burned against his palms, but they responded. Not much — but enough. The Ghostframe lived. Barely.

"How bad?" he asked.

Eve shook her head. "Worse than bad. It's tearing through us. Cutter's last fallback line just broke. The defense squads are buying time, but—"

He touched the Heartcoil housing. It was hot, cracked. No balance. The lines were overdrawn. Whatever buffer he'd managed in the last fight was gone.

He met Eve's eyes.

"I'm okay," he lied.

His vision still swam. Every breath ached. But worse than the pain was the fear — not of dying, but of failing. Of letting it end here.

She didn't believe it. But she nodded.

"You can't—" she started.

"I have to."

Not because he wanted to. Because if he didn't, no one else could. Not now. Not with that thing still tearing through them like paper.

She clenched her jaw. Looked back toward the plaza.

"I'm not letting you do this alone."

Link gave her a tired smile. "You already didn't."

Then, softly: "Get as far from this thing as you can. Please."

Eve hesitated.

Then nodded, though her eyes lingered a second longer — full of something between fear and protest. One step back. Two.

"I'll be waiting," she said.

Her voice was soft, but not weak. A promise whispered into the din — not just that she'd wait, but that she believed he'd come back.

Link turned back to the controls. But before his hand moved, his eyes drifted up — just high enough to catch the edge of the battlefield through a shattered viewport.

Guild forces swarmed. Steamwalkers and shock infantry flooded the streets. One of Free Steam's patchwork machines was on its knees, sparking. Another detonated in a burst of flame near the west wall. Bodies moved in blur — scattered, regrouping, falling. The air was alive with war.

And then, in the chaos — Eve.

She hadn't run far. Just beyond the lip of a broken barricade, she turned. Looked back. Not at the battlefield.

At him.

Then she was gone.

His thumb pressed to the manual ignition seal.

The Heartcoil thrummed — not with harmony, but with hunger. It pulsed like something alive and waiting, eager to be called upon again despite the cracks in its shell.

He reached forward — wincing — and rested his hand on the central core panel.

"Okay, buddy," he whispered. "We're not done yet."

His fingers brushed the scorched panel beside the core. Not just metal — not to him. The Ghostframe had carried him farther than he ever thought he'd go. It was bruised, battered, but still here. Still willing.

So was he.

The Ghostframe roared to life.

And dove back into the fire.

Chapter 42
The Colossus Rises

V altor did not speak as the Colossus marched.

The air inside the control chamber was dense with heat and the slow, rhythmic exhale of pressure vents. The smell of iron, sweat, and old steam hung close. Every step of the machine beneath him resonated through the deck plating — a bone-deep drumbeat he could feel in his teeth.

He stood in its reinforced control chamber, one hand resting on the thick spine of the command rail. Below him, the city shuddered with each of the machine's steps. Pipelines burst. Streets cracked. Walls of smoke drifted upward like banners torn from ruined towers.

Through the vision slit, he saw them scatter. Rebels. Children. Barely-armed fools in patched suits.

But one machine still moved.

Valtor narrowed his eyes.

The Ghostframe.

Valtor's jaw flexed. Not because he feared it — but because he'd already calculated the risk. The others didn't matter. Not the rebels with their coils and wrenches, not the screaming crowds. All irrelevant. This one machine was the center now. The point on which everything else would turn.

He leaned forward slightly, observing the way it limped through the fire, battered and burning, but not broken. Its lines were sharper now. Faster. Like the pilot had stopped fighting to preserve it and started fighting *with* it.

A pulse of heat passed through the Colossus' core. The control panels hissed, pressure building.

Valtor's voice was quiet, but the engineers below straightened at once.

"Bring us to full forward position. Engage main limb servos."

A beat.

Then, more to himself: "Let's see if the boy earned all this noise."

The Colossus advanced.

The ground trembled in rhythm.

Inside the cockpit, Valtor's hands moved with fluid precision — no wasted motion, but not without effort. His shoulders ached beneath the weight of his armored coat. The years sat in his spine, not in weakness, but in strain endured. He adjusted the shoulder bracing and recalibrated the impact diffusers, not just out of habit, but necessity. He'd overseen the Colossus' design personally. Not just a weapon.

A test.

Not for the rebels.

For him.

And now, as the Ghostframe cleared the burning line of wreckage, Valtor felt it — the quiet thrill.

He hadn't had a worthy fight in years. Most battles had been theater — crushing insects beneath boots of protocol and show. But this? This was something earned. Something real. And more — this opponent fought with clarity. With pain, yes, but with purpose. Not showmanship. Not pride. There was a discipline in it, a restraint. And in a quiet place Valtor rarely let himself acknowledge, he respected that.

Because it was everything his son had never understood.

Not since the Ash Rebellions. Not since the Twin Siege.

He almost smiled.

Almost.

The two machines faced each other across the ruins of Eastland.

One, polished, brutal, unyielding.

The other, cracked, scorched, breathing smoke.

Valtor lowered the primary control grip into strike position.

And spoke, just once.

"Come on then, boy."

He moved first.

The Colossus surged forward, hydraulic limbs pounding into the broken street like piledrivers. Steam vented in violent bursts along its shoulders as the arms extended — one clawed, one blunt and weighted like a battering ram.

Valtor aimed low. Testing. Not a killing strike — not yet.

The Ghostframe dodged.

Barely.

Soot and pressure exploded where Link's machine had stood a heartbeat before. It countered with a lunge, fast and crooked, like a beast fighting through broken ribs. Its arm swung wide — a slicing arc meant to dissuade, not disable.

Valtor blocked with the Colossus' forearm and twisted, turning the deflection into momentum.

Blow after blow followed — the sound of metal on metal like thunder folded in on itself. The Colossus' claw caught the Ghostframe's shoulder once, sending sparks shearing across the plaza. A counterstrike slammed into the Colossus' side, enough to jolt Valtor in his harness.

Every clash shook the air.

And yet —

The Ghostframe held.

Valtor's mouth twitched, almost a grin. Not quite.

"This one's not dancing for glory," he murmured. "He's fighting to survive."

The Colossus stepped in again.

A flare from the left — a fuel tank detonating near a support column — sent a shockwave rattling across the battlefield. Glass rained from a distant skybridge as the Colossus' wake toppled a building already leaning from weeks of shelling. Civilians scrambled from the wreckage, some too slow. Free Steam fighters tried to hold a line just beyond the square, but even from here Valtor could see them faltering.

One of his engineers' voices buzzed through the valve speaker behind him. "Pressure spike in lower piston three. Outer limb plate sheared near joint delta."

"Recalibrate and reroute," Valtor replied coolly. "Maintain stride priority."

He flexed his fingers along the control grip, watching the Ghostframe rise again. Slower this time. Stubborn.

He squinted through the haze.

This boy — this machine — it was becoming something more than a nuisance. It was forcing the Guild's hand. Forcing *his* hand.

If he won, it didn't just break the rebellion.

It broke the shape of the world.

And the real duel began.

The Colossus shifted left — piston arms rotating with a deep groan as its bulk twisted, feinting high before driving its claw down in a hammering arc. The Ghostframe darted inward, using the momentum to slide beneath the strike, scraping along torn concrete, sparks erupting from shoulder plating already weakened. Its counter was sharp, sudden — a jab of its claw-arm to the Colossus' midsection. Not powerful, but disruptive.

Valtor grunted as the feedback kicked through the rail.

He pivoted. The Colossus followed — a full-body spin that drove its weighted arm in a horizontal arc, cutting through a collapsed tram line like paper. The Ghostframe ducked low again, stumbling this time — one knee hitting the street with a hiss of overpressure.

For a breath, they circled.

Not giants.

Hunters.

The Colossus advanced with a fencer's patience. The Ghostframe answered like a wounded wolf — fast when it needed, feral when cornered.

Each blow rang out like a dropped furnace.

The plaza floor cracked. Buildings leaned. Every slam of iron on iron sent shockwaves up the broken walls, making rubble shudder and banners fall.

Valtor adjusted course — guiding the next strike toward the Ghostframe's weaker left leg. The machine twisted mid-leap, turning the blow into a skid that sent it carving a crescent scar into the stone.

Steam burst from its vents.

And it came back again.

But this time, Valtor met it with full force.

The Colossus dropped low and surged forward — not elegant, but devastating. Its claw-arm caught the Ghostframe mid-motion, slamming into its midsection with a sound like a forge cracking open. The blow lifted Link's machine off its feet, drove it back through a ruined barricade, and sent it sprawling through the wreckage of a collapsed statue.

Valtor didn't let up. He brought the Colossus' foot down — a stomping strike meant to pin, to break — but the Ghostframe rolled just out of reach, skidding sideways in a hail of sparks.

Valtor's grip tightened.

He'd been waiting for this.

Chapter 43
Ash and Echoes

Pain. That was first.

Not the sharp kind — the kind that burned low and wide, like fire eating its way through his ribs. Link sucked in a breath and it rattled in his chest.

The cockpit was dark. Cracked. Steam hissed from ruptured vents above his head, and warning glyphs pulsed red across the lower panels. One control lever was bent nearly in half. Blood, his, streaked the inner glass. The harness was tight across his chest. Too tight. He loosened it with shaking fingers.

Outside, he couldn't hear anything but wind and metal.

Then the ground shifted.

A tremor.

He blinked. Forced the viewport shutter aside — manual, because the pneumatic seals were blown. The viewport cleared just enough for him to see what he already felt.

The Colossus.

It moved like a god through firelight — smoke curling around its shoulders, steam pouring from its knees, every step echoing through the stone and up Link's spine.

He coughed, spat blood. Then tried to move.

The Ghostframe groaned in protest. One leg was jammed. Armor plates along the left side hung loose, warped from the last hit. The Heartcoil flickered — not steady anymore. It pulsed like a wounded animal, heat radiating in slow, uneven waves.

Link pressed a palm to the housing.

"Come on," he whispered.

No reply. Of course not. But the warmth deepened — not a response, but a rhythm, like a breath caught under strain. The casing trembled slightly beneath his fingers, as if the Heartcoil was struggling to draw air the way he was. A low hum returned, ragged but steady.

"We're not done," Link murmured. "Not yet."

He slammed the ignition grip forward.

The Ghostframe screamed to life.

And the Colossus turned.

Link braced.

The first blow came down like a falling world.

Steel shrieked against steel. The Ghostframe reeled, arms thrown up in a desperate crossblock as the Colossus' claw slammed into its bracers. Pain flared through Link's chest as the shock rattled the entire frame. His vision blurred.

Another hit followed — this one a low sweep that sent the Ghostframe skidding across the plaza. Link's shoulder harness bit deep as the machine slammed into a half-toppled tram station. Glass cracked. Somewhere deep in the left knee actuator, something popped.

"Pressure loss," Link hissed. He coughed again — this time darker. Copper rose in the back of his throat.

He blinked hard. Refused to black out.

Every nerve screamed. But he wasn't done.

He surged forward again — weaving between broken pylons, making the Colossus turn, burn fuel. Drain its rhythm.

He baited a vertical strike. Let it miss.

And when the opening came — just for a second — he drove the Ghostframe's right claw into the Colossus' side panel.

Metal tore.

Not deep. But real.

And the Colossus flinched.

Metal shrieked as the Ghostframe caught it crosswise, staggering back through rubble. The second hit missed — Link dropped the right knee just in time and surged low, aiming for the Colossus' exposed elbow joint.

Contact. Not deep enough.

The Colossus retaliated with a sweep that rattled Link's teeth. The viewport cracked further. Light bled in through the seams.

"He's faster than before," Link muttered, rerouting what little pressure he had left. "Or I'm slower."

Either way, it didn't matter.

He shifted tactics.

Let the Colossus chase. Let it strike wide.

He became smaller. Unpredictable. Darting between rubble heaps and scorched husks of trams, kicking up dust and flame to cloud its sensors.

The Ghostframe wasn't meant for this. Not really. It was a scrapper's machine — salvaged parts, desperate welds, barely balanced power routes. But when Link leaned in, when he whispered to it — it responded. With resistance. With heat. With the groan of ancient joints grinding forward anyway. It wasn't designed for war.

It just refused to stop fighting.

Like he did.

Each time they clashed, Link felt the cost. Heat spiked. Fluid leaked across the leg joints. The left arm barely responded now. But he kept moving. Not because he could win. Because he couldn't let it end here.

He ducked under a high swing. Fired the shoulder spike. Scored the Colossus across the collar. Sparks flew — minor damage, but enough to make the giant turn again, recalibrate.

"Yeah," Link muttered through gritted teeth. "Feel that."

He didn't know how long they could hold. Free Steam. The others. Cutter, still limping from the collapse. Walder, somewhere shouting blueprints over falling steel. And Eve — he caught her face flicker across memory, fierce and watching. He forced it away. He couldn't think about her now. Not while the cockpit creaked like bone.

But if he could keep the Colossus here — away from the fallback lines — he could buy them time.

He glanced at the Heartcoil. It was burning hot now. Breathing harder than him.

He curled a bruised fist around the control grip.

"I've got one more in me," he muttered.

Even if it cost him everything.

Through the fractured viewport, he saw the Colossus pause — just for a breath — then raise its clawed arm again.

Coming for him.

Hard.

Link didn't flinch.

The Ghostframe's systems screamed warnings. One last pressure valve failed with a sharp hiss, and a gout of scalding steam erupted from a joint near his elbow. Link didn't even blink. His focus tunneled — the cockpit narrowed to a blur of flickering gauges and raw, vibrating metal.

His hands ached against the controls. Not from the fight — from holding on.

A tremor ran through the Ghostframe as the Colossus stepped closer, raising both arms now. The air shimmered from the heat. Dust curled. Rubble shifted.

Link could see his own reflection in the inner glass, barely visible through blood and soot.

He whispered it again — not to himself. Not to the machine.

To the silence. To the city. To every soul still hiding, hoping, bleeding behind him.

"Not yet."

He leaned into it.

His knuckles were white on the controls now, sweat and blood slicking the grips. He didn't blink. Didn't breathe.

Just waited.

And when the Colossus moved — he moved too.

Chapter 44
The Godbreaker

T hrough the slats of the armored visor, Valtor watched the Ghostframe rise
again.

Smoke billowed between them in erratic gusts, stirred by the heat of their
engines and the crumbling wind of Eastland's dying breath. The smaller machine
staggered upright, its plates scorched, its joints leaking fluid like blood from an
opened throat. Still it rose. Inside the Colossus, Valtor felt a twinge — not pity,
not hesitation, but a flicker of recognition. The boy wasn't just rising; he was
enduring, clawing his way up through ruin on something deeper than will. And
somehow, Valtor knew: this wouldn't end clean.

He leaned forward in the Colossus' cradle.

Not in anger.

In focus.

"He's not yielding," one of the engineers said quietly from the side compart-
ment, reading damage feeds from the projection coils.

Valtor didn't answer. He didn't need to.

He adjusted his grip on the manual core levers, turned one brass dial a fraction
to the right. The Colossus responded with a pulse of pressure through the spine
and shoulders — tighter, coiled now. Ready.

Link was smaller, lighter, faster. But fast meant reckless. The Ghostframe
fought like a scavenger that had survived too many fires.

Valtor respected that. He didn't admire it — but he understood it.

The Colossus stepped forward.

The Ghostframe met it.

They clashed with a sound that rippled through the bones of the city. Valtor tracked each motion with ruthless precision, already calculating the angle of the next strike — but somewhere behind that focus, a sliver of unease whispered. Link wasn't fighting to win. He was fighting like someone who had nothing left to lose.. Sparks fell like shattered stars. Pressure lines burst from the ground. Every blow felt like it could bring the street down with them.

Valtor fought as he lived — efficient, absolute. Even as he struck, his mind remained cold, clinical — but some small part of him, buried beneath command instinct, wondered: what would it take to actually stop this boy? No wasted strikes. No movement without purpose.

The Ghostframe danced, but every time it tried to dart wide, he turned its momentum against it. A missed jab. A rotating shoulder strike. A body check that sent the smaller machine spinning sideways into rubble.

Still, the Ghostframe didn't stop.

It lunged again.

Scored the Colossus across the helm.

Valtor blinked.

It hadn't just survived the last strike.

It was adapting.

His engineer's voice crackled in his ear. "Primary actuator reports flux strain. Outer shell buckling at shoulder plate delta."

Valtor didn't look away. "Maintain aggression. Lock pattern. Prepare steam backflow ejector."

The Ghostframe came again, reckless now — not out of desperation, but intent.

It wanted to finish this.

Valtor braced and struck low, using the Colossus' knee bar to catch the advancing leg — the Ghostframe tripped. Just for a second. That was enough.

The Colossus surged forward and slammed both arms down.

The ground beneath them cracked. The Ghostframe buckled. Its left arm crumpled inward. Steam burst from its back as if the machine itself had cried out.

But it didn't fall.

It rolled.

And from the ruin of its arm, the shoulder spike fired.

The Colossus rocked sideways as sparks sheared up the right flank.

Valtor gritted his teeth.

He could end this. One more strike. One good hit to the coil chamber.

He reset the dial.

Then, through the thinned smoke, he saw something that froze his hand mid-motion.

The Heartcoil.

It was no longer flickering.

It was shining.

Not with warmth — with pressure. With purpose.

The Heartcoil blazed white-blue now, so bright it cast the Ghostframe in a halo of light that shimmered through the soot and ash like a storm waiting to scream. Arcs of electricity crawled across its plating, leaping from joint to joint, cracking through the steam like veins of lightning in a stormfront.

Lines of copper glow threaded out of the Ghostframe's open side, coiling like veins along its plating. Energy bled from the joints. Not controlled. Not clean.

It was unstable.

Overloaded.

Valtor narrowed his eyes.

There was no technique left in the Ghostframe's stance — just raw intent. Not improvisation. Instinct. The kind that couldn't be taught. Only survived.

It wasn't an attack.

It was a fuse.

And it was about to go off.

Link's body was screaming. He couldn't think — only endure. The pain was a wall, and behind it, a single thought clawed its way to the surface: if he blacked out now, it would all end — not just the fight, but the future they hadn't yet earned.

Blood ran down from his temple, warm and thick, seeping past his eye and down his cheek. His right arm trembled uncontrollably, the nerves refusing to stabilize. Every inch of him felt blistered and splintered — skin peeled raw beneath soaked layers, bruises blooming in purple and black where the harness had thrown him against the console. His ribs burned. He wasn't sure if one had cracked — or broken. The cockpit hissed around him, filled with flickering blue light and the sharp, metallic scent of overtaxed copper. Steam dripped down the bulkheads like sweat. The pressure was unbearable.

He didn't dare blink.

His breath came in ragged gulps. One eye was nearly swollen shut from a blow earlier — he couldn't remember which strike. Didn't matter. Pain was everywhere, and it was personal.

The Colossus loomed ahead — a shadow behind the glare, unmoved, coiled, waiting.

But the Ghostframe... the Ghostframe wasn't done.

The Heartcoil pulsed beneath him like a second heartbeat, no longer flickering. It surged. The console lights were white-hot. Electricity crawled across the armature supports, danced across the cracked gauges.

He could feel it through the soles of his boots. Through the harness digging into his shoulders.

He gripped the control bars tighter.

"One more," he whispered, voice torn and low. "Just give me one more."

The Ghostframe trembled — not in protest. In readiness.

He thought of Eve. Of the council. Of Cutter's busted shoulder. Of the way the city used to smell before the smoke took everything.

This wasn't victory. It was refusal. To stop now would mean letting everything they fought for dissolve into ash — the council's trust, the memory of old streets, Eve's unwavering faith. He couldn't betray that. He didn't know if he'd survive it — only that he couldn't stop it now.

And then he let go.

There was no fear. No last-minute prayer. He had already made peace with the price. But that didn't make it easy.

He hovered for one heartbeat, hand tight on the release — feeling the pulse of the Heartcoil surging beneath him like it knew what was coming. The cockpit rattled around him, and his vision blurred from more than just pain. A thousand futures blinked out behind his eyes. If this failed, there wouldn't be time for regret. Only silence.

His knuckles whitened on the lever. Somewhere inside, the voice that once told him to hold back — to protect, to wait, to survive — had gone quiet.

He wasn't waiting anymore.

He didn't shut the valve.

He opened it wider.

The overload sequence cascaded through the Heartcoil in waves. The power loop cracked open. White-blue light spilled from every crevice of the machine like it was shedding its skin of steel and smoke.

The cockpit roared.

Link screamed.

Then the Ghostframe charged.

Chapter 45
After the Storm

E ve stood just beyond the crumbled edge of the city's southern rise — a ragged bluff of broken stone and iron-split concrete where the warfront had peeled the skin off Eastland. From here, the battlefield stretched out below her: a sprawl of burning wreckage, steam-shattered towers, and distant silhouettes still locked in battle.

She should have been giving orders.

But all she could do was watch.

The Ghostframe and the Colossus towered above the smoke, but even from this distance, Eve could tell the Ghostframe wasn't whole. Its plating shimmered with unstable light, copper veins pulsing like arteries across its frame. Lightning danced along its limbs. It didn't look like a machine anymore — it looked like something burning through the last seconds of its own existence., locked in a final embrace of violence and light. Around her, Free Steam fighters shouted across the rubble line, some firing down at Guild soldiers still advancing through the outer ring. Others stood with her — Cutter among them, one arm in a sling, face half-wrapped in gauze — staring with the same sick mix of awe and dread.

Everyone watching knew the truth — this wasn't survival, it was sacrifice in motion. A machine burning itself alive. A pilot with nothing left to give but everything.

It wasn't just a battle.

It was a reckoning.

The Ghostframe lurched forward — not cleanly, not like any tactic they'd drilled for. It staggered, half-limping, trailing sparks and smoke. Then, with a shriek of metal and a burst of unstable light, it threw itself into the Colossus.

Eve's breath caught as the collision hit — not like a single strike, but a hundred impacts at once. Pieces of plating sheared off. Pressure lines exploded beneath them. A sonic shockwave burst outward, warping the air.

The machines locked — not with grace, but with violence so raw it looked like they were tearing each other apart. Metal groaned like a dying animal. One of the Ghostframe's arms twitched violently before locking. The Colossus' shoulder joint buckled sideways, sparks fountaining into the air. The whole structure beneath them cracked like ice underfoot.

Eve felt the impact in her ribs. The ground lurched. Her knees nearly gave. Someone screamed behind her — she didn't know if it was fear or awe.

No steam.

No sound.

No breath.

The world held its inhale.

She saw it then — the Ghostframe's arms clamped tight around the Colossus, plates flaring with uncontrolled energy. For one terrible second, the light grew so intense she could barely see — just silhouettes.

And then she saw it.

The hatch.

It burst.

A figure ejected into the air, trailing fire and smoke.

"Link!"

The name tore from her throat.

But the sound didn't come — not really. The air had been sucked out of the world. Eve knew what was coming, even before it hit. She'd seen the Heartcoil burn too hot before, watched Link push it past safety margins in training — but never like this. The overload had breached containment. The machine wasn't just collapsing — it was detonating, the way a cracked boiler rips through a hull. The

246

Heartcoil was never meant to survive this — just like him. It had always been a blueprint for rebellion, not endurance.

A pressure wave hit like a hammer to the chest, and for one impossible second, everything was light. Blinding, devouring light that swallowed the horizon. No sound. Just the vibration — deep and physical — like the bones of the city crying out. She *felt* it.

Only saw it — light swallowing the sky, steam and flame rolling outward in a dome that collapsed the ground beneath it. The Guild's forward tower began to crumble in the distance.

She was already moving.

The air stank of burning metal. Rubble shifted beneath her boots as she scrambled down the slope, footing sliding on scorched concrete and half-melted rebar. The heat clawed at her skin, smoke choking every breath. Voices called out behind her — she didn't answer.

The emergency chute had half-deployed — burned, torn, but enough to slow his fall. Barely.

Behind her, Cutter stood frozen at the bluff's edge, one hand clutching his sling, the other hanging limp. No orders. No cheers. Just the weight of survival settling in.

She saw the crater.

And in it — a tangle of limbs and torn fabric, body crumpled as if the crash had tried to unmake him.

Link.

She dropped to her knees beside him. His chest rose — barely. One eye swollen shut, skin blackened and bloodied. Burns along his jaw, across his ribs. The harness had melted against him, straps fused to skin. It took everything not to recoil.

He opened his mouth. No words came. Just a rasp.

Eve gripped his hand.

"You absolute idiot," she whispered, voice shaking. "You took it too far." Her voice cracked — not from anger, but from how close she'd come to losing him. "You weren't supposed to go out like that."

His fingers curled weakly around hers.

"You'd have done the same," he rasped — voice rough, but steady enough to sting her with truth.

She exhaled — a fractured sound, torn between disbelief and fury. Her legs trembled beneath her. Only adrenaline had carried her this far. Relief cracked open in her chest like a dam giving way, and with it came the ache of everything she'd almost lost.

Behind them, the city groaned.

The Guild tower groaned — not the scream of metal under stress, but something worse. A final exhale from a dying god. Its core supports had been ruptured in the blast, foundations buckled beneath the weight of power it no longer held.

Eve turned, still kneeling by Link's side, and watched as the steel colossus began to lean — slowly at first, like it was resisting the inevitable. Then, with a shuddering crack, it gave way.

The tower fell like judgment.

Windows burst in cascading waves. Steel ribs snapped one by one. A plume of ash and debris surged upward as the upper tiers sheared free, collapsing down through the body like a spine unzipping.

It hit the ground with a sound that wasn't sound at all — a rupture, a void collapsing in on itself.

Across the battlefield, the Guild soldiers faltered. Some lowered their weapons. Others simply stopped moving, gazes locked on the collapsing tower as if watching their own breath leave their bodies. Whatever commands had once driven them forward crumbled with the steel. Their leader was gone. Their gods had fallen.

A few dropped to their knees. One wept. Another just stared at his own shaking hands, as if unsure they were still his.. Others simply stopped moving, gazes locked on the collapsing tower as if watching their own breath leave their bodies. Whatever commands had once driven them forward crumbled with the steel. Their leader was gone. Their gods had fallen.

Eve stared into the rising cloud, into the silence that followed.. Her heartbeat was the only thing she could hear now.

She looked down at Link — broken, breathing. She thought of the names carved into the old trainworks wall. They'd lasted long enough to see this.

She looked up at the ruin — the place that had haunted every plan, every dream, every loss. Gone. Eastland was gutted now. But maybe, finally, it could begin to heal.

"It's over," she said — to him, to herself, to the ghosts still listening. The tower, the screams, the silence that had ruled them. Done.

And for one breathless moment, the war obeyed.

Chapter 46
Ashlight

L ink stirred in the haze of half-sleep. Not the medicated fog they'd kept him in those first two days, but the slow kind — the kind that came after pain had stopped screaming and started whispering.

The ceiling above him was cracked plaster and exposed beamwork — not a hospital ceiling, not really. This wasn't a hospital. It was a converted rail station, he'd heard. It used to carry freight. Now it carried the wounded. Maybe that was the shift — not what moved, but what it moved for. Heat radiated from a nearby engine core they were using to power field units. Every breath tasted like iron and dust. Clear tubes ran to one arm. A burn wrap covered half his chest, stiff against each breath. Someone had scrawled a number across the metal rail at his bedside — triage code, probably.

Footsteps approached.

He didn't move. Just listened. Through half-lidded eyes, he caught a glimpse of her before she spoke — standing at the edge of his cot, trying to look casual. Her shoulders were too straight, her jaw a little too tight. She wore a half-smile meant to reassure, but it didn't quite reach her eyes. She was worried. He saw it — in the pause before she spoke, in the way her hands flexed at her sides. Pain lingered low and deep, a quiet presence beneath every breath. His ribs protested the weight of stillness, and the dull ache in his side reminded him that survival had come with a cost.

Then a familiar voice, soft but firm: "Still pretending to be asleep?"

Link opened his eyes. She reached toward his hand, then stopped — maybe unsure if touching him would hurt.

He didn't move. Just listened.

"You say that like it's news." His voice cracked on the way out. The ribs still hurt when he breathed too deep.

Eve sank onto the crate next to him. "Three days. That's how long it's been. You slept through the Guild's surrender."

Link blinked. "Makes sense," he said. "The moment the tower fell, they lost their spine. Still... part of me didn't think they'd surrender without dragging more of us down."

She nodded. "After the tower fell... they stopped fighting. Completely. No orders. No reinforcements. The remaining officers signed the terms yesterday."

"And Roland? Don't tell me he vanished like a ghost."

"He was found," Eve said, her voice softer now. "Buried under rubble near the central stairwell. Alive... somehow."

Link looked at her, searching.

"He's not the same," she continued. "No speech at first. Eyes hollow. They said he just sat there for hours, watching the dust settle. Now he's... working. Helping clear debris. Helping rebuild."

Link raised an eyebrow.

Eve gave a faint shrug. "He doesn't talk much. Doesn't give orders. Just works. Like he's trying to find a version of himself that's worth saving."

He absorbed that in silence. The idea of Roland vanishing had once unsettled him more than the man dying. But now — seeing what remained — it was almost worse. A leader turned to wreckage. A man unmade and still walking.

Eve glanced down. "They're setting up a provisional council. The idea came from Garra — she was the one who kept saying the city had to govern itself or it would all just repeat. Cutter backed her, and so did half the ward captains. The vote passed two days ago."

She paused.

"Seven seats. Three from Free Steam, two elected from the civilian districts, and two engineers with no prior allegiances. All decisions need a five-vote quorum."

She looked up at him. "They want the city to run itself — not under fists, but hands."

Link closed his eyes briefly. "Good," he said, though the word sat heavy. Hope was harder to carry than he expected.

"Better than good. Hopeful."

He opened his eyes again and turned his head — slowly — toward her. "And the Heartcoil?"

Eve hesitated before answering. "It's... complicated. They've been arguing about it since the second day. Garra says it's the only thing that makes sense — clean energy, decentralized. Cutter's wary, thinks it's too volatile to rely on. But the civilians? They're the ones who pushed it forward. Said if something that powerful could end the war, maybe it could light the homes we fought to keep."

She paused, watching his face. "The council asked if it could power the city. Maybe all of Eastland."

Link let out a slow breath. Not fear — not really — but the weight of implication. The Heartcoil had never been meant for war — not at the start. It was supposed to be the first clean engine of its kind. A way forward. But when the world demanded a weapon, it became one. That was what haunted him now — not the machine's power, but how easily purpose bent beneath pressure.

"They want to turn the first spark of peace into the backbone of a future. And they want you to lead the way."

He didn't answer right away. His mind drifted — back to the cockpit, to the moment before he let go of the safety, when Valtor's face filled his viewfinder. Not rage. Not fear. Just a flicker of something almost...respect.

He remembered thinking he wasn't going to make it. That the best he could do was buy them a shot. He'd felt peace in that moment, not because he wanted to die, but because he believed it might matter. Maybe Valtor had seen it too — not surrender, not defeat, but the beginning of something neither of them had words for.

Now, somehow, he was still here.

He turned back toward Eve. "I'm not sure I can build another Heartcoil. Not like that one."

She met his eyes. "Then don't build *that* one. Build something else. Something that outlives the war."

He watched her for a moment.

Then nodded.

"Yeah," he said. "But it won't be for them. Not this time."

Also by

Stand Alone
FOR SCALES ALONE
LUX MENDACIUM

The Vaeritas Saga
THE SOUL-SUNG

About the author

Daniel Sheley has been telling stories for most of his life, shaped early by myth, folklore, and writers such as Thomas Malory and William Shakespeare. Those influences, combined with lived experience, inform his focus on character, belief, and the cost of choice.He served in the U.S. Navy in both technical and leadership roles, experiences that deepened his understanding of systems, pressure, and human behavior. He is the award-winning author of Heartcoil, Lux Mendacium, and For Scales Alone (2026 Indies Today Awards - 2nd Runner-Up in Urban Fantasy). His forthcoming novel, The Soul-Sung, was a finalist in the Writers' League of Texas Manuscript Contest and launches The Vaeritas Saga.Daniel lives in Midland, Texas, with his wife and blended family and continues to explore the space where myth, memory, and meaning meet through his fiction.

www.ingramcontent.com/pod-product-compliance
Lightning Source LLC
Chambersburg PA
CBHW050156120726
47903CB00002B/642